EQUATION

A. M. Burrage
WARNING WHISPERS

Other ghost-story collections by A.M. Burrage

Some Ghost Stories (1927)
Someone in the Room (1931)
Between the Minute and the Hour (1967)

EQUATION CHILLERS

WARNING WHISPERS

New Weird Tales by A. M. Burrage

Selected and Introduced by

JACK ADRIAN

EQUATION

This selection first published 1988

Stories © J.S.F. Burrage

Selection and editorial matter © Jack Adrian 1988

British Library Cataloguing in Publication Data

Burrage, A.M. (Alfred McLelland), *1889-1956*
Warning whispers, new weird tales.
I. Title II. Adrian, Jack, *1945-*
823'.912[F]

ISBN 1-853360-83-X

Equation is part of the Thorsons Publishing Group Limited,
Wellingborough, Northamptonshire, NN8 2RQ, England

Printed in Great Britain by Richard Clay Limited, Bungay, Suffolk
Typeset by MJL Limited, Hitchin, Hertfordshire.

1   3   5   7   9   10   8   6   4   2

CONTENTS

A.M. Burrage.

INTRODUCTION

LET me nail my colours firmly to the mast. A.M. Burrage wrote superlative ghost stories. His two principal collections, *Some Ghost Stories* (1927) and *Someone in the Room* (1931)—along with the posthumous *Between the Minute and the Hour* (1967), which contains reprints from the earlier collections as well as five previously uncollected stories—place him, I believe, fairly and squarely amongst the handful of front-rank writers of short weird fiction in the classic English tradition this century has produced.

Conan Doyle, who knew a thing or two about the storyteller's craft, admired Burrage immensely. M.R. James, who was immoderate in his praise of authors long dead but disliked intensely being put on the spot about the merits or otherwise of his peers, once admitted that he 'would have to find a place' for Burrage on any list of 'present-day authors' he was forced to compile who were worth serious attention. On another occasion he grudgingly allowed that *Some Ghost Stories* was 'not altogether bad', which, from James, was almost extravagant praise.

And yet you will look in vain for Burrage's name in any of the major, or indeed minor, critical works on weird fiction published over the past fifty years or so, either in this country or in America. In the field of the classic English ghost story James will be discussed, analysed, dissected (and rightly), as well as E.F. Benson, Algernon Blackwood, Oliver Onions, W. Fryer Harvey. Even the James *pasticheurs*, such as R.H. Malden, A.N.L. Munby, William Croft Dickinson, Christopher Woodforde, and others, will get more than a passing mention. But Burrage? Rarely a footnote. In Julia Brigg's *Night Visitors* ('The Rise and Fall of the English Ghost Story') he doesn't even rate that.

Why is this? Why should it be that the man who wrote two of the most anthologized ghost stories of the past half-century—'The Sweeper' and 'Smee'—and whose craftmanship and story-telling abilities were admired by contemporary editors and readers alike should now be so forgotten or ignored?

It's true that both Burrage's core-collections were never reprinted and are now very scarce books indeed, much sought after by enthusiasts and highly-prized even in the most dismal condition. And neither, more to the point, were published in America.

H. Russell Wakefield, another fine ghost-story writer to a certain extent still unrecognized in this country, was lucky in this respect. His work was published in America and was taken up not only by the critics but magazine editors and publishers after the Second World War. His high reputation as a writer of weird fiction, at least in America, is assured; his stories even now accorded status in academic overviews. By comparison Burrage's name, let alone his output, is virtually unknown there.

But that is not the only reason for Burrage's neglect. The trouble with Burrage is that he was what none of the other major ghost-story writers of his generation were. He was a writer of popular fiction. Worse, he was a writer of cheap popular fiction. And worse even than that, he was a prolific writer of cheap popular fiction.

Even with his ghost stories—in a sense his most serious work—he was stubbornly fecund. Twenty-seven stories appeared in the two collections published during his lifetime, but research has uncovered over forty more—and that was only hunting through about a third of the vast quantity of periodicals to which he is known to have contributed. A final figure of well over 100 ghost stories would surely not be a wild over-estimate of his total output.

It is always difficult to take seriously any writer whose output is prodigious. Received opinion is that the man, or woman, who is capable of banging out 3,000 words of trash (even trash that is ingeniously constructed and highly readable) in the time it takes for the serious writer carefully to craft half a dozen paragraphs cannot, by the very nature of things, be accorded anything but the very lowest critical judgement. And so it has been with A.M. Burrage.

Alfred McLelland Burrage was born in 1889. It is doubtful that he could have escaped becoming a writer even if he'd wished to.

His father was A.S. Burrage, a prolific producer for the Victorian boys'-fiction factories. His uncle (AS's brother) was the astonishingly fertile E. Harcourt Burrage, who spent over 45 years gratifying the desire of Victorian and Edwardian youth for vicarious excitement. From 'Handsome Harry of the *Fighting Belvedere*' to 'The Lambs of Littlecote', EH churned out hundreds of serials, millions of words. His most famous character was the wily Oriental youth Ching-Ching, whose dialogue, it's true, was at best almost totally incomprehensible but whose breezy resourcefulness in the face of outlandish dangers in far-flung climes generated so much reader-enthusiasm that he became the only serious rival to Bracebridge Hemyng's indomitable Jack Harkaway (for a while he even had his own paper, *Ching-Ching's Own*). EH's son, A. Harcourt Burrage (AM's cousin) also toiled in the fields of juvenile literature, although by no means as mightily as, and a touch more priggishly than, his father.

Burrage himself, who could not have failed to have been affected by all this feverish mass-production, entered the cheap-fiction business at an early age, his first story appearing in *Chums* when he was sixteen (even so, he was slower off the block than his father, who'd sold his first story at the age of fifteen).

In the juvenile fiction field *Chums* had more than a whiff of superiority about it; it was only a little below *The Captain* and *Boys' Own Paper* in the parental-popularity stakes. Because of this it was also something of a closed shop and although Burrage had successfully cracked it, it proved a limited source of income and he very soon discovered there was a good deal more work available in the downmarket weeklies issued by Newnes, Aldine, Henderson, Trapps Holmes, and what was to become the biggest pulp-fiction factory in the world, the Amalgamated Press (AP), run by Alfred Harmsworth (later Lord Northcliffe).

Long before he reached his majority Burrage was a busy professional writer earning excellent money, and by the age of twenty five he was not only turning out stories and articles for *Boys' Friend Weekly*, *Boys' Herald*, *Gem* (writing as 'Cooee'), *Comic Life*, *Vanguard*, *Dreadnought*, *Triumph Library*, *Cheer Boys Cheer*, but, unlike his father and uncle, had branched out into the even more lucrative adult market.

He began to break into the better monthlies—the *London*, *Pearson's Magazine*, *Cassell's*, the *Royal*, the *Storyteller*—although his bread-and-butter came from weeklies such as *Tit-Bits*, *Answers*, and the AP's *Short Stories Illustrated* (seldom an issue of which went by without something by him in it).

Like Edgar Wallace, and at around the same time, he found a sympathetic editor in the wise and gifted Isabel Thorne, who presided over the fiction side of a small but bustling outfit in Hind Court run by an old Fleet Street hand called Harry Shurey. Shurey's Publications was always on the look-out for new talent to supply the quantities of stories and serials it needed for the *Weekly Tale-Teller*, *Yes or No*, *Dainty Novels* and three or four other papers which were low in price, modest in payments, but whose readers were avid for romance, thrills, sensation, strong characterization, and neat plotting.

Edgar Wallace created probably his best, certainly his most famous, character for Mrs Thorne, Sanders of the River. In 1910 Wallace had no more than a handful of novels to his name and a by now fading reputation as a Boer War correspondent, but when pushed into writing the Sanders stories by Isabel Thorne he suddenly found his voice, his style; suddenly found the fluency and self-confidence that were to transform him into the most spectacularly successful, and best-loved, thriller-writer of his day.

Although certainly not in the Wallace league, Burrage too benefited enormously from his association with Shurey's, for Mrs Thorne had a fondness for tales of the supernatural and he discovered not only that he didn't mind writing them but that he had a natural bent for the genre. At the same time his work had attracted the attention of David Whitelaw, arguably one of the greatest British magazine editors of this century. Whitelaw was then editing Harmsworth's *London Magazine* (he was later to control all of the AP's magazines: the *London*, the *Premier*, the *Red*, and an assortment of lesser periodicals), and, like Isabel Thorne, he recognized raw talent when he saw it and was happy to educate the younger writer in the subtle art of writing successful popular fiction.

Now in his mid-twenties Burrage was reckoned to be not merely a fine storyteller (and he was pretty sure of this himself, since his work was now regularly being pirated by American editors) but dependable: a man who could be relied on for copy, and plenty of it. This latter quality—the ability to churn it out—was a virtue more highly prized, by often harassed editors, than gold.

The Great War drastically changed his life. Like many of his Grub Street peers he joined the Artists' Rifles, for the duration. He still wrote—there was always time to dash off the odd story in between drilling, fatigues, and button-polishing—although as the war dragged on it became increasingly more difficult to summon up any enthusiasm for the job. Burrage spent a year and a half in France, during some of the fiercest and most atrocious battles on the Western Front, and was finally invalided out, exhausted, in 1918.

Possibly he thought that work would be thin on the ground, that it would take time for publishers to get back to the great days of 1910-

1914, when monthlies were good and fat and healthy and a magazine such as, say, *The Storyteller* featured, every month, twenty to thirty pages of advertisements and in between 100,000 and 120,000 words of fiction (and with Christmas issues, of course, those figures were nearly doubled).

But in fact the end of the First World War saw the biggest boom in magazine publishing in Britain this century has experienced. In the space of two years, from 1919 to 1921, not just scores but hundreds of new periodicals flooded on to the market. It was a Golden Age for anyone with a fertile imagination and strong fingers. Burrage had both.

His forte now was the light and frothy romance of no more than 5,000 words: boy meets girl, boy has a row with girl, boy makes up with girl, wedding bells. Burrage ingeniously and successfully cranked the handle on that tired old plot in issue after issue of such lowbrow monthlies as the *Grand Magazine*, the *Happy Mag*, the *Merry*, the *Sunny*, the *Novel*, as well as scores of cheap-and-cheerful weeklies.

Too, he played the field. He was a dab-hand at the short series of no more than six connected stories, and knew precisely how to hit an editor twice, even in a short space of time—the trick being to write the same kinds of stories, featuring comedy, suspense, and romance with a neat little twist in the tail, but against slightly different backgrounds. For *Lloyd's Magazine*, for instance, he sold two series in rapid succession: 'The Amateur Arcadians' (a bunch of amateur actors tramp the roads from town to town having adventures), and 'The Strange Career of Captain Dorry' (an ex-officer, out-of-work and down on his luck, turns 'highwayman', driving from town to town having adventures).

He wrote weepies and soul-stirrers for the women's papers (the selfish and rackety Bright Young Thing turning over a new leaf after befriending the lonely and careworn old widow came out of his inkwell in one form or another on not a few occasions), and rollicking farce with more than a tinge of the fantastical for the sevenpennies (a series featuring Sir Archibald, a henpecked knight in Camelot, ran for nearly five years, on and off, in the bi-monthly *Yellow Magazine*). He hammered out serials and popular journalism by the ream, as well as historical yarns, detective stories and thrillers (under one of his pseudonyms he even wrote a couple of Sexton Blake stories), novellas, novelettes, and a fair amount of light verse.

And he wrote quantities of ghost stories.

In the early-1920s David Whitelaw, now controlling editor of the AP's

magazine empire, noticed that *Hutchinson's Magazine* had secured E.F.
Benson to write 'spook' stories for it. *Hutchinson's*, one of the main rivals
to Whitelaw's own prestigious *London Magazine*, was run by the somewhat erratic publisher Walter Hutchinson, one of whose many eccen-
tricities was that, although at daggers-drawn with Whitelaw in the
matter of periodicals, he was perfectly happy to include his rival in
his book-lists when Whitelaw was wearing his novelist's hat. Hutchinson also published many of Benson's books and had discovered that,
as well as writing amusingly waspish society novels, he could turn his
imagination to powerful and disturbing tales of the supernatural. At
one stage, and for over a year, Benson was writing one a month for
Hutchinson's.

Any good editor ought to be able to spot a likely prospect, and
Whitelaw was a great editor. Benson's tales in *Hutchinson's* were highly
popular, but Benson himself was unpoachable. Not that it mattered.
Whitelaw had his own tame spook-merchant and he encouraged him
to set to with a will, to such good effect that in the end Burrage out-
stripped the older novelist. In the seven and a half years from April
1922 to December 1929, Benson wrote 27 'spook' stories for Hutchinson. In the five years from October 1925 to September 1930, Burrage
delivered 28 to David Whitelaw (not to mention another twenty or so
to other editors), a number of which appeared in his first collection,
Some Ghost Stories.

Burrage was not much of a book-producer. For him, as for many
of his fellow-scribes, books were all very well but you had to wait far
too long for the rewards, if any. In those days most newspapers and
general-interest weeklies ran serials, more often than not extremely
long serials, the writer making absolutely certain his story reached the
100,000-word mark at least; preferably well over it. You were, after
all, paid by the thousand words, roughly thirty shillings per. You then
sold the story to one of the publishers—Ward Lock, say, or John Long,
or Hurst & Blackett—who specialized in producing books for the bulk-
buying circulating libraries such as Mudie's and W.H. Smith's.

But there was a snag. To be sure, the more your wrote, the more
money you received from the newspaper. But the more you wrote,
the more work you had to do to cut an unwieldy manuscript down
to a manageable 70,000-odd words, which would then fit neatly into
the 288 octavo page-count that was all most publishers allowed for the
popular library novel.

There were writers who could do that sort of hack-work in the twink-
ling of an eye. Or at least in a couple of weeks. Burrage was not one

of them. Apart from anything else, fiddling around with a manuscript took up valuable time that could be better employed in writing another serial, or short-story series, for which, in any case, you received a cheque every Friday lunchtime from the Bought Ledger department. Or even, if times were hard and your sob-story well-rehearsed, cash in hand across the editor's desk.

And for all his industry, times were quite often hard. In his history of the *Strand Magazine* Reginald Pound, one-time editor, recalls an occasion when Burrage, confronted by an irate subscriptions secretary in the Savage Club, called for an open cheque-form at the cashier's desk. He took his time in making it out, so much so that fretful noises could be heard from the queue behind him. Burrage murmured an abstracted apology. 'It's just that I'm trying to think of a likely bank.'

This is not to say Burrage published no books at all, apart from his two ghost-story collections. But his hardback output is decidedly meagre when placed against the millions of words he actually produced. His longer work for juveniles may be found in various pre-1914 paperbacks, published by Henderson's or Trapps Holmes, but these are now, after two World Wars and two ruinous paper-salvage drives, pretty thin on the ground. John Long issued a couple of mild melodramas in the 1920s, *The Smokes of Spring* (set in Burrage's beloved Cornwall) and *Courtland's Crime*; Newnes published his still very funny *Poor Dear Esmé* (which owes something, though not much, to F. Anstey's *Vice-Versa*).

His one great success, the grim and passionately written *War Is War* (1930)—an account of life in the muck and blood of the trenches by one who experienced those horrors at first hand—had to be issued under a pseudonym, 'Ex-Private X'. Victor Gollancz, who published the book and greatly admired it, had to point out that the critics would hardly take the book seriously if it became known that its author earned his living producing two or three slushy love stories a week. In the event, *War Is War* became a bestseller.

Burrage quickly issued his second volume of ghost stories, *Someone in the Room*, under the 'Ex-Private X' by-line, but by the time it appeared his cover had been blown in the press and although the book (which contains some of his finest work) did well, critics by and large tended to be dismissive. The general feeling was that while *War Is War* might have been an impressive achievement, mere ghost stories were really not worth bothering about.

And yet Burrage worked hard at his trade. He worked hard at the potboilers and the serials and the facetious love stories, but he worked especially hard at his weird fiction, of all fictions the most difficult to carry off successfully, even at a time (the 1920s and 1930s) when the majority of the population still lit their homes with candles and paraffin lamps and shadows were longer, and thicker.

In an age when everyone seems to have a home degree in amateur psychology, there's not much to Burrage, perhaps another reason why he has been so ignored.

The confirmed bachelorhood of Monty James and many of his clerical adherents is nowadays highly suspect; there are nasty streaks in the fiction of both Benson and Arthur Machen which may be traced back to an odd childhood or peculiar personal tastes, or both; Blackwood's feyness, Wakefield's boisterous tendencies, the mild (the very mild) obsession of Walter de la Mare with physical deformity—all of these contain rich pickings for the Freudian critic, or the post-graduate knuckling down to a lengthy dissertation on the wilder shores of literature.

But the worst that can be said of Burrage was that he was a storyteller. It is true that he was a staunch Catholic (educated at Douai School), who once admitted that one of his main hobbies was 'attending "churchings"', but one can surely forgive him this since his other main hobby was cricket. In any case his religious convictions never intrude upon his best tales. Quite the reverse.

During the 1920s, his most creative period, his range, in the field of the supernatural, was vast, his imagination unfettered by convention. Urged on by his mentor David Whitelaw (who, Burrage once complained, thought ghost stories 'easy to write') he was forced to improvise, forced to ring the changes, forced to deliver the psychical goods in as unpredictable a manner as possible, and at a fairly rapid rate.

The pressure certainly paid off: not for Burrage a continuous stream of mere hauntings. In his stories the boundaries between past and present and future often become blurred, then disappear altogether. Men dream of leading other lives, not in the past or even in the future, but in the here-and-now; a murderer is troubled not by someone who is dead but someone who is alive; in an appalling moment of self-revelation a general in the British Army suddenly recalls his past lives, his past crimes—not against humanity but against God.

And even while keeping Whitelaw happy (in both the *London* and the *Premier*) with a steady stream of superior weird tales, Burrage could still find time to indulge his more populist side. He turned out ghost stories for the women's market, humorous ghost stories for the popular weeklies; the bibliophile Ayresome Johns has stumbled across a fascinating series about a psychic detective, 'The Strange Experiences of Francis Chard', in one of the downmarket monthlies—written at the same time that he was creating some of his finest short stories for Whitelaw: 'The Gambler's Room', 'The Green Scarf', 'The Yellow Curtains', 'The Acquittal'.

Always the images—the effects—Burrage works at are disturbing; many are deeply so. Some are truly hair-raising.

An obsession with a figure seen in a moonlit garden and the subsequent lifting of a veil affect one character so profoundly that afterwards he cannot bear to be touched 'or to hear anybody laugh'. The careless waving of a scarf from the upper window of an old house summons not simply a horde of harsh-voiced and vengeful militia from another age but the ravening powers of darkness themselves: 'Hatred, Bloodlust, Intolerance...Treachery'. And perhaps the most chilling image of all is that of a child's footprints in the snow—for *we* know that, however innocent of evil or horror that image may be, it caused 'a whole inferno of terror' to be concentrated on a dead man's face.

None of the stories in this collection has appeared in bookform before. They range from the genuinely horrifying (whenever I think of it, the final image in 'The Acquittal' is still disturbing, even though I first read the story ten years or more ago) to the, it must be said, genuinely comic.

There are often distinct bonuses to Burrage's stories, bonuses which have nothing whatsoever to do with the supernatural, the weird, the blood-curdling. It is why it is always such a pleasure to read him. It is perhaps yet one more reason why he has been so ignored for so many years—for your inveterate ghost- and horror-story addict, especially today, is impatient of tales that do not contain a full meed of rot-eating ghouls, yammering cretins with blood-spouting eyes, the rank fetor of putrescent flesh; and nothing else but.

The ghost in 'For the Local Rag' is hardly one to chill the blood: that has to be admitted—yet as an affectionate portrait of small-town journalism of the inter-War years, as a beautifully-wrought character study, the story is worth much. The spirit in 'For One Night Only' is a melancholy thing—but what a marvellous evocation of pre-War music halls, slightly seedy digs, second-rate performers on the variety treadmill is contained within the story's bounds. As for 'The Imperturbable Tucker', who can read of the eponymous hero's curious nocturnal experience, and not smile?

It would be wrong, however, to give an impression that certain of the stories here collected are, somehow, not quite the genuine article. Burrage was a thorough-paced entertainer, his genius taking many forms, and all aspects of his art are here; all the stories unequivocally weird.

Burrage's purpose, as he once said himself, was to give the reader a pleasant (and occasionally a decidedly unpleasant) shudder late at night. My own purpose, in searching out his forgotten tales, has frankly been to redress the balance; to rescue the reputation of a writer who has, for all the wrong reasons, been grossly neglected over the past fifty years. And at last, it is to be hoped, to place him in the pantheon of classic English ghost-story writers, where he surely belongs.

L.P. Hartley, himself no slouch when it came to awakening a tingle in the spine, a lurking unease in the psyche, once wrote of the ghost story that 'if not the highest, it is certainly the most exacting form of literary art, and perhaps the only one in which there is almost no intermediate step between success and failure. Either it comes off, or it is a flop.'

There are no flops here.

JA
April, 1988

THE ACQUITTAL

T HEY kept Frenchal waiting below-stairs a long time—a very long time. Evidently the jury was not finding it easy to make up its individual minds. It must have been three hours before the ten men and the two women were brought back, closely guarded by those ridiculous javelin men, and ranged in neat rows in the little tiered box on the right of the judge's throne.

It had been a long trial, interesting enough to the newspaper students of such matters, who have only the tit-bits served up for their delectation by expert journalists; but those compelled to be in court, and the sensation-seekers, who had come for entertainment, had found long periods barren of drama and even of interest.

It was a poison trial. John Frenchal stood indicted for the wilful murder of his wife by administering arsenic. The evidence was all circumstantial and almost entirely technical. Two pathologists with conflicting opinions had each spent hours in the witness-box and given evidence which counsel, jury, and probably even the judge, had failed wholly to understand. The summing-up had been neither for nor against the prisoner, and the scales were evenly balanced when the judge said his last words to the jury. Only the newspaper men, highly experienced in such matters, knew during those long three hours what the verdict must eventually be. 'Oh, of course, he did it. But they haven't quite brought it home. The jury are bound to funk it. They'll have to let him off.'

Frenchal sat and sweated. He had no means of telling whether this long deliberation of the jury was in his favour or against him. He had borne himself all through the long trial with a calmness and dignity which had compelled a certain amount of admiration. Now, when at last they tapped him on the shoulder, he wondered if he would be able to walk.

Yet, once he was upon his legs, strength and the power of emotion returned to him, and he walked firmly up the wooden stairs between the two warders. He had scarcely reached the rail of the dock when a door opened on the other side of the court, and all around him sounded the rustling and scuffling of people rising from their seats. Through a mist he saw the judge in scarlet and ermine seating himself on the throne under the Royal arms; very far away, it seemed, he heard voices. The members of the jury were answering to their names. Well, one way or another, it would all be over in a few seconds now.

'Members of the jury, are you agreed? Do you find the prisoner at the bar Guilty of wilful murder or Not Guilty?'

'Not Guilty.'

He wondered for one aching moment if he had heard aright, if that short first word had really been uttered. Then one or two sentimental women, high up in the gallery on his left, began to clap and were sharply reprimanded.

What was happening now? The judge was speaking to him. He saw a faintly cynical smile on the thin, hard lips. Then a finger touched his arm and a voice whispered: 'Come along, sir. Better come downstairs and wait a bit.'

Inherent courtesy made him bow to the judge. Then he turned and walked downstairs in almost a state of trance. He did not need the supporting hands on his arms. He was strong enough, but nothing just then seemed real.

The warders, who had been sternly respectful, were now more friendly. But there was something cynical and restrained in their manner, as if they thought him a lucky man, as if they *knew!* They brought him brandy which brought new life to him and gave his surroundings more of the deeper colours of reality. He lit a cigarette and handed his case to the two men in blue, each of whom selected a cigarette and put it in his pocket. His counsel came down to congratulate him and receive his thanks, so did his solicitor, who had worked wondrously hard. But on the faces of each of them he remarked that smile, a little like the judge's, a little like the warders'—as if they thought him undeservedly fortunate.

Presently he remembered that now, after long weeks of confinement, he was free. He got up and spoke of going. His solicitor bade him wait a moment, and went to confer with a policeman standing near the door.

'Better wait a little while. You're not in a hurry. There's a crowd outside. Presently there'll be a rumour that you've been smuggled out, and then they'll go.'

A crowd! That meant a crowd which might possibly be hostile. So they thought he did it, did they? Well, confound them, they were right. Everybody knew, except those twelve fools who, faced with a responsibility beyond their powers of endurance, had given him the benefit of the doubt. The prosecution had bungled its work badly; *he* could have told that harsh-voiced, eminent K.C. where he had got the poison and how it had been administered.

The policeman came forward.

'Your car's just been round to the back, sir. I sent it away and told the man to come back in about twenty minutes.'

'My car?'

'A taxi, sir. He said it'd been ordered.'

Frenchal turned to his solicitor.

'Did you order me a car?'

'No. I was going to, of course.'

Then who had? Some friend of his who was present in court, he supposed. But he had seen no friends. Even Edith—but, of course, it would have been too much for Edith. And the train of thought, starting on a new trail, ran on. Did Edith know? Thank heaven that *something* hadn't come out at the trial. If the fools who, as the defence triumphantly proclaimed, could find no adequate motive, had known about Edith and put her in the witness-box, the trial might have come to a different end. Edith's circumspection, the secrecy on which she had insisted through their intrigue, her slavish worship of the conventions, and the outward show of respectability which had helped bring about the crime, had at least saved him from the consequences. This handsome young widow, his neighbour and his wife's friend, had not been mentioned at the trial.

The tale was as old as passion and crime, the yearning for romance of an unscrupulous man, who, tied to a wife who bored and irritated him, felt the sands of his youth already beginning to slip away. If Edith Longley, who came to live in the grey house across the common, had loved him a little more and her own reputation a little less, the affair might have ended less tragically in some other court.

Frenchal was in the forties, and he had been married for nearly twenty years to a woman who had begun to bore him on their honeymoon. He was not capable of giving a love which outlived passion. His wife was; and she was sentimental and clinging rather than ardent.

He soon came to hate her. He had hated her for years, and it was her relentlessly continuing to love him which had lit an ugly red fire in the ashes of boredom and indifference. If she'd only been indifferent, too, if she'd only left him alone instead of fawning around him and making his flesh creep with her caresses and endearments! Like a great ugly cat, she was, he thought, purring and nudging against him for caresses! Her little attentions to his comfort, and she was forever warming his slippers and filling his pipe, sickened him because they spoke of her unwanted love. He had borne it wonderfully, he told himself, and might have gone on bearing it indefinitely if the whisper had not come that life—as he counted it—with its ardours and capacities, was draining away. And then had come Edith Longley, young and warm-blooded and widowed, to bring him once more the thing he called love.

Oh, yes, she loved him—in her fashion. But she would not burn her boats. She did not like to think of certain houses being closed against her, and of having to find new friends among people who were not quite—you know! If he were free as she was it would, of course, have been so different! No more of the simple and ugly story need be told.

The court-house stood among narrow streets in the older part of a cathedral city. It was at a few minutes to six on a damp, dark autumn evening when Frenchal stepped out quickly and quietly through an arched doorway and into the taxi-cab which awaited him. He had trouble in fastening the door, and the driver, perhaps because he was anxious to get a view of his fare, left his seat and came round to help him.

'Farnham House, Benford Common,' said Frenchal.

'Yes, I know, sir.' As if everybody in the county didn't know his address by now!

'Wait a moment. Who ordered you?'

'A lady, sir.'

'Oh, really! I wonder who. Tall, dark lady with black hair—?'

He was describing Edith Longley. The man shook his head.

'No, sir. She was fairly tall for a lady, but from what I could see of 'er 'air it was fair and goin' a bit grey. I didn't notice what her clothes was like. They wasn't any particular colour.'

'Thank you. All right.'

Who could it have been? Not Edith, certainly. It was more like— hang it all, it might have served for a description of Mary—Mary dead and in her last resting place. What a strange spark that fellow's words had struck, half ghastly and half humorous. If one believed in ghosts! Faithful and affectionate wife arranges for the comfort of her husband after his trial for having murdered her. Just what Mary might be expected to do if she could! She had always tried to live up to copy-book maxims on the subject of forgiveness and returning good for evil.

It was a whimsical thought, but it began to give him discomfort, and he tossed it away. Not that he believed in anything of that sort. He held that dead men and women were as dead as dead dogs. Nor had his conscience given him the least trouble. All he had endured since his arrest was an agony of anxiety regarding his own fate. That anxiety was past now, and into its vacant place came crowding a host of other and smaller cares. His financial condition was a worry. He had been compelled to spend on his defence much more than he could afford. And Edith? How would Edith feel towards him now, when he came back with the stigma of his trial. For he was well aware that he had no more proved his innocence than had the prosecution succeeded in proving his guilt. And—hang it!—who was that woman who'd ordered the car for him immediately after the trial? Hair beginning to turn grey, clothes not any particular colour. . . Just like Mary; you never noticed her clothes. Why couldn't he get that silly bizarre thought out of his head? He began to sweat again and felt weak.

The car swung out into a broad, lighted thoroughfare and turned south. Frenchal tapped at the glass in front of him and spoke through the tube.

'Drive straight on until six o'clock,' he said, 'and then stop at the first inn. I want a drink.'

Six o'clock found them on a lonely stretch of road, but within a minute or two the lights of Carncross village shone mistily at them out of a hollow, and the driver slowed down and pulled up before an inn which stood a little way back from the road on the outskirts of the hamlet.

Frenchal got out and took a step or two towards the door, only to discover suddenly that he had a shrinking fear of being recognized, and needed the moral support of the driver.

'You'd better come in and have something,' he said.

The driver followed him. They entered a brightly-lit tap-room where some half a dozen rustic workers were already assembled. One or two of them made way for Frenchal before the narrow counter, on the other side of which a fat, florid landlord stood polishing glasses.

'A large Three Star brandy,' Frenchal muttered, 'and—what's yours?—oh, and a pint.'

The landlord brought the drinks, and stood for a moment trying to look over the heads of his customers and then craning his neck to right and left.

'Well, that's a rum 'un,' he said. 'Wasn't there a lady come in with you?'

Frenchal started and spilled some of the spirit.

'No,' he said, and almost snarled the word.

'Well, I could have sworn I see a lady follow you in.'

'I thought I see one, too,' remarked an aged farm-labourer from a far corner. 'Must have been shadders.'

The landlord laughed uneasily, and delivered himself of the inevitable joke.

'Well, you and I had better take more worter with it, George, 'adn't us? You ain't got an evenin' paper on you, I s'pose, sir?' he added, addressing Frenchal.

'No.'

'Ah! I wanted to know 'ow the trial of that there Frenchal's gettin' on. You don't happen to know if it's over?'

'Yes, it's all over.' Frenchal tried to speak indifferently. 'He got off.'

There was a low, growling chorus and then a laugh.

'There, 'Arry!' said a voice. 'Wot did I tell yer?'

'I don't care wot you told me,' the landlord retorted hotly. 'I reckon they didn't ought to 'ang nobody after that!'

'You'd 'ave liked the job of 'anging 'im yerself, 'Arry,' chuckled the old labourer in the corner.'

''Anging 'im! I'd like to burn 'im! 'Ires this 'ere Sir James Champion to defend 'im. Bin a pore man, 'e'd have swung all right. All I've got to say is, if 'e didn't do it, nobody did.'

Frenchal had the wit to perceive that he had not been recognized. His identity was known only to the embarassed driver, who shuffled beside him awkwardly, sipping his beer. So this was how the Man in the Street regarded him. Well, it was more or less what he had expected. He braced himself, knowing that the driver would have a tale to tell before closing-time that night.

'Possibly,' he said coldly, 'if you'd attended the trial you might have come to another decision, the same as the jury. After all, my friend, you've only read bits of it in the newspapers.'

'I've read quite enough, sir, and nothing won't alter my opinions. You mark my words, there was a lady in that case which nobody knows nothing about. 'Ushed up, somehow, that was. Bin a pore man, now—'

In spite of himself, Frenchal was put out of countenance. A lady in the case! Strange how a stupid, vulgar mind, which did not know how to begin to reason, had stumbled upon the truth! He turned to the driver, trying to smile.

'You ready?' he asked. 'Good-night, landlord.'

He wanted to snarl an insult at that fool of a publican, and yet felt that he might be grateful for the warning. How closely the eyes of his little village world would watch him now! If he married again too soon, if he saw too much of Edith, the self-appointed critics would draw their own conclusions. He cursed them in thought as he clambered into the car. Let them think and say what they liked; prove what they liked now. Not again could he be tried for his life because of Mary. And yet he knew in his heart that popular opinion mattered much to him, that he could not bear social ostracism. During his time of waiting he had dreamed of a popular acquittal, of people coming out to cheer him as he drove back to his home. He knew already how this dream was to be fulfilled. People knew! He was returning to them, not stainless, but having the benefit of a shadowy doubt.

If only he could get away! But financial ruin already stared him in the face. He had been living beyond his income for years: and the price of his defence had added very materially to the encumbrance on his small property. To sell now would leave him poor indeed. He saw himself tied fast to his little house, the 'gentleman's farm,' with its memories of Mary and its circle of hostile neighbours.

Nobody except the driver saw his arrival home. The car purred up the short drive, turned in the circle of gravel, and stopped outside his door. He saw a light in the dining-room and the flicker of a fire on the blind. They expected him then!

He got out and tipped the man, handsomely. The man thanked him hoarsely, and shame-facedly wished him luck. 'He don't look like a murderer,' the driver thought, forgetting that no murderer ever did.

His indoor servants, a married couple named Townsend, both came to welcome him. The door opened as he set foot on the steps, and revealed them standing in the lighted hall. They were both obviously embarrassed, and had spent long hours in discussing how they should receive him if, and when, he returned. They were agreed that it was unnecessary to make any speech of congratulation, and yet they could scarcely behave as if nothing had happened. Their both being in the hall to receive him was a tacit vote of confidence, for they were both loyal believers in his innocence. How could he be a murderer when they had been with him so long and knew him so well?

Frenchal was a little cheered and reassured by the sight of them standing there, with the shy, tremulous smiles on their old faces. Like them, he found it unnecessary to refer to the ordeal through which he had just passed, but he shook hands with them in turn.

'Well, Townsend, how are things?' he asked, trying to assume a bluff heartiness of manner.

'Pretty much as usual, sir. Dick Baines is comin' up early tomorrow mornin' to see you about the stock. Dinner's all ready for you, sir, and Mrs T. have done the chops the way you like 'em.'

'Dinner ready! How did you know—'

'We was rung up, sir, just before six, and told as you'd be home about seven.'

Frenchal frowned, and, because he was bewildered, his over-strained nerves snapped the thin thread of his temper.

'But hang it, I didn't know that myself, then. The—the—*it* wasn't over until after five. Who rang you up?'

'A lady, sir. She just said that you'd be in for dinner at about seven. Nothing more than that. And then, of course, sir, we knew—'

'What lady was it?'

'I don't know, sir,' Townsend faltered. 'It gave me rather a turn. I thought it sounded like—'

'Hush, T!' his wife interposed sharply.

She might have added that she, too, had received a 'turn,' when her husband had rushed to her white-faced and said that the voice he had just heard on the 'phone was so like the old Missus's that he didn't know how to hold the receiver to his ear.

A chill struck Frenchal, accompanied by a sudden spell of giddiness. He knew exactly what Townsend had been about to say, and found himself not daring to ask the man to end the interrupted sentence.

'Oh, somebody who knew me, I expect,' he said, with a quaver in his voice. 'We shall find out tomorrow, I dare say. Did you say dinner was ready, Mrs Townsend? All right, I shall be ready, too, in a couple of minutes. I'm just going up to wash.'

He went upstairs to his dressing-room, where a fire, blazing in the little grate, gave him a welcome with which he would have gladly dispensed. The sight of that fire burning there reminded him of Mary. A fire in his dressing-room was one of Mary's little 'attentions,' which used to irritate him because they proclaimed her unwanted love. For such he was expected to kiss her and say, 'Thank you, darling!' A wave of anger swept over him. What right had Mrs Townsend to light fires without orders? He was a very poor man now; he must make sweeping economies.

He was half-way to the linen cupboard in search of a towel when he glanced back at the hearth and uttered an ugly little choked cry. Just inside the fender were his slippers and pyjamas, and nobody but Mary had ever dreamed of laying them there. Seeing them there made him think that after all she couldn't be dead, that she was in the next room on the other side of that half-open door, preparing for dinner. He who believed in nothing but the plain creed of materialism glanced stealthily and uneasily at that door, and involuntarily his ears listened for once familiar sounds—footfalls, the rhythmic sound of long hair being brushed, the tinkle of hairpins in a china tray.

He went downstairs again, stumbling and cursing. In the kitchen he found Mrs Townsend and rated her wildly. What the devil had she meant by lighting that fire? He couldn't afford fires in his dressing-room. And what the devil did she mean by putting out his pyjamas and slippers like that? When he wanted a valet he'd engage one, he told her.

Mrs Townsend looked startled and abashed.

'I lit the fire because I thought you'd like it, sir,' she said. 'You often used to have a fire. And I'm sure I didn't touch your pyjamas and slippers, sir! No, that I didn't!'

He turned to Townsend, who had come in in time to overhear.

'Then it was you,' he said.

'No, sir. I haven't been upstairs all this evening!'

Frenchal included the pair in a snarl.

'Well, one of you must have done. One of you is lying. I found them there!'

He turned away muttering, trying to shut out from his mind the dreadful thought which now clamoured all the more insistently. Suppose neither of them had put his shoes and pyjamas there to warm? Suppose they had been put there by the same woman who had rung the Townsends up on the telephone and sent the taxi round to the Court House at Hanchester. Suppose it were true, after all, that people had souls which survived their bodies? Suppose Mary still hovered about him, unseen by him as yet, forgiving him for what he had done, still anxious for his comfort, still loving him and angling for his love in the ways which had irritated and nauseated him while she lived?

He grappled with the thought and flung it away. It was too fantastic, too utterly appalling. He told himself that his brain must have been affected to create a fancy so hideous, so utterly unfit for any man's mind. But thoughts, once begotten, bred quickly, and their dreadful freakish offspring over-ran him.

He found himself unwilling to go up to the dressing-room again, and dispensed with washing. Instead, he passed through the gloomy hall into the dining-room. The hall was only dimly lighted, and for him the great, shapeless blots of shadow were the lurking places of other shadows. Now that he had begun to imagine things he could feel Mary's presence. She was watching him sorrowfully, hungrily, always somewhere behind him, and cunningly eluding his gaze whenever he gave way to his sick fancy and swung about, staring this way and that.

The dining-room was more cheerful. It was brightly lit up, and a fire burned cheerfully in a wide, old-fashioned grate. A place was laid for him at the end of the table where he had always sat. Here there was little at first to remind him of Mary, but he noticed, as he was about to sit down, the empty chair at the opposite end. He got up and pushed it back against the wall. He was a sick man, he told himself, his nervous system had been deranged by what he had already endured, and his fancy was likely to play him tricks. Suppose he looked up suddenly at table and saw in that opposite chair—No, he dared not think of it!

With Mary's chair out of its accustomed place he was satisfied for a moment or two. Then, with a curse, he realised that this slight re-arrangement of the furniture would not escape the notice of the Townsends. They might even divine the motive which had made him move it, and begin to suspect, and whisper that the master was haunted by his conscience. So he returned the chair to its old place, found himself weak and perspiring, and went to the sideboard for brandy. As he helped himself liberally he was conscious of a Presence which was aware of his misery—although, perhaps, not comprehending the cause—and was nauseatingly sympathetic and trying to caress him.

He thought, quite reasonably, that he was going mad. Never in his cell had he been tormented like this. There he had faced another terror in single combat. He made a supreme effort to reason with himself as he drank the spirit and felt a little of his courage ebbing back. Very soon he would find out who had ordered that taxi for him and rung up the Townsends. All these sick fancies had sprung from the fact that some good-natured busybody had tried to befriend him. And, of course, one of the Townsends had put his slippers and pyjamas in front of the fire upstairs, and afterwards forgotten all about it. They were a pair of fools, and the sooner he got rid of them, the better.

He began to be angry with that perverse imagination of his. If it had to whisper to him that Mary was near him, why couldn't it have been logical and told him that she hated him and wished him dead. He could have endured the imagined presence of a vengeful spirit, but not the spirit of Mary, forgiving and smarmily loving as she had always been. And suppose his imagination went further, learned new tricks? There was no knowing where it was going to stop.

Sooner or later he would have to go to bed, to sleep in that dressing-room which led into another room where, lying in the double-bed, she used to come in and say good-night, bending over him and brushing his face with her long, loose hair. She had never plaited it, and some-times, after she had washed it, it was dank and sticky. Suppose he were to fancy—Ugh! It did not bear thinking about!

Mrs Townsend brought him in soup, and then a brace of chops. He ate little, and was careful never to raise his eyes to that chair at the other end of the table. He drank unsparingly, keeping to brandy, but it seemed to have no more effect on him than water. Only when one of the Townsends was in the room did he look straight and calmly at that chair at the far end of the table.

Townsend came in after the plates had been removed.

'Some letters for you, sir,' he said apologetically. 'I'm sorry. I forgot them.'

He took the little bundle and turned the envelopes one by one until he came to one addressed to him in a thick, round, feminine hand. As the door closed he tore it open feverishly, and stared out of hot, dry, feverish eyes at Edith's unsigned note.

'In the event of your being acquitted, please do not make any attempt to see me. I wish neither to see you nor speak to you again.'

So Edith knew! He realised now that all the time she, of all people, must have known. And this was how she now felt towards him—she for whose sake he had risked everything. He stared at the written words in an agony of frustration, of foiled desire. His heart seemed to rise and swell as if it would choke him. Then terror had him by the throat and he stood rigid in an agony of fear.

High up near the right shoulder he felt on his arm the sympathetic pressure of slim fingers. Somebody, some woman standing behind him, was touching him, fondling him, being sorry for him. It seemed to his stricken senses that the air close to his ear was faintly stirred by a fluttering warmth of breath. This—*this* was no fancy. *She* had touched him like this a score of times when he was angry, when things had gone wrong, when he was disappointed and unhappy.

He could not move nor cry out. He knew that she was there, that, could he turn his head, he would endure the culminating horror of seeing the presence which he already felt. She was being sorry for him, 'smarming' him, because his poor heart had been bruised by her rival! He suffered physical besides mental nausea. He stood there in indescribable agony of mind, while his life and reason rocked and reeled on the edge of some fathomless abyss.

At last the hand on his arm relaxed its pressure. He felt himself being softly patted twice. Then he reeled to the side-board, clutched it, buried his face in his arms and crouched there, moaning.

He had at last to face the dreadful prospect of going to bed, and although he drugged himself with all that was left of the brandy, he walked upstairs as sober as any living man.

The fire in the dressing-room was nearly out, but there was still a glow in the ashes, and he thought of trying to revive it. But a fire sets shadows in motion all about the room, and he could not face the prospect of a wakeful night in such a company. He undressed, with his gaze for ever turning sidelong to the door which led into the room which had once been Mary's.

The electric light switch was by the door, and he kept the light burning when he got into bed. Then it seemed to him, as his courage revived a little, that he might have some chance of sleeping if he turned it out. Besides, in the dark, one might feel and hear; but at least one could not see, and all the man's five senses had become his enemies.

In the dark he returned to bed, thankful for the closed door between him and that other room. But he was hardly in bed for the second time when it opened with the click of a slipping latch, setting his heart jumping and his nerves tingling.

He remembered that this was an old trick of that particular door, and wished that he had remembered to find the key and lock it. He could hardly endure the thought of it standing a few inches ajar, but to get up and close it—no, he could not quite do that. He began to sweat again at the thought of all manner of hideous possibilities which began to jostle like gamins to attract his attention.

For a full hour he lay tossing and turning, hearing the bed creak under him at every turn. It was a noisy spring mattress, and when Mary was alive she always knew when he was wakeful and often came in to ask why he could not sleep. That thought instantly begot another which was unspeakably hideous. He wished he hadn't remembered. He plunged over from his left to his right side, as if to shake himself free of it. The bed creaked—and an answering creak from the bed in the next room brought the sweat from every pore in his body.

He had heard that sound before when Mary was awake. He used to lie still then, lest she should come in to him with her tender inquiries and her irritating nerve-destroying solicitude; but never did he lie as still as he lay now.

Frenchal, rigid as a corpse, scarcely dared to breathe. His pyjamas, sodden with perspiration, clung to him and irritated his skin. He found himself in an attitude quite unendurable, but dared not stir. When at last he moved, it was as if his tortured nerves had rebelled and shifted a leg and elbow. The tell-tale bed creaked, and sharp upon the sound he heard an answering creak from the bed on the other side of the wall.

He was quickly losing control now, and a low moan escaped him, and it was answered by a familiar sound in the next room—the soft, shuddery sound of somebody turning over in bed. Sparks of light now began to dance before the man's eyes, keeping time with the galloping of his heart. He stuffed bedclothes into his mouth and bit into sheet and blanket. He writhed this way and that, and the tell-tale mattress creaked and tinkled.

In the next room a pair of feet thudded softly on the carpet beside the double-bed. Footfalls came softly to the door. The hinges creaked, and the footfalls crossed the threshold. The window fronting Frenchal's bed was a dimly luminous rectangle. For a moment it framed part of a human shape which moved, looming nearer. He closed his eyes. He was far gone now, and capable of no other movement. He heard the sound of breathing drawing nearer, and then, close above him, the soft, dreadful voice he knew so well.

'Can't my darling sleep? Oh, what's the matter with my darling?'

And there fell upon his upturned grimacing face a soft rain of cold, damp tresses.

When Mrs Townsend brought Frenchal's morning tea at eight o'clock, she knocked without being able to make him hear. Presently she walked in and pulled up the blind. Then she turned, looked at the bed, and uttered scream after scream, which brought her husband to her side.

It was a doctor who, speaking in low tones to others in the room, presently drew down the blind again.

WARNING WHISPERS

Beach and Dolby were hanged at the County Gaol at eight o'clock on a Thursday morning; and the village, if it made somewhat more than a nine days' wonder of the crime, slowly reassumed its normal air of sleepiness. Indeed, as Beach and Dolby were not natives, but casual labourers who had strayed thither from the teeming port some thirty miles distant, only one or two of the villagers were closely concerned with the tragedy. One of them was Martha Speed, the mother of the poor murdered girl.

John Archelaus Hoskins was probably the person most closely and lastingly affected. For one thing, he was the hero of the hour; and for another, he was one of the very few to whom good had been blown by this particular ill-wind. It was his evidence which had tied the nooses around the necks of Messrs Beach and Dolby, and it was he, or rather his mother, who received the reward of one hundred pounds, which had been, perhaps, a little too hastily offered. At the time he was a very promising boy of eight.

Nothing could shake young Hoskins' testimony. Certainly the two barristers could neither bully him nor cast a doubt upon his word. He was clear, cool, intelligent, and his little piping voice penetrated to the farthest corner of the hushed court. As he was passing Tumbledown Barn he had heard two men coming out, and had hidden behind the opposite hedge until they were gone. He had hidden because he had been poaching trout in Squire Pollard's stream, and he didn't know who was coming. He recognized Beach by the black patch he wore over his left eye, and Dolby by his stoop and slight lameness.

He had seen the two men dabble their hands in a ditch not twenty yards from where he was hiding, and heard one say—he didn't know which—'You'll 'ave to burn that coat o' yourn.'

Small wonder, in the circumstances, that John Archelaus Hoskins, the orphaned son of a butcher's assistant, became the hero of his native village. An older head than his might easily have been turned, for there was not a man, woman or child but made much of him. In a community of thick-wits his precocious intelligence shone like a candle flame in a dark room.

Three days after the trial old Squire Pollard came plodding down the village street on a cob which looked ridiculously small for him. He was elderly—a childless widower, and something of an eccentric. It pleased him to appear in public looking like a small farmer on the verge of bankruptcy, but he was well known to have more money than he could conveniently spend. Narrow and fanatical in his religious views, he was also hard and mean in nine-tenths of his dealings, but indulged now and then in surprising bursts of generosity.

Outside Mrs Hoskins's cottage he dismounted, and was received by the smirking matron, who dusted a chair for him in the front room and fussed around him like a distracted hen.

'Well, Mrs Hoskins,' said he, 'all the excitement over now, eh? Settling down again to ordinary everyday life? Excitement bad for all of us. How's the boy?'

'Oh, he's at school, sir,' said Mrs Hoskins. 'He's still a bit excited-like. But we can't expect old heads on young shoulders, can we, sir?'

The squire nodded. 'He's a smart lad for his age,' he said, thoughtfully.

'Ay, he is that, sir. He's the apple of 'is mother's eye. You wouldn't believe what a good boy 'e is.'

'Hum! I have an idea he'd been poaching in my stream when he saw those two miscreants——'

'Ah, sir, if I'd only known that at the time! But we can't expect old heads on young shoulders, as I said before, can we, sir? And if 'e *'adn't* been fishin' that evenin——'

Squire Pollard nodded again.

'Just so! Poaching's wrong, though. Wicked. Stealing. Still, we'll say no more about that.'

'Thank you, sir. The pore little man's been punished enought already. He can't get out of 'is 'ead the way them two villains scowled at him while he was givin' evidence against 'em. He 'ad a nightmare about it last night. I'm sure, sir, if they could do him a mischief they would.'

The squire smiled wryly.

'Well, they'll never be able to hurt young John or anybody else. Make him understand that. When do you expect him back from school, Mrs Hoskins?'

'In about half an hour, sir.'

'Very well, I'll wait. Does he know his catechism?'

The woman smiled broadly.

'Why, sir,' she said, 'you examined the children yourself and give my Jacky first prize.'

'Bless me! So I did. Knows his catechism, eh? Well, I've been thinking! He seems a very bright boy indeed. Ought to have a real chance in life. I don't want to take him away from you, Mrs Hoskins—only to go away to school. And I'll see you don't lose by it. I haven't a son of my own——'

He broke off abruptly and hitched his cloth gaiters. Mrs Hoskings flinched and coloured as if the hand of prosperity had struck a sudden blow at her.

'He's a good boy,' was all she could say.

When Master Hoskins arrived home half an hour later, kicking another boy's cap down the garden path, he was surprised to find an august presence in the front room.

'Come here,' the squire greeted him. 'Come here and tell me what happened in 1815.'

'Battle o' Waterloo, sir,' said Master Hoskins, promptly.

The year before a very much older boy had received a shilling from Squire Pollard for answering the self-same question. Since then not a boy in the village but knew the date, for other shillings might be forthcoming. But the squire had forgotten, and the triumph of John Archelaus Hoskins was complete.

Next day, when the new favourite of fortune met Anne Peters, a damsel of his own years, he haughtily declined to play with her.

'I shan't be able to play with you no more, Anne,' he said. 'Haven't 'ee heard as Squire Pollard be goin' to make a gentleman of me?'

Miss Peters put out her tongue at him and made a remark which would have staggered her Sunday School mistress.

'Mother says,' she added, 'that your luck come to you by an evil road and you'll get no good of it.'

'Sour grapes!' retorted young Hoskins.

The first step towards raising young Hoskins from the level of the peasantry was taken at once. He was provided with stiff clothes and made to wear every day the hard, wide collars he had hitherto worn only on Sundays. He was then sent to a distant vicarage, where a large family of children bullied him and derided him until his nouns agreed with his verbs and, bit by bit, he lost most of his broad country accent.

At the age of ten he was sent to an establishment where boys were prepared for the Navy and the Public Schools. There he gave out that his parents were both dead and that he was the nephew of Squire Pollard, a most important man, from whom one day he would inherit several millions of pounds. That kind of braggadocio was, however, kicked out of him before he was ready to take another step.

Squire Pollard had entered the boy at Charterhouse, but, when he was fourteen, and ready to sit for the entrance examination, the old man had a sudden fit of economy, and young Hoskins was despatched to King Edward the Sixth School, Somewhere-or-Other.

It was a good school, although inexpensive and its endowment provided for half a dozen scholarships at Oxford and Cambridge. Young Hoskins, at the age of eighteen, took one to the value of one hundred pounds per annum, and duly went up to one of the smaller colleges at Cambridge.

The scholarship was his crowning triumph in the sight of the squire, who was now turned seventy and beginning to feel his years. He regarded the young man more than ever as a son, and sent him up to the University with an allowance which he regarded as princely, and which really was quite reasonable.

Meanwhile young Hoskins had spent half his school holidays with his mother and half at the Hall. Old Mrs Hoskins, who had a gift for attracting charitable notice, now occupied a very superior cottage, and imitated the dress and manners of the vicar's wife. Squire Pollard had duly seen that she lost nothing by the partial surrender of her son. She was painstaking, if not always correct, in the use of her aspirates, and inclined to patronise her less fortunate neighbours.

The village had not forgotten the murder, but it had grown used to the distinction conferred by it. Tumbledown Barn was still pointed out to strangers, and, of course, it achieved a reputation for being haunted.

One night, in the long vacation at the end of his first year at Cambridge, young Hoskins was standing at the door of the superior cottage, talking to his mother. He was then just twenty, and had grown into a tall, slim youngster with nothing of the stolid heaviness of his labouring forebears apparent in his build. Dark-haired, dark-eyed, and rather pale, he had his full share of good looks, and these were of a

softer and more feminine type than one would have expected after seeing the photographs of the bright boy about whom all England had
talked for a day.

'Who is she, mother?' he asked, with a careless nod towards the back
of a girl who had just passed the gate.

'She? You used to know her once. You used to play with her when
you was both children. But you've forgotten her now. And very right
you should, I'm sure.'

'That's not her name, mother,' he said, laughing.

'To be sure. Her name's Anne Peters, and a nice, fast piece of goods
she is too, I've heard.'

'Anne Peters!' He was stroking his chin as old men stroke their
beards. 'I remember, of course. I'm afraid we quarrelled after—that.
She's grown up rather pretty.'

Mrs Hoskins sniffed.

'I hope,' she said, 'my Jacky won't have any truck with the likes
of her. The squire wouldn't like you to mix with village people.'

He laughed, and bent to kiss her.

'You needn't worry, mother,' he said. 'I wouldn't offend the old boy
for worlds. Besides, I prefer the society of ladies.'

'You're not going out now?'

'Yes. I promised I'd look the old boy up before he went to bed, and
he goes pretty early now. I shan't be long.'

He disappeared into the dusk, and his way happened to be up the
hill whither Anne Peters had gone.

'Anne!' he called to her, softly. 'Anne!'

She turned and saw him abreast of her, his hat lifted.

'Don't you remember me, Anne?' he asked, with a little laugh.

'It's Mr Hoskins,' she said.

'I thought you'd forgotten.'

'I thought *you'd* forgotten, Mr Hoskins. What do you want with me?'

She did not speak at a cultured pitch, but her accent was almost
pure. Like many village girls of this generation, she had striven after
that mysterious thing which she called refinement.

'Nothing,' he said, in answer to her question. 'But we're going the
same way, and we're old friends. Won't you let me walk with you?'

He saw her profile cut clear in the faint light which pierced the ragged
foliage overhead. Almost Greek it was, to an eye already critical of
women, save that the chin was a thought too prominent and the lips
were pouting.

'I can't stop you, can I?' she asked. 'But you're a gentleman now.

Why do you want to walk with me?'

'Where are you going?' he asked, ignoring her question.

'Never you mind.'

'Is it to meet somebody?'

'Perhaps. Why?'

'Only because I'm jealous, Anne.'

She laughed quite prettily. She could take a hand in this game as well as he.

'You're at Cambridge College, aren't you?' she asked. 'Do they learn you to flirt there?'

'It's a natural gift. I've been taught, however, to recognize beauty when I see it. You're a lovely kid, Anne. I expect a dozen of these louts have told you that a hundred times.'

'It doesn't follow as I believe them.'

'But you believe me. I'm an expert.' He laughed, and linked his arm in hers. 'You're not going out with any of these ticks tonight. You're coming for a walk with me.'

Her quick little brain busied itself in an instant with a hundred possibilities. Nowadays the village despised young Hoskins for a gentleman who was not a real gentleman. But there was glamour about him—a nice surface polish—and one day he was going to be very rich. If a girl were only clever enough——'

'What would squire say,' she inquired, archly, 'if he knew you were taking me out?'

'What the eye doesn't see—you know, Anne.'

She made a half-hearted attempt to rid herself of his arm 'There you are!' she said. 'He wouldn't like you to be flirting with a girl like me.'

'I don't see eye to eye with him in everything. He ought at least to admit my good taste, Anne. You are a dear, you know.'

He disengaged his arm from hers, and this time slipped it around her waist. She, on her part, let her head fall back against his shoulder, as she would have done with any other rustic swain with whom she walked on a dark evening. Thus they descended the hill to where a five-barred gate gave entrance to a farmyard, and, close to one of the granite posts a black barn thrust one of its corners through the ragged hedge.

Anne halted, and brought him to a halt.

'You remember?' she asked.

'God! Yes!' He drew and expelled an audible breath. 'There's the spot over there where I hid that night.'

'Have you been inside?' she whispered.

'Never since. Come on.'

She uttered a little provoking laugh.

'You're as nervous as a thoroughbred!' she exclaimed, and he affected to ignore the double meaning. 'They say the place is haunted. You don't believe that, do you?'

'It ought to be!'

'What? You at Cambridge College and believe in ghosts?'

'Why not? There are a lot of men up at Cambridge who do. There's a little society of us who investigate such things, and I can tell you there is a lot in it. There's a Scotsman up at Trinity who is what they call a clairvoyant. Do you know what he told me, Anne?'

She shook her head. She was smiling, and her eyes were full of amusement and unbelief—tenderly contemptuous they looked in the dusk.

'He told me, Anne,' young Hoskins continued, in a strained, hushed voice, 'that two evil spirits dogged me, seeking to hurt me. One took the shape of a man with a black patch over his eye. Do you remember Beach, or were you too young?'

She nodded, but she was still smiling.

'The Scotchman knew about you,' she said, 'and tried to frighten you.'

'No. Nobody up there knows that I'm the boy who got those two fellows hanged.'

Anne plucked at his sleeve.

'Come and peep inside.'

'No. The dog would bark and rouse people.'

'They keep him the other side, where the fowls are.'

'Aren't there fowls roosting in the barn?'

'They say fowls won't roost there. There's only a couple of old carts and some straw.'

'Anne,' he whispered, 'the place *is* haunted!'

'Are you afraid to peep inside—even with me with you?'

'Of course not! Only I——'

'Come on, then!'

Unwillingly he pushed open the farm gate and led the way on tiptoe to the door of the Tumbledown Barn. He held the door open for her to enter first, and followed, striking a match.

The barn smelt damp within, and was in an advanced stage of disrepair. The faintly luminous sky shone through a dozen gaps in the roof. The match, flaming bravely in the still air, lit up the place and showed the two old farm carts, a litter of old rubbish, a pile of straw.

Hoskins lit another match when the first burned out. His hand was not quite steady.

'Why don't they burn the place?' he demanded, in a harsh whisper. 'It's full of evil! I can feel it! Can't you feel it too? Oh, let's go!'

'Why,' said Anne, 'you're afraid.'

'Only because I understand—and feel! *They*'re here—Beach and Dolby! Don't you feel that the place is devil-ridden? It's bad—bad! I could be cruel here—cruel as hell—damnably cruel! I could——'

He broke off suddenly. Before the match went out the girl could see little spots of moisture shining on his brow.

'Why,' she whispered, with a little, soft, wheedling laugh, 'you don't want to hurt me, do you?'

She stood before him, dimly revealed in the deep gloom. The soft bright in her eyes mocked the light of love. The shadows which hid part of her beauty hinted at an even richer loveliness. Something in him, beyond his control, responded to the silent call of her.

'Hurt you?' he heard himself cry. 'I hurt you? I who love you—love you—love you! Little Anne!'

His arms were around her. His lips found hers and clung to them. In the darkness she gave him kiss for kiss, until she felt his body start like a hooked fish, and he seized her and blundered wildly with her towards the gleaming rectangle of the open door.

'Didn't you hear?' he stammered as he faced her, gasping, in the clean air outside. 'Oh, God, didn't you hear? *Somebody laughed!*'

When Hoskins finally came down from Cambridge two years later, he went to stay with Squire Pollard, whose remaining days were not many. The old man had already spoken to Hoskins quite openly about his will.

'I hope you'll take the old name when I'm gone,' he said. 'You're fit to bear it. You're a clever boy, and I think you've been a good boy. Only one breath of scandal about you has reached my ears, and that I wouldn't believe.'

There was a hard light in old Pollard's eyes, and the younger man coloured uncomfortably.

'What was that, sir?' he asked.

'Oh, never mind! People wag their tongues a deal too much. I've already told you I don't believe 'em. If I did, you wouldn't set foot across this threshold again. I'd not go to my God—as soon I must— and have to admit that I'd connived at wickedness in others. A hussy like that Anne Peters deserves to be——'

'Ah!'

'What do you mean by "Ah!"?'

Young Hoskins knew how to assume the *rôle* of an injured innocent.

'Because I've spoken to her when I've met her out!' he exclaimed.
'I suppose that was enough to start a rumour in this scandal-whispering
hole. I used to play with her when we were both children. Thanks to
you, sir, my position's changed since then. But one doesn't like to cut
people one used to know. It would seem too foolish and snobbish, since
not a soul in the village but knows my history.'

The old man nodded, and the younger one wished his eyes were
not so alert and keen.

'I shouldn't speak to her any more,' he said. 'It is her own fault if
she has placed herself beyond the pale.'

The conversation ended there, but a new dread was born in the
young man's heart. Except for an accident, old Pollard's money was
now as good as his own. He told himself that he had been a fool to
risk so much for this rustic light-o'-love who, after all, had served no
more than to dispel some of the dullness of his vacations.

For a long time past he had contemplated breaking off his association with Anne Peters. Now he saw the necessity for such a step. If
rumour grew into a circumstantial story, built up out of evidence, he
knew old Pollard's will would be in the fire and a new one drafted.
For a man who firmly believed that he was dogged by two evil spirits
which were determined to compass his ruin, he had to admit to himself that he had behaved like a fool. So, on the following night, when
he went to meet Anne Peters at Tumbledown Barn, he had decided
that it was for the last time.

Of course, he expected trouble. Anne would object to being cast off,
and he might have to make her a present in money. This, although
he was not famous for being open-handed, troubled him very little,
since he had over three hundred pounds in the bank, which he had
thriftily put by out of his allowance. All he needed to do was to keep
her quiet temporarily until the breath was out of his benefactor's body.
He might even make her a vague promise of subsequent marriage
which he need not fulfil.

It was as if by some queer process of telepathy Anne Peters was aware
of his intention that night, and had determined to profit herself by
striking the first blow. He saw that something was amiss with her while
he stood in the entrance to the barn, a lighted match between his hol-
lowed hands. She did not trip towards him and offer to kiss him, as
was her wont, but sat aloof on the dropped pole of an old wagon.

'You're late, as usual,' she greeted him. 'You're late every time. It's no way to treat a lady. I suppose you're afraid to be here a minute by yourself. Afraid the ghost with a patch over his eye will get you!'

He grimaced at this loose reference to one of his personal devils in that of all places. Then he smiled, and, as he struck another match, managed to answer lightly:

'What's the matter with you, old thing? You've got a grouch on you tonight.'

'I'm sick of it all,' she answered. 'Sick and tired.'

So was he, but he could not say so. His voice mocked the accents of a lover as he crossed the barn towards her.

'Poor little old Anne! Never mind, poor little girl. Very soon now——'

She stood up and faced him purposely. He could see that she had been lashing herself into a fury by the mental repetition of her real or assumed grievances.

'For God's sake, don't give me any more promises!' she cried. 'I've been listening to 'em, off and on, for two years, till I'm sick. Promises aren't solid things to live on—yours especially! I've had enough of it.'

'Anne!' he exclaimed.

'Yes, Anne!' she mocked.

'What do you want?'

'What I'm going to get. You're going to marry me.'

'Of course,' he murmured. 'Some day.'

'Not some day. At once.'

Fear began to tingle in his blood. He leaned against one of the wheels of the wagon and avoided meeting her eyes in the gloom.

'Is there any reason,' he asked, 'why we should be married soon?'

A moment elapsed before she answered: 'Yes'.

'That's a lie,' he said; and he knew suddenly in his heart that she was lying. A sudden fury shook him, for that she should try to deceive him—a man of the world, as he accounted himself—by this threadbare trick.

'Lie or not,' she answered, 'you'll marry me within three days, or you'll regret it.'

It was strange how suddenly he hated her, how hard he found it to school his tongue in replying.

'Then you'll marry a pauper. He'll disinherit me.'

'Because I'm not good enough for you?' she sneered. 'Because I'm a common girl and you're a gentleman?'

She had stung him again. In cold fury he answered:

'Don't hold me responsible for his views. Why can't you wait until he's dead? It won't be long.'

She broke out into ironic laughter.

'You think I'm a fine fool, don't you? I don't want your promises. You'll marry me in three days, Jack Hoskins.'

'He——'

'He needn't know. We can be married by licence over at Towcester.'

'That couldn't be done in three days.'

'Haven't you heard of a special licence?'

He turned at bay then, openly savage.

'Why can't you wait until he's dead?'

'Because a dead man can't alter his will. A lot you'd care then! Do you think I don't know you? You'll marry me within three days or I'll go to him and tell him everything.'

Vaguely he was aware that his control had slipped from him. He was like a ridden horse mastered by strange hands. Feebly he strove against something that he knew to be evil. When he answered it was as if he listened to a strange voice which spoke for him.

'Of course, he'd take your word against mine!'

'He'd have to, with the letters I've got to show—the letters posted from Trumpington, in case anybody in the village should see the Cambridge postmark.'

'Anne! Anne!' He heard the name slide out of his mouth all oily and wheedling. 'You wouldn't ruin me, would you, Anne?'

She mocked him, mincing her accent in imitation of his. Strange, he thought, that she did not realise her peril; strange that she did not see the change in him. He felt himself moving in a black cloud which should have been visible to her. It seemed to him that the darkness around him was riven continually by small, swift flashes of light, so that he saw eyes watching him, grinning lips, twisted, malevolent features which he remembered across the years. For one immeasurable fraction of time he was back in the witness-box; his little, piping voice filled the great room; and these same eyes which gloated over him now shot hatred at him across the well of the court.

Anne was speaking again. He could hardly hear her. There were voices whispering to him that if she were dead she couldn't speak at all—couldn't even tell old Pollard the story of this liaison. Her words blent with these whisperings into a murmurous babble.

'You never meant to marry me!' he heard her say.

'Marry you!' Was it his own voice—that sneering snarl? 'You, a village slut with a kiss for every Tom, Dick, and Harry! Marry you!'

She would have answered him in kind, but he had drawn near to her; and in the gloom she saw his face, all wrung and devilish.

'Jack!' she cried. And in that, the last coherent word she ever uttered, there was a wail of terror and dismay.

Presently it was all so still and silent that the rats came out of their refuge in the heap of straw.

Next morning the village was electrified.

All previous excitement was surpassed a thousandfold when it became known that Tumbledown Barn had claimed a second victim; that Anne Peters had been strangled there, and that 'Mr Hoskins' had been arrested in connection with the crime.

A hundred rumours were current during the day. Among them, the most persistent and—as subsequent events proved—the best founded, was to the effect that Hoskins had already confessed. At six o'clock the tap-room of the inn was filled by an eager crowd of yokels, most of whom remembered the previous crime, all eagerly discussing the new sensation.

Old Gaudy, the badger, voiced the sentiments of most of the others.

'I mind them other two very well,' he said. 'Beach with his one eye, and Dolby with his stoop and shamblin' limp. Bad men they was both, as most of us knowed from the moment they set foot in the village. But who'd ha' thought it o' young Hoskins? Why, not a man or woman here that thought him worse nor a stuck-up calf! Truly the ways of men be past understanding.'

The entry of the village policeman created a hubbub in the crowded bar. Police Constable Clarke had been absent all day at the county town, whither he had taken his prisoner. He was new to the neighbourhood, and therefore able to be more impressive than a native. With promotion already within his grasp, he entered the house with a swagger which was almost pardonable. He was the man of the hour.

'I can't tell none o' you nothing,' he said, as he accepted a pint of beer, and made his voice carry above the clamour of a score of questioners. 'It ain't accordin' to regulations. You'll hear all about it in good time.'

For five minutes he was adamant, until Seeley, the grocer, spoke to him.

'But Mr Clarke,' he said, 'if it be true that you went into the barn and found him in the act of burying the body in the straw—that's what we've heard tell—what made you go to the barn at all?'

The constable coughed and expanded his chest.

'I don't mind tellin' you that,' he said, 'as there's two missin' witnesses I've got to make inquiries for, and p'raps some o' you can put me on the right road. Not as these 'ere witnesses are necessary in view of what's happened, but it's regulations. Two men came round to my cottage yesterday evenin' and told me there was trouble up at the barn. Two tramps, I think they was. Leastways, I haven't seen them hereabouts. They'd gone by the time I'd got my boots laced, and I didn't see 'em very clearly through the window.'

'Wot was they like, these two?' questioned Seeley.

The constable considered.

'Well,' he said at last, 'it seemed to me that one wore a black patch over his left eye, and the other 'ad stoopin shoulders and seemed to limp.'

CROOKBACK

TREMLETT told us the story around the drawing-room fire one Sunday night. For some reason the half-dozen of us who made up the weekend party had risen above frivolity and entered upon a state of high seriousness, which was very unusual on such occasions. I don't know who gave us the lead. I only know that we drifted from a desultory conversation about the relationship between spiritualism and the churches into a discussion on spiritualism itself.

The believers and unbelievers were equally divided, and the argument that ensued was about as heated as the circumstances permitted. Everybody was deadly serious. Such humour as there was had a savour of bitterness.

Young Parslow wanted to know how anybody could follow a cult which claimed to produce the miraculous, and only succeeded in satisfying the blindly credulous with a few transparent frauds. What could any man with a sound and logical mind believe, in view of the fact that every medium who had come prominently before the public, had sooner or later been caught in the act of cheating? Sift the evidence, and you found none, unless you took the word of a fraud and a self-deceiver. If the dead could speak to us, he said, we should know all about the next world from the first voice beyond the grave. Surely we thought better of our dead than to suppose they would return and shake tambourines for our amusement at the bidding of some vulgar hireling. What was not vulgar about the proceedings was farcical.

He went on to remark that there was no real evidence of continuity. Occasionally one heard of a ghost story which seemed possible to believe; but nearly always a thorough search yielded an explanation. If it were possible to get a sort of trunk call through to the other world, our dead would surely have something better to tell us than the inane stock phrases which the charlatans kept for their customers.

I saw Mrs Richardson quivering slightly. Her lips were drawn in a tight line. She was one of those women who had outworn many creeds, and now clung tenaciously to the last, as if fearing to be left with nothing. I could feel a tension in the atmosphere, and knew that there would be trouble unless Tremlett interposed.

I glanced across at our host, and found myself meeting his gaze.

'What's your opinion about it?' I asked, before Mrs Richardson could mass her forces for attack.

He shook his head and laughed.

'No, you don't, young man. I decline to be drawn into this. I believe in what I call ghosts, which shows that I have a highly unscientific mind. Parslow has just been saying that there is an explanation to every ghost story—I suppose he meant a material one—if one searched for it enough. I think I could tell him something which came under my notice, and happened in this very house, which would trouble him to explain away.'

Mrs Richardson was diverted from her intended attack, as I think Tremlett intended she should be. She looked across at him eagerly. Parslow took up the challenge by demanding to hear the story. A desultory chorus from all of us seconded him.

Tremlett lit a cigarette, and gazed thoughtfully into the fire.

'I haven't told the story for years,' he said. 'One is liable to be disbelieved or laughed at. However, if you want corroboration my sister Muriel and Arthur Brinkner will tell you the same extraordinary things, although neither of them cares to talk about it.'

Tremlett cleared his throat, and, after a moment's consideration, began the story which I am about to repeat in his own words as faithfully as I can remember them.

We used to come here as children (said Tremlett) when there seemed little chance of our ever inheriting the property. The house belonged to our uncle Wilby, who was really no uncle at all, but a distant connection who liked to consider us as his nephew and niece. He was devoted to children, and used to fill the house with us and our small cousins.

I remember him as a very tall grey-haired man with a very kind face, and a very gentle voice, about the last man in the world you would take for a retired colonel. The most delightful time of the day was always the hour before bedtime, when he would have us children into his study—it's the morning room now—and tell us stories. The room was always like an oven, for he had been too long in India to keep warm at home without enormous fires, and it smelt deliciously of his cigars. I can see us all now in a half-circle around the fire, gradually creeping farther and farther away from it, and hugging our little roasted legs.

He had a delightful way of telling stories, and his repertoire was long and varied. Nearly always, if one looked for it, there was a moral, although the pill was always too thickly coated with sugar for us to realise it. He had a great horror of cruelty, and he was always driving it into our heads to be kind to each other and to animals.

I suppose he made up most of his stories, for he was clever enough to intrigue our interest by giving them a setting familiar to some or all of us.

I wish I could remember in detail a story he told us about this very house. We children used to love the place, partly because it was just the sort of house one used to read about in wildly exciting mystery stories. We thought it was at least a thousand years old, and of course, part of it *is* pre-Elizabethan.

Muriel has only a hazy recollection of the tale he told us about the poor hunchback youth who was heir to a great property some time in the seventeenth century. His uncle, who was the next heir, had at least one good reason for hating him, and caused the wretched youth to visit him in this very house, after which he was never seen again. I know it reminded us all a little of the Babes in the Wood. I know the exciting part of the story, and incidentally the moral, consisted of the dreadful things that happened to the uncle and all who had a hand in the murder—for, murder it doubtless was, although the assassins were never brought to book. Muriel and I both forgot the story too long for either of us to recapture more than a vague recollection of it.

I was twenty-eight and Muriel was twenty-two when poor uncle Wilby died, and I found myself to be heir to this house and the greater part of his property. I had a clerkship in the Foreign Office at the time, and Muriel was keeping house for me in a small flat off Sloane Square. Arthur Brinkner was then our most frequent visitor, but although we had been friends ever since either of us could remember, I did not flatter myself that he came to see me. Anybody could tell in what direction those two were drifting.

It was late in September when Muriel and I came down here to take up the reins. Mrs Watts, the housekeeper, received us in a most stately manner, and showed us all round the house as if we had never been in it before. She had an enormous bunch of keys, every one of which was labelled, and she took us into every room, expatiating on its merits or its demerits.

I said every room. I meant every room except one. There was a bedroom in the front—the one next to yours, Parslow—which we found locked, and for which she had no key.

'Colonel Wilby was always funny about that room,' she said. It had always been kept locked, and if there were a key to it, it certainly was not in her possession.

I remember Muriel and I were a little amused about it, and even made jokes about poor Uncle Wilby keeping a Bluebeard's chamber. I was indifferent as to whether the room was opened or not, but Muriel said she couldn't endure the thought of living in the same house as a room which she knew nothing about. I daresay feminine curiosity had a great deal to do with it. Anyway, I gave way to her and sent for a locksmith.

If we had expected anything in the nature of a find we were doomed to disappointment, although, except that it had no dressing-room, it was one of the best bedrooms in the house. We found inside a stripped double bed, some heavy old-fashioned furniture, a few early Victorian novels, which seemed to indicate the period when the room was last used, and any quantity of dust.

Nobody seemed to know why the room had been kept locked, and we accepted the most feasible explanation—namely, that the key had been lost, and Uncle Wilby, having already more bedrooms than he required, had never troubled himself about it. Muriel took rather a liking to the room, and as we still had some workmen on the premises she had it redecorated and made it what she called 'Pretty.'

We had been in possession about three weeks before Muriel had the house more or less to her taste; and during those three weeks she had been telling me about five times a day that we ought to ask some people down.

I was not in those days a very gregarious animal, and I rather shrank from the idea of a house-warming. Fortunately, I had a safe card to play in resisting Muriel's suggestion.

'We'll have a crowd down later at Christmas time,' I said. 'Meanwhile I'd rather we only had Arthur.'

Muriel's argument against 'only Arthur' was a mere pretence, and Arthur Brinkner duly arrived one Wednesday in the middle of October. It was amusing to watch Muriel playing hostess to him in this new environment.

'I've put you in the Mystery Room,' she said, as the three of us sat at tea in the hall. 'You won't mind, will you?'

'The Mystery Room?' said Arthur. 'What's that?'

'Oh,' returned Muriel, 'it's a room Uncle Wilby always kept locked, because it's haunted by all sorts of dreadful apparitions, and everybody who sleeps there either goes mad or becomes white-haired in a single night. But I know you're not afraid, Arthur.'

'Being a very courageous man,' he laughed, 'perhaps I shall only go iron-grey.'

'Don't let Muriel fill your head with a lot of nonsense,' I said. 'We found the room locked for the simple reason that the key has been lost. It's like Muriel to invent a ghost story about it. If you don't like the idea of it, there are plenty of other rooms. I don't know why Muriel put you in there.'

To this day I believe that Muriel had in the back of her mind some faint suspicion that the room had once been supposed to be haunted, and that she put Arthur into it by way of an experiment. Arthur, as you all know, was a hard-headed brute who had very little fear of anything which was tangible, and still less of anything which was not.

'That's all right,' he said good-humouredly. 'If I don't like the room, I shan't be afraid to shout.'

As a matter of fact he liked the room very much. It faced south, and got all the sun, and all through that October we had been having glorious weather.

Next morning when he came down to breakfast he found Muriel already at the table, and she greeted him with a laughing, 'Well, Arthur, seen the ghost?'

'Four altogether,' he replied in the same tone of badinage. 'The mediaeval gentleman,' he added, turning to me, 'who walked about with a sword stuck through his chest was easily the worst. Really, Dicky, you ought to get him exorcised.'

'Most people,' said I, 'prefer him to the Jacobean lady who wrings her hands.'

'Oh, ' he answered, 'she was only on duty for about five minutes. Rotten lot of ghosts you keep here. Four of them and not a decent hollow groan between the lot.'

I think Muriel was a little disappointed at her Mystery Room having apparently failed to provide our guest with an uncanny experience. After breakfast she collared one of the grooms and drove over to Gaybury to do some shopping. Arthur, I knew, would have liked to go with her, but he had to put up with my society instead for the morning.

I subjected him to the usual infliction which a guest has to endure when paying his first visit to a country house, particularly when the property is still a new toy to his host. I showed him round. Together we inspected fields and farms, cattle and horses and pig-stys.

I noticed that he yawned several times and thought it rather unfriendly of him to be bored. As we were crossing a field of stubble I said to him suddenly:

'You look rather tired, old man. Is this boring you to death?'

'No, it's not that, but I *am* a bit tired,' he admitted.

'What's the matter? Didn't you sleep well?'

'Not very,' he replied, 'but then I never do for the first time in a strange room. I always have to be fagged out before I can drop off to sleep at an hotel, for instance.'

'No ghostly disturbances?' I asked, smiling.

'I was unusually restless,' he said, acknowledging my worn-out pleasantry with a faint smile, 'and I had very little sleep indeed. I—'

He ended abruptly, and I saw his expression suddenly change. He was looking ahead into a grass field which we were approaching, and following the direction of his gaze I saw a cow with some strange malformation of one of its forelegs.

'Look at that brute of a cow!' he exclaimed in a voice which rang with disgust.

'I suppose it's nothing very serious, poor devil,' I said, 'or they'd have to have it destroyed.'

'I hate anything deformed or misshapen,' he said between his teeth. 'I could kill any monstrosity. I'd like to kill that infernal cow!'

I looked at him queerly. I thought I knew Arthur almost as well as I knew myself, and I was a little surprised, not so much at the words but at the tone in which they were uttered. I had previously heard him express repugnance for anything freakish or malformed, but it had always been repugnance mingled with pity. But his tone and expression now implied hatred, a passionate, bitter hatred. For a moment I saw Cruelty peeping out of his eyes. This was very strange, and—it wasn't Arthur!

A moment later, he laughed and said: 'I know you've always thought that there was a queer kink in me. We've all got our pet abominations.'

This was the first straw which afterwards showed me which way the wind had begun to blow. A strange depression settled on me for the rest of the morning. I had an uncomfortable suspicion that Arthur was not the fellow I thought he was, that there was a bad streak in him somewhere, of which for the first time he had just given me a glimpse.

During the next week, when Arthur and I were pretty constantly together, I saw, or thought I saw, a number of little changes in him, probably because I had set myself to look for them. He had not sought as much of Muriel's society as I had expected, and seemed to look more to me for companionship. He had been with us exactly a week when there came a sudden sequence of happenings which shook me more than a little.

I had just finished dressing for dinner, that is to say, except for my tie. I could always tie my own bows at a pinch, but I always preferred somebody else to do them for me, as my own efforts were never too successful. I never kept a valet, but one of the men had a spare-time job of brushing my clothes and putting them away. Arthur had lately been knotting my tie for me, so I went round to his room.

But this evening he had forgotten my needs and gone downstairs, so I walked along to Muriel's room and called to her to come out. She came out promptly, and I was shocked and surprised to see that she was crying. But in the midst of her tears she was smiling, and I heard her utter a little puzzled laugh.

'I don't know what's the matter with me, Dicky,' she said before I could utter a word. 'It all came on me just a moment ago. I felt so terriby sorry for something.'

'Sorry for what?' I exclaimed.

'I don't know.' She laughed again and dabbed at her eyes. 'That's the absurd part of it. I feel that I've seen somebody in the most dreadful trouble, and—well, of course, I haven't!'

Now Muriel was never an emotional or imaginative sort of girl, and I thought I saw through a rather shallow artifice. I came to the conclusion that she had had some row with Arthur which neither of them had told me about. However, to humour her and not let her see what I suspected, I said:

'What an extraordinary girl you are, Muriel! Has anything of the sort ever happened to you before?'

'Yes,' she answered after a moment's hesitation, 'two or three times in the last few days, generally when I've been going to bed. I've had a most intense feeling of pity come over me. I don't mean depression, Dicky. I mean *pity*. For some reason or other I believe my nerves have all gone to pieces.'

'You with nerves, Muriel!' I exclaimed.

'Well, what else can it be? There seems to be something that seems to nudge up against me, something terror-stricken, that comes to me for protection, and looks to me for pity and love. That's how I feel.

And if that isn't a case of nerves, I should like to know what is!'

'My dear old girl,' I said seriously, 'you'd better see a doctor to-morrow.'

But I am afraid I didn't feel as serious as my voice implied. I still thought that she was throwing dust in my eyes to prevent my seeing that she had had some misunderstanding with Arthur. But if that were the case, I couldn't help wondering why Arthur hadn't told me, or why he hadn't left us. I went down to dinner pretty thoughtfully that night. I had noticed some subtle changes in Arthur, and I hated the feeling that there were many things of which I knew nothing going on around me below the surface.

We had been spending very quiet evenings. Generally Muriel played and sang to us for a little while and then went early to bed. Arthur and I generally played a hundred up, and were in our rooms before eleven. This evening was no exception as regards Muriel's departure.

I followed her up the stairs about two minutes later, for I wanted to show Arthur a letter I had just received from an old friend of ours, left in the pocket of a coat which I had discarded before dinner. I had reached the landing when I suddenly heard Muriel's voice from the passage leading to her room.

'Oh, you poor, poor darling,' it said. 'What is it then? What is the matter with you?'

I thought she was talking to some stray cat which had found its way into the house. She spoke in that crooning tone in which she addressed animals. But what she had told me before dinner was fresh in my mind, and I hastened to the corner of the passage.

There was no light burning in the passage, and the only illumination was a dull glow from the night skies diffused through the long row of windows.

Muriel was standing about half-way down the passage, her head slightly bent as if she were in search of something. And I saw, or thought I saw, something crouching against her skirt, something broken and misshapen, but not inhuman; something in an attitude of terror and supplication.

It was gone even as my heart leaped at the sight. A moment later I could scarcely have said what I thought I saw. What it actually was I could not guess; a trick of the eyes perhaps, or part of Muriel's shadow which had fallen strangely in the dim light.

'Muriel!' I cried sharply.

She started, turned, and came towards me. There was distress visible in every step, in every movement of her slim body. When she had come up to me she touched my sleeves with her hands, as a child waking from a bad dream might touch something solid and comforting.

'Oh!' she gasped, and I felt her breath fan my face.

'What's the matter, Muriel?' I asked, and my voice sounded dry and troubled.

'It came over me again—that feeling. Something tortured by fear was fawning upon me for pity and protection. Can't you feel it too? No, I can see you can't. What does it mean, Dicky? Am I going mad?'

'You are going straight to bed,' I said, 'and tomorrow we will get a good doctor to run the rule over you. Something's happened to your nerves.'

'Yes, I know that,' she agreed drearily. 'But it's over now, for the time being. I'm quite all right again now.' She smiled tremulously. 'I know I'm worrying you, Dicky, and I'm so sorry. Perhaps I shall be better tomorrow.'

Now that I was convinced of the truth of what she had previously told me I was hard put to it to know what I had best do. To make a fuss, to suggest that she ought not to be alone, might only have the effect of frightening her into the belief that she was worse than she was. I did suggest that she should send for her maid, but she shook her head.

'I'm going straight to bed,' she said. 'It won't come over me again tonight. Good-night, Dicky.'

She kissed me, took a step away from me, and then looked hurriedly back.

'Dicky! You won't say anything to Arthur about this, will you?'

'Of course not,' I said.

I went downstairs feeling pretty bad. That the bright and practical Muriel should show symptoms of a diseased imagination was something I had to dread. Here was no neurotic from whom one might expect an occasional mental relapse. I don't mind admitting now that the dreadful word Madness began to whisper itself to me, and would not be shaken from my mind.

Arthur read the letter which I had brought to show him, and we chatted awhile over its contents.

'Going to play me a hundred up?' he asked at last.

I nodded, and we went into the billiard-room. Neither of us was a great performer, and tonight we were worse than usual. After a quarter of an hour we were still in the twenties, and Arthur at last, having missed an absurdly easy losing hazard, laid down his cue.

'Let's chuck this, shall we?' he said. 'We're both hopeless. Besides, I want to talk to you before I turn in.'

I went to the rack to put away my cue, and he came and stood, hands in pockets, close behind me, resting his back against the table.

'Dicky,' he said suddenly, 'I don't know how to put this to you. Do you know, when I came down here, I came with the intention of asking Muriel to marry me?'

'I did suspect something of the sort,' I answered dryly.

'And I haven't done it. I wonder if you can guess why.'

During a bad moment I wondered if he knew of the change in Muriel.

'Old man,' he said in a shaken voice, 'I wonder if you've noticed anything peculiar about me?'

Well, I had; but apart from his little outburst out in the fields my impressions were all too vague to wear a label. So I said No.

'The fact is,' he said with a sort of dreary calmness, 'I have every reason to believe that I am going mad.'

So that was it. And there were two mad people in the house instead of one! I'm afraid my 'Nonsense, Arthur!' did not ring quite true.

'I don't mean that I'm dangerous,' he continued quietly; 'at least, not to you or Muriel, or I should have put myself out of harm's way before this.' Then his voice suddenly rose. 'But you show me anything ugly or deformed, and by God I could tear out its heart!'

As he spoke his fingers hooked involuntarily and his eyes dilated.

'Dicky,' he said, in a lower tone, 'have you ever known me to be cruel?'

'You're about the last man,' I said.

'Well, I'm not now. I could be hellishly cruel. I could be a devil to anything mis-shapen. I lie awake at night, imagining my fingers around the throat of a cringing hunchback. Yes, I don't wonder that you look at me like that. That isn't me, you know, Dicky.'

'It certainly isn't,' I agreed.

Back into my mind came the memory of the shadowy thing I thought I had seen crouching against Muriel's skirt in the passage.

'When did all this begin?' I asked.

'When I arrived here. I remember telling you I didn't sleep very well that first night. Well, lying awake, I got a sort of obsession. You know how I've always shrunk from the grotesque? I found myself actively hating something that was mis-shapen—not the hatred that one might have for an enemy, but a sort of frenzied abhorrence mixed up with—I don't know how to put it—a sort of personal grudge. And this hatred varied between all malformed beings and some particular personality which I imagined. I'm sorry to be so vague, and I'm afraid I've shocked you, Dicky. Believe me, I don't like myself a bit.'

I felt chilly and uncomfortable as I listened. I could not help remembering that this thing had come upon him in that room which Uncle Wilby had shut up. And back across the years came the vague memory of a story of his about a hunchback youth who had been done to death in this very house. Had he made up the story? Or was it true? And again, there was the strange shadow I had seen. All against my will my thoughts were leading me across the frontier of a strange territory.

'And have the same thoughts been tormenting you ever since?' I asked.

'Yes, but with a difference. My hatred has been directed almost entirely against this one particular personality. I can see it at times, but not with these eyes.' He pointed at his eyes with an excited gesture. 'It's a crookback idiot who's terrified of me, and yet he's always close by me at night, as if he can't get away. The terror of the thing and its slobbering inanity simply infuriate me. I've gone around my room, slashing with the poker, hoping to smash in its ugly skull, and always just missing the slobbering thing that blubbers and flinches and runs away from me. And all the while the saner side of me knows that it isn't there.' He uttered a short mirthless laugh. 'Well, what do you think of me, Dicky?'

'I think,' I said, 'that you ought to see a mental specialist at once.'

'Meaning that I oughtn't to stay on here? All right, I'll go to-morrow. Only it'll go with me, and I thought I had more chance of fighting it here, living with you and Muriel.'

What was that nebulous Something for which Muriel was moved to pity? Something that went from him to her for love and protection? Or was I too going mad?

'Wait a moment, old man,' I said. 'We'll suspend our judgement a bit before we decide that there's anything wrong with your head. You're pretty self-critical for a man with a mental disease. Most men afflicted in that way don't know it. Do you think it's the room which has caused all this?'

'The room?' he repeated. 'What can the room have to do with it?'

'It was shut up, and very likely with a purpose. Uncle Wilby may have slept there for all I know, and come under the same sort of influence. I remember his telling us a story once about a hunchback youth who was murdered in this very house.'

'Oh, ghosts again!' he exclaimed impatiently. 'My dear Dicky, I simply don't believe in that sort of thing. And I don't see anything—at least not in the accepted sense of the term.'

'It's strange I should have heard the story of a hunchback being killed in this house.'

'Not a bit! I'd have killed him myself!' His eyes dilated again, and he clenched his hands until his biceps quivered with the strain. 'If only this thing which obsesses me were living, tangible, Dicky, I'd tear it to pieces!'

I am quite incapable of reproducing his tone or giving the least impression of it. It literally chilled my blood.

'Arthur,' I said, 'I'm coming with you to your room. I want to see if I too am affected in any way.'

In Arthur's room I sat in an armchair by the fireplace, and he sat on the edge of the bed.

'I don't feel that way now,' he said quite calmly; 'or, if you prefer it, it isn't here. You'll feel nothing, Dicky, unless I infect you with my madness. You'd better go before I get worked up. I warn you I shan't be a pretty sight.'

'At all events I'll wait,' I said.

One can form theories very quickly, and I had already blundered a little way on the right track. I did not expect to be affected in the same way as Arthur. I never had, to begin with, his artistic sense of repulsion for what was freakish. Neither had I Muriel's keen sense of pity for those so afflicted. These different senses in them both had, it seemed to me, been intensified and distorted. It was as if both of them shared, in a sense, the same thought.

Here was Arthur hating and loathing and longing to do violence to something imaginary. There was Muriel, pitying at the same time something imaginary which came to her as if for love and protection.

We sat on smoking in silence for a long while, during which my thoughts raced ahead of me, and had to be called back from all sorts of mental labyrinths. And suddenly I began to notice that Arthur was getting uneasy. Presently he slipped down from the edge of the bed.

'Are you—?' I began.

I couldn't find the words I wanted to complete the question, but I knew he understood. He took no notice of me, however. He was staring into a corner of the room by the floor, and I saw his eyes kindle and his upper lip lift with the lust of hatred. Then from his mouth came hissing a string of lewd epithets. The change in the man, from one of the best fellows in the world to a devil incarnate was as sudden as it was startling and beastly.

I have seen a man in *delirium tremens*, but his behaviour was nothing compared with that of Arthur's. Still glaring malevolently at the corner, in which I could see nothing, he sidled to the grate and picked up the poker. Then, suddenly springing, he slashed wildly at the empty air.

'I'll have you yet!' he breathed in a dreadful whisper. 'You foul, elusive beast! I'll smash ... and smash ... and smash ...'

He was slashing this way and that as he spoke, leaping about the room, dodging and wheeling. The poker hummed in the air as he struck and struck. Under one of these blows the brass rail at the foot of the bed smashed like a glass tube. I sat like a man transfixed, unable to move or speak, as I watched that ghastly pantomime.

Suddenly he made a dash for the door as if in pursuit of something. He wrenched it open with one jerk of the hand and arm and was out and across the landing. Then I found a use for my limbs and followed him.

He was running towards the passage leading to Muriel's room, cursing and flourishing the poker as he ran. And as I turned the corner behind him, I saw Muriel standing fully dressed outside her door.

What else I saw I saw but very dimly; but I swear I saw it. Crouching against her, its brow touching her instep, was the grotesque figure of a hunchback dwarf, in the same attitude in which I had seen it before. And on the instant Muriel's voice rang out.

'Don't, Arthur! Don't! Oh, don't hurt him for my sake, Arthur!'

He had his back to me, but I was somehow as well aware of the sudden change wrought in him as if I had seen his face. He seemed to trip and stumble into a walk. He ceased to brandish the poker, letting it swing gently for a moment, and then dropping it almost noiselessly upon the carpet.

'Muriel!' he said, in a queer, strangled sort of voice.

It seemed that to those two, who had never previously uttered a word of love, had suddenly been given a perfect understanding. When he reached her he took her quite naturally into his arms, and the Shape at her feet melted away like mist from a glass.

The house was no place for either of them. We all three went away on the morrow to Bournemouth, and while we were there we reasoned the thing out amongst us as best we could. Arthur and Muriel were both quite normal as soon as they had left the house. Muriel had been feeling too upset to go to bed that night, and had had a sudden impulse to rush out of her room and protect the Thing that had been seeking her pity and protection when she met us both in the passage.

Now we all three decided that Uncle Wilby's story about the hunch-back was at least founded on fact. At some time during the history of the house some afflicted youth had been sent here to be murdered. Probably the poor wretch more than suspected his fate, and his terror whetted the hatred of the fiend who subsequently murdered him.

We agreed that the murder probably took place in the room in which Arthur had slept, and that certain forces had lain dormant there ever since—fiendish hatred and loathing on the one hand and gibbering terror on the other.

People of certain temperaments who used the room were liable to be affected. There was Arthur, with his natural repulsion for what Nature had mis-made, an easy victim to the force that overwhelmed him. His hatred re-created an object in the spirit of the poor mur-dered youth, who fled for pity and succour to the kindest and sweetest spirit in the house. Perhaps in those last terrible days of his life there had been a woman in the house who pitied him and yet could not save him.

It is almost useless to theorise over these things. We shall never know in this world.

When we returned I had the walls of that bedroom taken down, and in one of them we found the bones of a boy or an undersized man. They were not the bones of a normally shaped person.

Arthur and Muriel married, as you know, and you don't need me to tell you that Arthur is one of the best fellows in the world, without a spark of cruelty in his composition.

I don't think it would hurt anybody to sleep in that room now. We don't keep it shut up, but we don't put people in there. I don't believe in taking risks.

And now I think I've propounded a riddle which it would puzzle any materialist to answer.

FOR THE LOCAL RAG

Early in December it was customary for Mr Marvell, the editor and proprietor of the *Foxbridge Independent*, to edge his way into the reporters'-room and say to Dorby:

'Oh, Dorby, about our Christmas supplement. We'll have a short story from you as usual this year. Have it ready in plenty of time, won't you?'

And Dorby would say: 'Yes, sir, thank you. The usual sort of short story?'

'Yes; something—h'm—sentimental, you know. Holly and mistletoe, and families being reunited and—h'm—enemies forgiving each other on Christmas Eve.'

And Dorby would go home and write something which he fondly believed Charles Dickens would have approved, full of the Christmas spirit, with aged and starving parents being surprised on the eve of Noel by the return of a prodigal son or daughter burdened with hitherto unsuspected wealth and laden with presents. For this he received thirty shillings—which relieved Mr Marvell from the embarrassment of feeling that he ought to have made his faithful employee a little present.

The total population of Foxbridge did not exceed eleven thousand, and the circulation of the *Independent* was proportionately small. Like more ambitious newspapers, it relied largely on advertisements for its revenue. Mr Marvell had no difficulty in getting sufficient of these to make a comfortable little income. Auctioneers' notices, servants wanted, agricultural implements, manures and land dressings, bargain weeks at the local shops, all were grist that came to that dusty little mill set in an alley behind the High Street. And, as Dorby could tell you, Mr Marvell kept the expenses of the paper very low.

But at Christmas-time Mr Marvell lashed out. He published a supplement as a kind of Christmas box to his readers. You could rely on finding some syndicated articles on Old Christmas Customs, Christmas Games, a revolting Household Hint or two on what to do with a stale turkey or how to make mincemeat go twice as far, and always a short story by Charles Dorby—with the title in huge Old English letters intertwined with holly and mistletoe.

Charles Dorby was the chief reporter. As a matter of fact, he was the only reporter, for you could hardly count Monkland, the pimply boy of sixteen who seemed to come to no harm through wearing canvas shoes all the year round. So far Monkland could only be trusted to report cricket and football matches. He had not yet learned to read his own shorthand, and he had a fascinating gift of misreporting speeches and, in the fresh innocence of his youth, making 'floaters' which, if undetected at the office, might have involved Mr Marvell in heavy legal expenses. The bulk of the labour therefore fell on Dorby's shoulders, and he was thus overworked besides being underpaid.

Dorby was a little man of indeterminate age, and he wore the dejected air of a dog which had been chained up too long. He was secretly proud of his calling, but used long since to being snubbed, patronised, and abused. He was proud of the *Independent* and simmered under the surface in mild rages when he heard it described as 'the local rag'. True, it wasn't run quite as he would have run it if he had had full control. It wasn't quite so independent as it sounded. He knew quite well that Mr Marvell increased his modest revenue by accepting presents for leaving something out or putting something else in. And the world's worst poetess since Eliza Cook enclosed a postal order for ten shillings with each of her effusions.

Dorby, then, was a small man of dejected aspect, and this was accentuated by a drooping moustache, which Mrs Dorby in her maiden state had thought silky and fascinating. He had married in his intrepid youth, when he still dreamed of coming to London and editing the *Times*, a local music-teacher, who was responsible for most of the desolating noises which the young bourgeoisie of Foxbridge knocked out of their untuned cottage pianos. The Dorbys were not more unhappy than the average married couple with a family and a very slender income. There were two boys who relieved Dorby of some embarrassment by winning scholarships to the local Grammar School. He wanted them to become journalists!

In his spare time—yes, he managed to find a little spare time—Dorby wrote short stories, and occasionally these were accepted by obscure publications. Dorby's chances came when the editor of a would-be popular weekly found himself short on the day of going to press. He was a really terrible writer of the worst kind of journalese, and all the most worn *clichés* were as dear to him as his wife and family. If your eye happened first to catch the substantive you could guess the adjective. A barrister? Well, of course, he was 'rising' and 'young.' A chasm? Naturally it was 'yawning.' A void? Not very surprisingly it was an empty void. And his characters all talked as if they were living in the eighteen-eighties—and proud of it, too!

But Dorby knew not of his own treasonable assaults on the King's English. In his own funny little way he was inordinately vain. If a friend met him at Christmas-time in the local Constitutional Club, and said, 'Oh, Dorby, old man, that was a jolly good yarn of yours in the supplement of the local rag,' he felt like a schoolboy who had just won the mile open, and forgot the offensive name by which his paper had been called.

I have been generalising, of course, meaning all the while to come to a certain day in Dorby's life. The boy Monkland, obviously, was not always sixteen. He had been younger, and he will unfortunately grow older unless his canvas shoes lead him to the grave by way of pleurisy and pneumonia. I do not know the exact date of the day I have in mind; I only know that it was early in December and that it was snowing. The time was early afternoon, but it was already dusk, for the clouds which were shedding the snow had shut out the failing sunlight. Dorby sat on a high stool in the reporters'-room, transcribing shorthand notes into longhand with the grudging assistance of a blue flicker of a gaslight overhead.

He had been to a wedding, and he hated weddings; still he had to go. The boy Monkland had once been entrusted with a wedding, and, quite innocently, had written in his report something so shocking that, but for the sharp-eyed compositor, the subsequent and inevitable legal proceedings must have ruined Mr Marvell. This had been a bad wedding, even as weddings went. The bride's people, a frugal family, had, it seemed, detailed a relative to steer the reporter away from the refreshment buffet. Dorby preferred funerals. At funerals the bereaved were generally so distressed as not to care what became of the ham sandwiches.

Dorby went through his notes. Had he a full list of presents? Yes, he had. Heavens, how many fish-slices had been bestowed on that happy couple? It looked like the shopping-list of a monastery in Lent. Could

he call it 'A Fashionable Foxbridge Wedding'? If he did the county
people wouldn't like it, and if he didn't the townsfolk would be offended.
Well, one can't please everybody in this complicated world.

Still, there was snow falling and Christmas was coming on. Dorby
loved the merry Yuletide—as he invariably described it. When he had
dealt faithfully by this hateful wedding, he knew that he would feel
quite Christmassy and sentimental. It was about time that Mr Marvell came in and reminded him about the Christmas story.

And it was at that very moment that Mr Marvell actually came in,
with the promptness of a familiar spirit responding to an incantation.

'Oh, Dorby,' he said, 'leave out that report about the affiliation case.
The man's people have been to see me and—h'm—you know—I don't
think any good purpose would be served by publishing it. You can fill
up the space by writing something about the real Father Christmas
who will be at Judson's Toy Bazaar. They've sent us a quarter-page
ad., and it won't hurt to write them up a bit.'

Mr Marvell edged himself a little further into the room. He could
not get in very far, because the room was merely a cubby-hole. There
was no available space for Dorby to entertain callers. He could not
spread his arms beyond the margins of the narrow desk without soil-
ing his elbows with the dust from old files of the paper which had been
kept for some unknown, but probably morbid, reason.

'And,' Mr Marvell continued, 'you'd like to do a story for the supplement as usual, I s'pose?'

Dorby looked up.

'Yes, sir. Thank you. Same sort as usual?'

Mr Marvell screwed up his liberally whiskered countenance and
rolled his eyes in an effort to concentrate his thoughts. He might have
been a publisher trying to make up his mind if it would be worth while
to bring out an *édition de luxe* of the works of some precious but not
too popular author.

'No,' he said slowly, 'I think not.'

Dorby had written the story for the supplement on each occasion
for the past twenty years, and year by year Mr Marvell had been growing more and more conscious of an element of 'sameness' about them.
Prodigal sons had returned home on Christmas Eve with a punctual-
ity highly creditable to the railway systems, which were generally dis-
organised at that time of year. Old enemies had shaken hands or
embraced according to whether they belonged to the same sex or not.
Peace children had brought the Christmas Spirit into sordid homes.

Church bells had pealed out their messages of peace and good will. Modest maidens had surrendered—verbally, at least—to dashing young men while the carols were being sung. On the whole Mr Marvell was conservative, but he believed in a change now and again.

'I tell you what,' he said. 'Write us a ghost story.'

'A what?' said Dorby. Dorby's face did not fall, because it had fallen years ago and had, so to say, stayed down; nor did his tone indicate the dismay in which the request had suddenly plunged him. It merely suggested that he thought he might not have heard aright. Mr Marvell might have said goats instead of ghosts. 'A what?' he asked again.

Mr Marvell responded quite airily.

'Ghost story,' he repeated. 'Christmas ghost story. You know, old country houses—panelled walls—spectre with clanking chains—missing will, or hidden treasure. You know the sort of thing.'

'Yes, sir,' said Dorby. 'Very well.'

If Mr Marvell had told Dorby to write a tragedy in blank verse after one of the Elizabethan models, Dorby would have said, 'Very well!' and gone home and had a shot at it; and he would have owned himself to be no journalist had he failed to produce something. Mr Marvell, quite unaware of the shattering effects of his order, then nodded and withdrew.

You must know Dorby a little better to understand why the blow that had fallen on him was indeed a blow.

First of all Dorby was proud of his old-fashioned Christmas stories. He secretly regarded himself as a second Dickens, but deprived of general recognition by the stupidity of the public and a general conspiracy on the part of most editors and publishers. He had looked forward to writing that Christmas story for the supplement and afterwards receiving the congratulations of a few sentimental old women and one or two insincere male friends. It was his star turn, and now he had been robbed of doing it by a mere editorial caprice.

In the second place, Dorby did not believe in ghosts. He believed in a great many things which leave most men sceptical, but not in ghosts. He was well-known in the town and had made no secret of his views. For so mild a man he had said some quite cruel things about superstitions and the superstitious, and said them publicly. Now there would be a great deal of ribald laughter in the town when it became known that old Dorby had written a ghost story.

Ghosts! How could such things exist? When you died you went to Heaven if you had been good, or to Hell if you had been wicked or

bad, or perhaps only just ordinary. How could anybody come back?
If you were in Heaven you wouldn't want to, and if you were in the
other place you jolly well couldn't! This was logic. Only the subscribers
to an almost unmentionable creed, and a few loose-thinking people
with practically no religion at all, believed in a middle state in which
souls were neither yet at peace nor eternally condemned.

Again, he did not know how to write a ghost story. He hated such
things and had never read one except on rare occasions when he had
been led astray by the dishonest methods employed by the author. Yet
what was he to do? Refuse the commission and lose the thirty shillings? That was quite unthinkable. Besides, to do so would be a tacit
confession of his failure as a journalist. A journalist, he held, should
be able to write something about anything on the shortest notice.

It was then, while he continued knocking his 'wedding' copy into shape,
that he renewed his regrets for having quarrelled with Rennick.

Rennick was the only man in the town in Dorby's station of life whom
he felt that he was meeting on terms of intellectual equality. The
interests of the local tradesmen were few and material, and instead
of looking up to Charles Dorby as a representative of the Fourth Estate
they were apt to pity him for being an over-driven and underpaid hack.
Rennick, though, was different.

Rennick was a little dried-up man of fifty, clerk to the principal lawyer
in the town. He, too, was poor, for although he knew most of the vil-
lainies perpetrated by his employer during the past thirty years, he
lacked the blackmailing touch, and his salary remained disgracefully
small. But he was not fond of money. His tastes marched a long way
with those of Dorby. He knew his Dickens and his Trollope, and spoke
highly of a certain Henry James, whose works Dorby often tried hard
to enjoy, but who invariably defeated him and sent him to bed with
a headache.

Also Rennick was a mine of odd scraps of local information and forgotten folklore. He knew how many horses had been stabled by Oliver
Cromwell in the parish church, and the site of a battle which had taken
place outside the town during the Wars of the Roses, and where the
Duke of Y and Lord X had fought a duel during the eighteenth century, and the spot where the last of the fairies was supposed to have
been seen by a plumber late on Boxing Night. Rennick was just the
man to know of some ghostly legend which could be twisted into a
tale. In that case there would be the added attraction of local colour.
But three months ago he had quarrelled with old Rennick, and they

were not now on speaking terms.

It has been said that only a fighting man should keep a fighting dog, because a dog of that nature is sure to lead his master into trouble sooner or later. Neither Dorby nor Rennick could have been described as fighting men, but their respective dogs were about as pacific as two adjacent Balkan States. Rennick owned an Irish-terrier which was a sort of canine Tybalt and regarded every other dog as a Montague. Dorby owned a pugnacious mongrel, with perhaps rather more bull in it than anything else, which he had bought as a pup under the delusion that it was a pure-bred fox-terrier. Of course, neither had the least control over his dog, and the result was inevitable.

The men and the dogs met one Sunday morning, and while the two men were discussing the unemployment problem the two dogs made acquaintance in the unconventional manner of their kind. Then Rennick's dog bristled all over and rumbled like an empty stomach, and Dorby's dog, having made a rude and quite unmistakable gesture of contempt, uttered distant thunder in his throat. Of course, both men shouted 'come here,' and, of course, neither dog took the least notice. A moment later events were moving at such a pace that it was impossible to distinguish one dog from the other.

That was perhaps how it was that Rennick came to smite Dorby's dog with his umbrella, and Dorby did violence to Rennick's dog with a rather futile little partridge cane. By why describe the childish scene that followed? Each man took his own dog's part, and each blamed the other for not keeping his dog under control. They quarrelled like a pair of flustered old hens giving each other little verbal pecks. They parted in anger, having said just enough to hurt each other. When they met again Dorby tried to look down at the drooping ends of his own moustache and Rennick looked pointedly in another direction. They had not spoken since.

Tomorrow was press day, and besides being chief reporter Dorby was also chief sub-editor and had to get everything ready for 'putting the paper to bed.' He finished his notes about the wedding, and wrote a few lines about Judson's Toy bazaar and his Father Christmas, to take the place of a police court case which Mr Marvell, on receipt of five pounds, had considered too unsavoury to be reported in detail. Where was Monkland's football copy? Oh, there it was. 'County Senior Cup—Foxbridge's Slashing Victory.' Same old stuff. Monkland was a partisan and had once been charged with the impropriety of booing the referee from the Press box. Foxbridge were always gaining slashing victories or suffering narrow defeats. Mustn't forget to leave room

for a report of the Wesleyan Mission Tea Social which would come
in this evening, and the Bowling Club annual dinner which would come
in tomorrow morning. Thank Heaven the Wesleyans and the Bowling
Club did their own reporting. It was quite slack for the day before press
day. He could go home quite early.

Yes, and then he'd have to tackle that beastly ghost story!

All the while he had been attending to the needs of the paper his
mind had been elsewhere. The quarrel with Rennick and the prospect
of having to write a ghost story were as two weights dragging at him.
The one affected the other. If he hadn't quarrelled with Rennick he
could have gone round to his house that evening and said: 'Rennick,
old man, give us an idea with a bit of local colour in it. I've got to
write a rotten ghost story this year, instead of one of the good old-
fashioned Christmassy sort.'

And then a happy thought struck him. If he couldn't write a sentimental Christmas story this year, at least he could *live* one. It had
never before occurred to him to forgive Rennick. After all, the quarrel
was very foolish and trifling. Why shouldn't he go round to Rennick
and say: 'Rennick, old man, it's getting on for Christmas, the season
of peace and goodwill. I'll own I was in the wrong'—although he didn't
really believe that—'let's shake hands and be friends again?'

He knew that Rennick would respond, just as he himself would have
responded if Rennick had made the first advance. Each had been looking for a sign from the other. It would all be very pleasant and very
Christmassy, and would more than compensate him for the pleasant
little task of which he had been deprived. After all, it is far better to
experience something delightful than merely to write about it. Then
he and Rennick would go off arm-in-arm to the Constitutional Club
and take something to moisten the new cement of their friendship. Or
perhaps Rennick would have 'something' in the house—which would
be even better.

Dashed if he wouldn't do it! It was a fine idea. What funny things
men were! Here was he, who had written scores of stories about quar-
rels being made up at Christmas-time, prepared until a minute or
two since to nurse a stupid little grudge and greet an old friend with a
scowl.

Dorby's heart lightened suddenly. Even the prospect of writing the
ghost story was not so dismal and irritating. Certainly he would go
and see Rennick. Wait a minute, hadn't he heard that Rennick was
laid up, or had been laid up? A cold or a touch of 'flu or something.
Well, that only made it the more likely that he would find him at home.

It was quite dark outside when Dorby left the office, and snow was still falling. As he came out in to the High Street the illuminated dial of the clock outside the town hall, shining like a full moon, informed him that it was twenty-eight minutes past four. Snow was beginning to lie on the pavements, but traffic had so far kept the roads clear. Dorby lived in one of a row of villas some half a mile distant on the outskirts of the town. He set off briskly enough, but after a few moments the sight of a grocer's window tempted him to loiter.

A grocer's window, well lit and packed with crackers and dried fruits, looked more Christmassy to Dorby than any other sight in the world. For a moment or two he stood gloating over it. Then a car drew up close against the kerb behind him, and a voice addressed him.

'That you, Dorby? If you're going home I can give you a lift.'

The speaker was young Mr Packham, the auctioneer, and to reach his home he must pass Dorby's. Dorby thanked him gratefully and climbed in beside him. The car went forward.

Two or three hundred yards distant, on the near side of the street, was the shop of Mr Munko, a dealer in second-hand furniture and books. When on foot Dorby always looked in at the window. It would not be safe to guess how many hundreds of times he and Rennick had turned over the contents of the threepenny box in the hope of finding a first edition worth hundred of pounds. Mr Munko, however, had other views.

The blood of nearly every known tribe of the human race was mingled in the veins of Mr Munko. It would be safe to say that none of his ancestors had married anyone hailing from within a thousand miles of his birthplace. Mr Munko, despite a tendency to scream when he became excited, had a level head. Such men are not fools in business. One never found anything in the threepenny box much more exciting than the sermons of some defunct and forgotten clergyman whose innocence had been exploited by wicked publishers. But he and Rennick had never quite given up hope.

The thought that he was approaching the shop put Dorby once more in mind of Rennick. Then, as the car drew near, Dorby was a little surprised to see Rennick standing bareheaded in the fluttering snow-flakes, peering in through the shop window. Rather silly of him, Dorby thought, to stand about bareheaded in the snow so soon after having had a chill or a touch of 'flu.

Dorby had no doubt but that it was Rennick even before the little man turned and faced the street. The shape of the figure, its poise with bent head and short-sighted stare were unmistakable. An instant later the car was passing, and then Rennick turned, looked straight into Dorby's face, and gave him the friendliest of friendly smiles.

Dorby acted on an impulse.

'Would you mind stopping just for one second?' he said to Packham.

'Eh? Oh, very well. Only do be quick!'

The car stopped. Dorby clambered out and ran back. Rennick was waiting in the ungenerous light which filtered through Mr Munko's dirty windows.

'I say, old man,' Dorby exclaimed breathlessly, 'I want to make it up! Sorry we had that stupid quarrel. May I come round and see you this evening?'

Rennick nodded and gave him again the very friendly smile. He did not speak, but the nod and the smile quite plainly said: 'All right, old man, come round by all means, but we won't talk about it now.' This was all Dorby wanted. Packham, he gathered, was in a hurry. He turned and trotted back to the car.

'Sorry to hurry you,' Packham said. 'Thought you wanted to buy something, not only just go and look in the window. But I promised to be home sharp at half-past four, and it's that now.'

Five minutes later, having shaken the loose snow off his coat, Dorby entered his small dining-room, where Mrs Dorby was hugging an economical fire. She rose immediately and began to prepare his high tea.

Mrs Dorby was a depressed little woman who believed that it was healthy and economical to feed her family on stuff that came out of tins. There was no waste, she would say; and there wasn't, because all scraps were eaten, even after they had been kept a perilous length of time. Still, none of them had yet suffered from ptomaine poisoning, and had Dorby been one of those men who aspire to breaking records he might have claimed to have eaten more tinned salmon that any other living man. It was tinned salmon this evening.

While he ate and drank, Dorby shared his new grievance with his life partner. Mrs Dorby was herself, and not without cause, a painstaking and highly efficient grumbler, and Dorby lost few opportunities of letting her know that *his* life wasn't all honey.

'A ghost story!' he exclaimed, disgust on his face and in his voice. 'Who believes in ghosts nowadays! It's childish. It's against nature and it's against religion. And I could have written something to make people feel that there's still some goodness in human nature. But, no—a ghost story!'

'Need it be about a real ghost, dear?' Mrs Dorby asked. 'I mean to say, I read a pretty little story in a ladies' paper once. It was about a young lady who was put into a haunted room. The room wasn't really haunted, of course, but supposed to be. And in the middle of the night the ghost came in and frightened her. But it wasn't a real ghost, it was a man dressed up in a sheet. So,' Mrs Dorby concluded simply, 'she married him.'

'Pah!' said Dorby.

'Couldn't you write something like that, dear?'

'No, I couldn't. I suppose if Marvell says he wants a ghost story he means a real ghost story. Why couldn't he let me write about something that I believe in? I believe in humanity, I believe in Christmas, I believe in Charles Dickens. But ghosts!'

'You're always saying that a good journalist ought to be able to write about anything,' commented Mrs Dorby.

'Oh, so I could, I suppose,' he answered moodily, 'but it doesn't say I want to. I suppose I shall get hold of some silly local legend and twist something out of it. At six o'clock I'm going to step round to see old Rennick—'

'Rennick? But I thought—'

'Pooh,' said Dorby, 'that's all over now. I met him in the High Street about half-past four, and he was quite friendly. I don't bear any malice. He knew he was in the wrong and he apologised.'

Dorby believed in maintaining his dignity in the home even at the expense of truth. It was his dignity which had caused him to select six o'clock as the hour of his call. Very soon his boys would be home from school, and the elder, Sidney—yes, I am afraid they called him Sid—was involved in the mysteries of quadratic equations. Dorby, who had lived most of his life under the delusion that algebra was an Oriental language, did not know what a quadratic equation was, but he was not going to expose his ignorance to a younger and critical generation. By six o'clock the boys would have had their tea and would start discussing their home-work; and that was the time for Dorby to go.

Events proved that he had timed his departure almost to the minute. At the first glance of a Hall and Knight and an exercise book Dorby rose and prepared to go out.

It was a wretched evening. It had stopped snowing, but the wind had veered east and cut through his thin overcoat like a cold knife. As he walked he huddled himself in his clothes.

What a life it was! An editor who wanted to make him write about

something he didn't believe in, a son who wanted to be told about quadratic equations, and now this brutal east wind! Still, he was going to
make friends again with old Rennick, and that was something. Dorby
estimated that Rennick's home was ten minutes' walking distance from
his own, but on this occasion, spurred by the desire to keep warm,
he covered the ground in eight.

The house was very dark and silent. Not a light anywhere. Dorby
pressed the electric bell three or four times without attracting attention from within, and shivered on the doorstep for four or five minutes
before coming to the conclusion that the Rennicks were all out. He
was in the act of turning when he heard flat and heavy footfalls
approach the door from the other side, and a faint and muffled voice—
Mrs Rennick's voice—called out: 'Yes? Who is it?' Dorby answered,
and the door was hesitatingly opened. Mrs Rennick stared at him across
the threshold. She showed him a face which was very white save for
the eyes, and these were red-rimmed and swollen.

   Like so many small men, Rennick had taken himself a wife of noble
proportions who had grown mountainous in middle age. Dorby had
now only to look at her to see that there was something wrong. The
long channels running down her flaccid cheeks were now watercourses
for tears.

   'Mrs Rennick,' he exclaimed. 'What's the matter?'

   'Haven't you heard?' she faltered. 'I thought that was perhaps
why—'

   'I haven't heard anything. Tell me.'

   'My husband. My dear husband. He took to his bed three weeks
ago. He thought it was only a chill. He wouldn't let me send for a
doctor. I d-didn't until—until it was too late. It was pneumonia.'

Dorby stared and then reeled forward. A kind of sickness seized him.
All that he had believed was shattered and came toppling around him
like the ruins of a falling tower. He buried his face in the wet sleeve
of his coat and leaned against the doorpost, whimpering. He knew
instinctively what he was going to hear. The voice of Mrs Rennick came
to him like something heard in a dream:

   'He died…at half past four…this afternoon.'

THE LITTLE BLUE FLAMES

FERRERS had been looking at the brass candlesticks for some time. Presently he rose, took them from my sitting-room mantelpiece, and held them in his hands appraisingly as if he were trying to guess their weight. He closed his eyes for a moment and frowned.

'Where did you get these?' he asked.

'Oh, I came by them honestly!' I laughed. 'I bought them at a second-hand shop. Why?'

'You don't know anything about their history?'

'One doesn't ask for the pedigree of almost worthless second-hand articles. They're of no intrinsic value, a bit battered, and not old enough to be called antiques. But I'm fond of brass, and I happened to like their shape. You apparently don't.'

'I don't object to their shape,' said Ferrers, 'but I don't like them. To me there's something repellent in the sight of them, much more in the touch. They've been connected with something ghastly.'

He put them back with a theatrical air of haste and wiped his perfectly clean fingers on his coat.

Ferrers was a very good fellow, but a bit of a crank and, I was sure, more than a bit of a charlatan. We were office mates. Like most cranks he played chess rather well, and although I believed myself to be fairly normal, I, too, played a pretty good game. Thus we often came to visit each other's rooms of an evening.

Ferrers was of the type much beloved of middle-aged, superstitious women. You know those dear ladies who have outgrown a faith which has supported millions during the past two thousand years, but can still believe that their futures can be ascertained by shaking up the dregs in a teacup.

'Dear Mr Ferrers is so clever! He is ever so psychic and susceptible to "atmospheres," but not *quite* a clairvoyant, my dear, because he will not develop his wonderful *gift*.' Ferrers was taken about and exhibited at quite a lot of tea-parties.

When he was taken to a house three or four hundred years old he generally had some shuddersome things to say about it. A tragedy had happened there. He couldn't say what it was, but there was a sinister atmosphere in one of the rooms. And since nobody could contradict him everybody accepted his word, and was impressed by his remarkable gift.

If on the other hand he went to a house which he knew had been specially built by the happy young married couple who still inhabited it he looked just as wise and discoursed on the benevolence of the atmosphere. Nothing tragic had ever happened there! Clever Mr Ferrers! For those who care to try it this is the simplest way in the world of getting kudos and free meals.

Please note the simplicity of his methods. He had first noticed that my candlesticks were fairly old and rather battered. After that he had ascertained from my own lips that I knew nothing of their history. All then was plain sailing. He 'sensed' something sinister about them, and although I might laugh at him I could not disprove his statement.

I did laugh at him.

'I've been lying to you,' I said. 'Those candlesticks were standing on a table in the room at Holyrood when Rizzio was murdered. Afterwards they came south to England, and provided the light by which Sir Edmondbury Godfrey was murdered. Afterwards they passed into the possession of Thurtell, the murderer of Weir. I forget how many other murders they've been connected with. They seem to *cause* murder. Very likely they will make me murder you. Have a drink, Ferrers.'

He smiled at me as a man will when he dismisses a weak joke.

'If I were you,' he said, 'I should get rid of them—sell them, or give them away, and get another pair.'

'What'll you give me for them? They're only worth a shilling or two.'

'Oh, I don't want them! I wouldn't live with them for anything!'

'Come off it!' I laughed. 'You're not in good psychic form tonight otherwise you wouldn't have lost the game, when you had it well in hand, by letting me take your queen.'

'It was those darned things,' Ferrers said, pointing to the mantelpiece. 'I couldn't keep my mind off them.'

'You've met them before,' I said mildly. 'They've been here for months, but they haven't worried you until tonight.'

'I know,' he answered. 'I don't pretend to understand it. There are no discovered laws about these things. Perhaps it is only at certain seasons of the year that they become repulsive to a sensitive like myself. Probably you're quite safe with them. If you've got a brick instead of a head you can't expect to feel much.'

I swallowed the jibe. I could always get my own back on Ferrers, the deluder of old maids who were always having their fortunes told, and were not in the least deterred by the fact that they came out different every time. I mixed him a drink, sat on chatting with him for another quarter of an hour, and then verbally turfed him out by telling him that I was jolly well going to bed.

But quite unconsciously I was affected by Ferrers' words. You know how it is when you meet a man and like him, and then somebody comes and warns you against him, whispering in your ear a word or two of unpleasant scandal. You may not believe it, but you haven't quite the same ease in his company afterwards. So it was with me and my candlesticks. Ferrers had uttered the poisoned word, and for two or three days afterwards I found myself disliking them and nearly following his advice. Then I forgot all about it.

It happened that about three weeks later I shuffled my household goods. Those who live, or have lived, in two rooms understand the deadly monotony of that sort of existence. You get sick of the sight of your small possessions. The best way to overcome that is to move them about—shift the bookcase from one wall to another, turn the table so that its long ends are where its flanks used to be, find new places for the pictures and ornaments.

Thus it happened that the battered, old brass candlesticks came to occupy positions on either side of my bedroom mantelpiece.

My bedroom was on the second floor and the one large window looked out across a street in Bloomsbury on the sooty facade of another house similar to the one in which I lodged. The window was flanked by the inevitable dirty 'lace' curtains, looped towards the lower ends and bearing the design of a shepherd boy surrounded by impossible flowers piping to invisible sheep.

My bed pointed straight at this window, the head of it lying flush with the opposite wall. There was a space on either side. The door was at my right hand when I lay on my back. The fireplace and mantelpiece were in the middle of the left-hand wall. Here my candlesticks rested, and on those mornings when the sun happened to be shining I could see the gleam of their brass by looking slightly to my left across the foot of the bed. These details of my bedroom are as necessary as they may be tiresome.   /

I never had candles in the sticks. I had both gas and electric light, obtainable through little boxes clamped to the floor which were always hungry for shillings at inconvenient moments. The candlesticks were merely articles of decoration and not of utility.

Most nights I went to bed early, but occasionally I went to a theatre and had a late meal afterwards. Late suppers never agreed with me and it was on those nights that I slept worst. It was on the occasion when I had been to see 'Journey's End' and taken a hurried meal afterwards—including lobster—that the first and lesser of my two unpleasant experiences befell me.

I want to be quite impartial, stating all the facts, and that is why I confess to the lobster.

I got into bed at about half-past twelve, having first turned out the electric light. The switch was by the door and out of reach from the bed. It was a black night, and while I undressed I heard the steady *whirr* of the expected rain on the road outside and a gurgling and choking of water running into gutters. The window was just a pale rectangle and I could hardly discern any of the bedroom furniture.

The lobster has his own way of taking revenge on mankind. The poor devil is plunged alive into boiling water. He therefore gets his own back on those who eat him. Mine arranged for me many sleepless hours. I kept my eyes resolutely closed, lay on my right side, and waited for sleep in vain. I heard the London clocks striking every quarter of an hour, the sonorous voice of Big Ben deepening or softening his tone at the wind's will. And still the rain droned and pattered outside, and still I could not sleep.

After a long while I turned over and opened my eyes. The best thing, it seemed to me, was to jump out, turn on the light and go and fetch a book. But when I opened my eyes I was astonished to see that a dim light already pervaded the room.

It was not moonlight. Besides, there could be no moon with that drenching downpour still going on. Nor could the light have come from the opposite window across the street, for my own window looked darker than ever.

I was idly curious at first. There was no smell of burning, nothing at which to take alarm. The light was very dim and bluish. Although the window was dark it must surely, I thought, be reflected into the room from outside.

And then I looked straight over at the mantelpiece and gasped.

Flickering just over the tops of my two brass candlesticks were two little blue flames. There were no candles in the sticks: indeed, so far as I knew there was not a candle in the house. These small flames seemed to be feeding on nothing, to have independent lives, to be hovering in the air like little phosphorescent moths. You know when sometimes you light a new candle and it seems uncertain for a few moments if the candle will burn. The little weak flame you see then is just like the flames I stared at from my bed.

To me—since I knew they could not be candle-flames—the oddest thing was that they were poised just above the candlesticks. Of course, it was a reflection, some sort of optical illusion, and the obvious step to take was to jump out of bed and walk across to take a closer view. It was only when I moved a leg, preparatory to doing so, that I found myself powerless. Fear leaped upon me like a wild beast out of a thicket. It was an inexplicable panic terror of which I was afterwards thoroughly ashamed, but which at the time I was powerless to combat.

In the midst of this sudden wild and galloping brain-storm I remembered what Ferrers had said about the candlesticks. There was something sinister and uncanny about them. And I knew with a certainty—which had grown, like my dread, out of nothing—that if I lay and watched I should see something unbearable. I did what I had so often done as a little frightened child when I woke in the night and thought I heard some strange noise in the dark. I plunged down into the bed and drew the clothes right over me.

I lay in mental torture for a period which threatened eternity. Once I thought I heard a scuffling in the room close to the foot of my bed. Then I suppose I must have fallen asleep, for I returned to consciousness when I heard a teacup rattling in its saucer close to my ear and the familiar friendly sound of my landlady's voice.

'Oh, Mr Roberts! Fancy! It's a wonder you didn't die of suffocation.'

It was a man with a headache and very little pride who got out of bed a few minutes later. What was I to think? Had any other man told me the experience which I have just described I should have laughed at him. I should have said: 'This charlatan Ferrers tells you some rot about those candlesticks, and eventually you get a bad dream about them after a lobster supper.' It was the feasible and only reasonable explanation, but such explanations, while they're always applicable to the other fellow, are no good to ourselves. Because it had happened to me, I couldn't convince myself that it was a dream.

I carried the memory of it all day like a burden, but the burden lightened as the day drew on. My work in the office lightened it, for one cannot concentrate one's mind on two things at once. By the evening I had decided that my last night's experience was just 'queer,' but capable of some absurdly simple explanation. My sudden terror was induced by the memory of what Ferrers had said.

That evening I went round to Ferrers' rooms to play chess, but I said nothing to him about the previous night. It would have been a score for him, and also it might have tempted him to enlarge on the subject to such an extent as to give me another beastly dream. I returned to my rooms at about midnight, entered my bedroom, and, walking about while I took off my collar and tie, I suddenly found myself confronting the two brass candlesticks.

The obvious thing to do, to insure against a recurrence of what had happened last night, was to dump them in the sitting-room. I had almost seized one of them, when I drew back. That would be cowardly. I had not yet recovered from the shame of my last night's fear, and I knew that the way to breed terror was to make concessions to it. What I had seen last night was capable of some simple explanation, and my fear had bubbled out of my subconscious mind for reasons already stated. Here was I, sane and sound and healthy, and what had I to fear from a pair of brass candlesticks?

Put them back in my sitting-room? Certainly not! They must stay in my bedroom and I must teach myself that what I dreamed or imagined last night was nonsense. It was that idiot Ferrers who dropped the germ into my mind. Let all his bogies come and do their worst—if they existed.

Eventually I switched off the electric light, jumped into bed, and was soon asleep.

I don't know what woke me, but when I did wake the room was once more illumined. I did not at once think about the candlesticks, for I had all the hazy feelings of one who becomes half-awake in a strange room. I began to ask myself where on earth I could be.

To begin with, the door was in the wrong place. It should have been at the end of the wall close to my right hand. Now it was diagonally opposite, set in the far corner of the left-hand wall and close to the window. It was standing wide open, so wide that it formed an acute angle with the wall. This was very odd!

Another odd thing was a change which had taken place in the window. It used to be high and narrow, now it was long and low. It used to be flanked by not too clean lace curtains. Now it wore a veil of pink-muslin, hanging down from brass rings along a curtain pole at the top.

Between my bed-rail and the window there was a table, laid for a meal. A woman stood with her back to me and seemed to be preparing food. She was poorly dressed and after a fashion which died before I was born. She wore a blouse, and a belt around her waist, and the hem of the blouse lay around her hips like a soldier's tunic.

My gaze travelled to the fireplace. It had become an open hearth with a log fire burning on it and a kettle stood suspended from a chain. On the high mantel stood several tawdry cottage ornaments—and my two brass candlesticks. There were candles in them now, burning faint and blue, but they brightened even as I watched, and these, together with the firelight, illumined the room.

I stirred, mystified, but as yet not fully awake. How had I got to bed in some country cottage? Where was I, anyhow? Yet the bed was familiar, indeed the bed was mine. And those candlesticks—

Then I began to remember. I had certainly gone to bed in my own room. Had I not been playing chess with Ferrers? Then what had happened, and who was this woman, and how had the room beyond my bed-rail become so changed.

I knew that I was not dreaming. In dreams one loses all one's critical faculty. The most impossible and incredible things happen without causing the least surprise. But my critical faculty was not lost. It was arguing passionately against the evidence of my senses. Still, I must own that when I tried to speak I found that I had no voice.

And then fear leaped upon me again. I knew that something unspeakable was about to happen. Some remorseless Power had decreed that this time I was to endure the whole horror of it, and my gaze was forced in the direction of the open door.

The door had thrown a black shadow on the wall, and in this dark angle I was aware of something crouching. I saw the gleam of a long knife, and once more I tried to cry out, to move, to do something to warn that woman whose back was towards me; but only a convulsion seized me, and the sweat poured from me.

I seemed to know already what must happen. The woman was not preparing the meal for herself. When all was ready she would blow out those candles, preparatory to retiring for the night. And then— oh, I knew what was going to happen then.

There was something particularly ghastly to me in the leisured movements of the woman. I wanted to shriek out to her, like a yokel at a melodrama who sees the villain about to pounce on the heroine. But could I have shrieked I knew that it would make no difference, for the tragedy I was watching did not belong to the present. It had all happened so very long ago.

Presently she stood upright and, still half turned from me, moved across to the fireplace. I never saw her face. She picked up each candle in turn and out it went, and now the room was lit only by the flickering blood-red glow of the fire.

I heard the door swing and close with a crash. Something leaped from behind it into the firelight. There was a scream and a snarl and a mad mingling and leaping of shadows. Then I fainted.

When I awoke in the morning my room was normal, and the brass candlesticks beamed innocently at me in the pallid sunlight of a half-hearted dawn.

Of course, I told Ferrers about it. He affected to understand these things, and I began to think that he was not such a charlatan after all. He began by making that particularly irritating remark:

'I told you so.'

'But what do you make of it?' I asked.

'I know as much as you do,' he replied, 'and I doubt if either of us will ever know any more. You're not likely to find out much about a cottage tragedy of the 'seventies or 'eighties. Such things were common enough and always will be.

'Influences sometimes cling to rooms, houses, country lanes, areas of open space; sometimes they cling to inanimate objects. I told you I didn't like your candlesticks. I should get rid of them if I were you.'

'I have,' I told him promptly.

'What have you done with them?' he asked.

'Chucked them into the dust-bin, and I didn't like even carrying them downstairs in broad daylight.'

'You should have slung them into the river,' Ferrers said.

Well, they've gone now, and I hope they were destroyed. But if the dustmen picked them out and sold them, I am afraid that there is a chance that somebody else may have a very uncomfortable time.

THE RECURRING
TRAGEDY

POST-WAR business brought William E. Fitchett to England, and
pleasure lured him from the great northern manufacturing city down
to Arborhaven, there to renew a friendship which had been broken
off at the end of his last term at Yale.

Standring was a specialist in nerves and mental diseases. Before the
war he had achieved a reputation. During the war his successful treat-
ment of cases roughly diagnosed as shell-shock had brought him world-
wide fame. He was still a youngish man, round-faced and kindly-
looking, with big searching grey eyes and a full head of dark hair flecked
here and there with white.

To Fitchett the Tudor mansion, designed in the shape of an E by
an architect anxious to do honour to the Virgin Queen, was a place
made out of dreams. The first sight one has of it, the gabled pile of
mellowed red bricks, standing at the top of long terraces across the
water meadows, is something not to be forgotten. The interior is a
wonder of crooked floors, oak panelling and beams, great stately rooms,
rooms absurdly small, with mysterious little passages and staircases
leading to unexpected parts of the house. Here it would seem that Time
had stood still, had not the men and women who trod the hollow floors
changed the fashion of their clothes and the manner of their speech
through the three centuries.

'They built real houses in those days,' Fitchett said. 'I don't remember your telling me in the old days that you had a family mansion.'

They were sitting alone in the long dining-room after dinner. The
table was an island of light set in a sea of shadows. The gleaming white
cloth, the shirt-fronts of the two men, the flowers and silver, the red
wine in the glasses, all stood out in shining contrast to the darkness

around them. Only an occasional reflection from the fire went questing into the mysterious dimness, and little focusses of light gleamed on the polished surface of furniture or panels.

'I hadn't,' Standring answered. 'I bought this place only six months ago. It used to belong to General Sir Thomas Shiel.'

'General Shiel.' Fitchett repeated the name as if he were trying to wake a memory. 'Now what did I hear about him? He's dead, isn't he?'

'Yes. Before he died he was one of my patients. I came down here to attend to him. I knew him slightly before. While I was here I fell in love with the house. After his death it came onto the market and I bought it.'

'Yes, yes.' Fitchett's brows were gathered up into a frown. 'But what did I hear about General Shiel? I know there was something.'

'He commanded one of our divisions over in France.'

'Yes, that's right. And didn't he get sent back for making a mess of things—losing a lot of men or something? Wasn't that it?'

'There were questions asked about him in Parliament, certainly.'

'Ah, I thought so.'

'Actually, though, he was invalided home with shell-shock.'

Fitchett laughed and turned a quizzical eye upon his friend.

'Well, that's just your British way of doing things,' he said. 'No general was ever sent back for being incompetent. He was always sick. It sounds so much better.'

The specialist smiled and sipped his wine.

'I can tell you,' he said, 'that the General was in a pretty bad way.'

'Oh, yes: I forgot. He died. And you couldn't cure him. So you're not infallible after all, Standring?'

'I haven't pretended to be. And, mind you, there were several forms of what was popularly known as shell-shock. There was the kind experienced by the poor devil who was blown up, or lay for hours under the wreck of a dug-out. There was another kind which was a polite name for funk. There was also, as you have remarked, the kind which afflicted generals who never went near the line, but about whom questions were asked in the House of Commons.'

'And he had that kind and yet—he died. You should have found him all the easier to cure, Standring.'

'You don't understand. Suppose you came to me and told me you suffered from delusions, and suppose when I inquired their nature you told me that all the grass you saw looked green—what then? Your delusion would consist in your thinking that it ought to be some other colour, and you would be much more difficult to cure. Even if I succeeded in making you think that grass looked red you would be very far from cured.'

Fitchett smiled and broke the long ash from his cigar into a little silver tray at his elbow.

'I see. And if a man tells you he's been seeing ghosts you can only cure him if he's been seeing imaginary ghosts—not real ones. Was that the General's trouble? Did he see ghosts?'

'He did not. At least he didn't say so. But in a sense I suppose he was a haunted man.'

He came to an abrupt pause. Fitchett regarded him with eyebrows slightly raised.

'Well?' he asked. 'I'm not going to pretend that I'm not curious.'

Standring lowered his gaze.

'I'm sorry,' he said. 'I can't tell you. There's such a thing as professional—'

'Professional secrecy. Professional humbug! Do you remember when we were at Yale, and bitten with the literary bug? I remember one evening we were talking about novels and short stories and the old gag about truth being stranger than fiction. We both agreed that every man, no matter how humdrum his life, had at least one experience which, if he cared to tell it, would make a tremendous story. You may also remember that we agreed to tell each other when the great story in real life came to each of us. Mine hasn't come yet. I rather think yours has.'

'Perhaps it has,' Standring agreed. 'I'm sorry, though, but I can't tell it to you.'

'All right.' Fitchett was plainly disappointed. 'If you can't, you can't. But listen. Years ago when we made that compact you knew me for a man who could keep his head shut. That was before you joined a profession which made you pigeon-hole your memories and label half of them "secret." I heard some sort of queer story about General Shiel in New York. Who brought it over I can't say. You tell me the truth, and I'll pass it along if that is your wish. If it isn't—next week I leave Liverpool for New York, and I won't say a single word in this country or mine.'

For a little while Standring seemed to consider.

'You can say,' he replied at last, 'that whatever were General Sir Thomas Shiel's faults he suffered for them.'

Fitchett inclined his head.

'I'll say that. And what are you going to tell *me*?'

'The whole thing if you're really so anxious to hear it and willing to swear to say not a word about it. The General is dead now, and his story—I don't know if that deserves quite to die. At least it's a queer story and there's certainly a moral in it.'

He sat silent a moment, the fingers of one hand on the stem of his half-empty glass, which he rocked slowly to and fro.

'I'd known the General slightly for some time. I knew him when he was a lieutenant-colonel in command of the first battalion of one of the county regiments. He had then the reputation of a martinet, nobody liking him except perhaps one or two of the senior officers. He gained promotion before the war and went out as a brigadier. Afterwards he was given the command of a division. I believe he was pretty thoroughly hated by the men. Every petty annoyance which he could devise to make their lives more miserable he inflicted at a time when life for them was little better than hell. His men all died with their buttons in a high state of polish, their equipment and shrapnel helmets shining. If it sounds splendid it seems at least purposeless. Too much of that sort of thing only harassed them, made them irritable and injured their *morale*. His orders about prisoners, care of wounded and so on were monumentally brutal. He was a specimen of our own home-grown kind of Prussian, of which there were, fortunately, few. On courts-martial he was extraordinarily severe. He thought only of himself and his own glory. Were it not for another picture which I shall always carry in my mind, I should think of him as a serio-comic goose-stepping figure, with a big sword and a mouthful of oaths. Well, as you know, he ended by losing nine-tenths of the *personnel* of his division and being sent home—'

'With shell-shock,' Fitchett interpolated drily.

'At least he came home a broken man. Lady Shiel came to see me after a time. She could not get him to put himself into professional hands. She did not tell me much. How much she actually knew I can't say. We made an arrangement. I was to come down to Arborhaven apparently as a guest, actually as a physician. I was to try to win the General's confidence and do what I could for him. In the end I agreed, mostly for the sake of acquaintance, which she was pleased to call friendship.

'I arrived here on a Friday, and Lady Shiel met me at the door. She took me into her husband's study—that small room across the hall—but he was not there at the time, and she went to look for him. While I was there alone I picked up an open book which evidently the General had been reading. The books a patient reads often afford a guide, or at least a finger-post, to his mental state. The book was Eugene Sue's

The Wandering Jew.

'When Lady Shiel returned with the General his appearance had a great and very disagreeable effect on me. I will not say that I was shocked, for that is no word for a doctor to use, and yet I do not know of any other word capable of conveying what I mean. To begin with he had aged terribly. From a red-blooded, middle-aged man typical of the Army he had grown old and haggard. Somehow he seemed to have shrunk inside his great frame, like a punctured football. His voice, when he greeted me, had lost its depth of tone. It was as if old age had come upon him in a night.

'Strangest of all he did not impress me as a sick man. His eyes certainly told their tale of suffering, but it was not physical nor yet of that mental kind which any physician may heal. Mind you, in describing this to one of my own profession I should have to consider my words and pick them carefully. To you I tell frankly exactly how I felt about him without stopping to consider any niceties of phraseology. Tell me, have you ever seen a man suffering terribly from remorse, from consciousness of sin? I don't use the phrase in a necessarily pietistic sense.'

Fitchett inclined his head. It was the first movement he had made for some minutes.

'I once saw a man who had been acquitted of murder,' he said. 'Nobody had much doubt about it, although the jury wouldn't convict. I know what you mean.'

'I think you've only a dim idea for all that. It was as if the General bore upon his soul ten thousand crimes, each one ten thousand times worse than murder. I never had much faith in God or devil, heaven or hell until that moment, when I knew that I looked into the eyes of a damned soul. I tell you, Fitchett, my own nerves are pretty sound, and I am not a man whom most would describe as "sensitive", but something like nausea overtook me as I made some kind of pretence to shake his hand.

'I will pass over the early part of the evening and the dreary dinner which followed in this room. There were no other guests, and the Shiels were a childless couple. I found myself dreading the departure of Lady Shiel to the drawing-room. I was almost childishly averse to being left alone with her husband.

'When she had gone, however, I resigned myself to the inevitable, and, at the General's invitation, mixed myself a stiff whisky and soda. I sat where you are sitting now. The General sat here in my place at the head of the table. The low shade of a lamp cut off the light from the upper part of his face, and, thank Heaven, I could scarcely see those dreadful eyes of his.

'He came very abruptly to the point before Lady Shiel had been absent a full minute. "I know exactly why my wife has asked you here," he said, with a kind of weary indifference. "If you cannot see it for yourself I suppose it is hopeless for me to tell you that I am no material for your skill. You will, of course, persist in trying to cure me?"

'"As you have guessed, that is why I am here," I answered.

'He poured himself out a stiff tot of whisky, and regarded me with a mirthless smile.

'"Of course," he said, "this is the first thing I am to give up?"

'"That and morbid books," I answered.

'"Oh, you mean *The Wandering Jew*? Do you know the story?"

'"I haven't read Eugene Sue's book, but I know the legend. He passes from life to life, doesn't he? And cannot die until Christ's second coming? I have heard various accounts of the legend. Christ on His way to Calvary had fallen under the weight of His Cross. One of the crowd struck Him and urged Him to go faster. Christ replied: 'I go on, but you shall linger until I return.' Some accounts have it that the Wandering Jew was Pilate's porter, others that he was one of the Pharisees, a shoemaker."

'"He was neither," said the General, as if he were stating an item of authentic news. "He was Judas Iscariot."

'"That is quite new to me," I said.

'"He was Judas Iscariot," he repeated. "He stood jeering with the crowd, and Christ fell at his feet—the Cross was so heavy—and Judas—Judas was so eager to show that he had renounced his Master. He kicked Him as He lay fainting and said: 'What are you feigning, Man?' And Christ, presently rising up, gazed at him and—and spoke that dreadful sentence."

'The General's voice shook terribly, and the words ended in a whisper.

'"Who told you that version?" I asked as lightly as I could.

'"Who told me?" he repeated. "Who told me?" He let his face fall between his hands and groaned aloud. "Oh, my God, if somebody had only *told* me!" He raised his face once more. "Do you know why Judas betrayed his Master? I can tell you that, too. It was pride. His some-time friends had jeered at him for a follower of the charlatan who pretended to be the Messiah, the King of the Jews. It wasn't for the thirty silver coins—it was all pride!"

'He spoke with an uncanny air of certainty and ended with a deep shuddering groan. Rather belatedly, perhaps, I thought it best to change the topic of conversation.

'"Come, General," I said. "I don't think too much theorising about Scriptural matters is good for you. I am here to try to do something for you. If you don't mind my asking a few questions so soon after dinner—"

'He cut me short with a motion of his hand.

'"My dear doctor," he said, "I will tell you the whole truth about myself, as far as I know it. If, after having heard what I am going to tell you, you still think that my malady comes within the scope of science, then—I was going to say for the sake of peace—I will submit myself to your hands. You will probably regard me as an interesting case, but you will not have much time in which to experiment upon me. First, I know, you require perfect frankness. You shall have it. And I had better begin by stating that just as a few rare men have never been able to understand the meaning of the word fear, so I have never understood the meaning of the word sympathy. I know it to be a sensation which makes people shrink from hurting others, but I never experienced it.

'"I have had the reputation of a hard, proud, ambitious man. I have earned it. The men under my command hated and feared me, not without cause. I wanted them to. I had my head full of the hard great men of old times: Moor, who lashed men for breaking step on the march; the swearing, steel-hearted Iron Duke. I wanted my name to go down to history coupled with names like these. My great aim was to win battles, to take ground, not for the sake of my country, but for the reputation of General Sir Thomas Shiel."

'"He had no heart, no feeling. He was an automaton, but what an automaton! What a soldier! Almost I could see the printed word.

'"To that end my men had to be the smartest in France. I caused them to be continually harried while they were resting. While they were in the line my brigade staffs continually went round to see that their buttons, boots, and equipment were as brilliantly polished as if they were parading on the barrack square. It mattered nothing to me what rest and sleep I deprived them of. Those last letters home, which might have been written and were not, troubled me not at all. I was the Iron General; they were my soldiers, my pawns. When men were sniped at night because of the moonlight shining on a polished shrapnel helmet it mattered nothing to me. Men were cheap enough. England was full of them; the bases were full of them; long processions of drafts thronged all the lines of communication. One asked for men and got them, as if one were indenting for quantities of soap or rifle oil. I did not mind sacrificing lives to enhance my reputation. I wanted to command an army; I might even rise to be Commander-in-Chief if the war lasted long enough. There was no end to my ambition.

' "I had orders at last to move my division on to the Somme, to take part in one of those attacks which proved so disastrous. My division had a certain objective. I gave my brigades orders that they had to take it. There must be no flinching or bungling. I warned them. If a unit failed to take its objective, whatever the cause, it must attack and attack again so long as there was one man left. I said it, I meant it, and I stuck to it. I was the Iron General until the end.

' "I had my headquarters in a little village called Flarincourt. There was a small white chateau a few hundred yards to the north where my staff and myself were housed. We arrived some days before the troops, and as the trains at the railhead disgorged them I myself took the 'march past,' sitting my horse at the roadside, my hand at the salute, while the doomed battalions tramped past me in columns of fours. There were motor-omnibuses waiting for them at the next village, and the men hated them as forerunners of disaster.

' "I had watched the last battalion of a brigade march past, and, knowing no other troops were due to arrive for some hours, rode off with an officer on my staff for lunch at the chateau. Opposite the chateau gates was a roadside Calvary, the Cross raised high and almost surrounded by poplars, but with an opening of the trees in front, made—so it seemed to me later—so that Christ might look down and marvel at the ways of men two thousand years after His own passion and death. Close against the Calvary, and in the shade of the poplars, a private soldier sprawled on the grass in an attitude of acute exhaustion. His face was pale and damp with sweat. To the sleeves of his tunic, below the numerals on his shoulder-straps, was sewn the divisional sign which marked him as one of my men and a straggler from one of the battalions which had just marched down the road.

' "Just then we were getting men from employment at the bases and from the non-combatant forces, men who had hitherto been declared unfit for service in the front line. They were hastily passed as 'fit' by medical boards and drafted into fighting units after a few days' training. Some of them were fit for the work and others were not. I had a reputation to retain with men who came under my notice for falling out on the march. I reined up at once. 'Hi, you, man' I shouted, 'what are you doing there?'

' "He neither stirred nor answered, and in a trice I was off my horse and standing beside him, shouting and cursing. The man was clean-shaven, and his short hair was auburn-brown. I started a little when I saw his face, for I fancied I had seen him somewhere before. I knew the wide brow and the pair of large, deep, sorrowful brown eyes which he opened to look up into my face. The lower part of his face I did not recognise, but that brow and those eyes were strangely, insistently familiar. There was something else which affected me queerly. I put it down to some optical illusion, due to the sun's rays and the shrapnel helmet. When I first looked at him it seemed as if blood were trickling down his forehead. Then, as I looked closer, it was gone.

'"'Why can't you stand up,' I bawled, 'when an officer speaks to you? *What are you feigning, man?*'

'"'I must have fainted', he answered in a gentle cultured voice. One hand strayed round to his shoulders and touched the great square pack which was strapped upon them. 'It is so heavy,' he said.

'"I cursed and kicked him, told him to get up at once and go on, and stood over him while he struggled to his feet. I did not care if he were shamming or not. If he were, he would go on his way with a wholesome lesson. If he were not, he might drop down again and die for all I cared. He was no use to the Army in that event, and I cared nothing of what happened to men who could not march and shoot.

'"With great difficulty and much obvious suffering he rose to his feet. Then he stood still for a moment and looked at me. 'This has happened before,' he said very slowly and distinctly, and added: 'You will remember.'

'"Something—I do not know what—prevented me from questioning him as to his words. It seemed absurd at the time, but an unaccountable sensation of fear stole over me. The curse died on my lips as the man turned his back on me and began slowly and painfully to limp down the road. I remounted my horse and rode up to the chateau for lunch—wondering.

'"'Next day occurred an incident which I forgot immediately afterwards for the time being. A party of men with a sergeant in charge was passing the chateau, proceeding on some duty or other. I came out immediately behind them so that, although they did not see me, I could hear them talking. 'Your pack 'urts you, does it?' shouted the sergeant to one of them. 'Well, you look up there.' He nodded towards the Calvary. 'Jesus Christ 'ad to carry something a blank sight 'eavier!' I do not know if he meant to be profane or if it were merely his rough way of offering consolation. But I remembered the incident later.

'"From the next day I was busy. Before dawn the muttering, rumbling and fluttering of gunfire began. It continued all day and the next night, increasing to drum-fire before the following dawn. Shortly afterwards the first reports came in. The day had gone ill with us. Our attack had broken down. I sent out the order: 'Attack again immediately. Every objective must be taken.' It was the sort of order that any of the great generals might have issued. It made me one with them— I, the Iron General.

' "All that day and the next panic reports came in from all the brigade headquarters. The enemy along our front was impregnably placed so long as he held out on the left and right. I knew it was so. I think a kind of madness seized me. To send the remnants of those battalions again and again to the attack was like flinging spray against a rock. But my pride weighed down all discretion. I was the Iron General who had never drawn back from what he set out to do. I cared for nothing but that reputation. From the safe distance of my chateau, far from the welter of mud and blood. I sent out the order repeatedly: 'Attack again! Attack again!' And my big battalions melted and melted and melted, and long processions of Red Cross vans thundered past the chateau, and still I sent to my rebellious brigadiers the same mad command: 'Attack again!'

' "You know how it ended, the thousands I sacrificed on the altar of my pride. That's ancient history now. When the final crash came, in the shape of a peremptory order from the Army Command, I was like a man dazed. Then, through my bewilderment streamed the light of old and dreadful memories. *He* had told me I should remember. I *did* remember! I *did* remember!' "

'The General's voice rose to a scream. His face worked horribly and he clenched his hands and beat them upon the table, close by where I am sitting now, in a kind of frenzy.

' "What did you remember?" I asked him.

' "It was the soldier's face first of all—the soldier who had fainted under the weight of his pack beside the Calvary. I thought I knew it. I did know it. Everybody knows it. O God, have mercy—mercy!" '

'I drew a long breath and sat still and staring. "Ye did it unto Me." The words shaped themselves in my brain and kept repeating themselves. The General's voice broke out again:

' "Don't you see? Don't you understand?" he snivelled. "It was He I cursed and kicked as He lay fainting by the roadside, just as I had cursed and kicked Him on His way to that other death two thousand years ago. Oh, yes, I remembered that, too! It all came back so clearly across the centuries, even to the memory of how the blood-money in my pouch had jingled as I asked Him what He was feigning. I remembered all—all. How they laughed at me for a follower of Him ... the leering High Priest of the Temple with his bag of money ... the kiss in the Garden. And I remembered passages out of other lives since then, for death with me is scarcely a breathing space between one life and another. And in each of these lives I have betrayed my fellow-man because of the pride that is my heritage and curse through all the ages. I can look back until my mind reels upon betrayal after betrayal in my many lives, down to the day when, because of my pride, I betrayed those thousands in that hell upon the Somme. For that is my punishment!—to go on living and betraying, to live in many lands and under many names, but always to be Judas."

'He fell forward and began to weep unpleasantly, great rending sobs that seemed to tear his throat. "If I'd only known Him," he whimpered, "when He lay by the roadside outside Flarincourt, He might have forgiven me at last! I might have saved myself! But I must go on ... I must go on to the same End which only marks another Beginning.'"

Standring brought his story to an abrupt conclusion. His cigar had gone out, and he sought for and lit another. Fitchett waited a little while, as if he expected more to come.

'Is that all?' he said at last.

'That is all the General's story, as he told it to me.'

'But what about the end?'

'The end? Oh, you know that. I treated the General, and failed. You knew that from the beginning. I think you remarked that I wasn't infallible.'

'But what did the General die of? One doesn't generally die of an hallucination, does one?'

'No. My dear fellow, surely you can guess. You remember what happened to Judas Iscariot, don't you?'

'Not—'

'Yes. The General hanged himself from that long beam out there in the hall.'

THE CASE OF THISSLER AND BAXTER

I KNEW all about Thissler's recurring or, rather, continuous dreams, for he had often told me about them. Indeed, unless carefully hand-led, he was apt to become wearying, like any other man who is always anxious to revert to one particular topic of conversation concerning himself.

The first time he told me about his dream existence as Mr Baxter, I now dare frankly confess that I didn't believe him. I thought he had invented it all with the purpose of becoming an object of half amus-ing, half uncanny interest.

'Directly I go to sleep,' he said, 'I become an altogether different man, and live in an altogether different place. I am a short paunchy man of fifty-five, a corn merchant, and I live in a small town called Thurlbury. My name is Baxter, and I am a big pot in a small way. I am an alderman and I have twice been mayor. I am married to a thin insipid woman of rather limited intelligence, and I have two grown-up daughters, Ethel and Clara. It is all as real to me as is my ordinary existence as Charles Thissler, stockbroker's clerk.'

'Do you mean to say,' I asked, 'that you dream this every night?'

'I don't think you understand,' he replied. 'I don't dream the same dream over again. Directly I fall asleep I *am* Alderman Baxter, and simply live through the ordinary petty details of his daily life. Noth-ing exciting or important ever happens. Our occasional family quar-rels are very mild. I am perpetually rebuking Ethel for being fast, and Clara for her temper. I am pretty well off, and not a little self-satisfied. It is only when I wake up as Thissler that I realise that, as Baxter, I am a pretty dull sort of dog.'

'I've never heard of anything so extraordinary,' I murmured, far too polite to call a bigger man than myself a liar.

'Nor have I. The dreams go on in an unbroken chain. Directly I fall asleep each night I go on where I left off on waking. I've been wondering lately if there is such a man as Baxter or such a town as Thurlbury. In my dreams it's a potty little place of about five thousand people, somewhere in the Midlands.'

'Look it up in the ABC,' I suggested. 'There's sure to be a station there.'

'Right, I will,' he said. 'And if there should turn out to be an Alderman Baxter, corn merchant of that town, I shall hand myself over to the Society of Psychic Research to see what they can make of me.'

'Are the dreams as vivid as your waking life?' I inquired.

'Absolutely.'

'Then you must wonder whether you're really asleep or awake—whether you're really Thissler or Baxter. And you can't be both?'

'Ah,' he returned, 'I thought you were going to say that. But I know I'm awake now, and really Thissler, because when I'm Baxter I have no recollection of being Thissler. But really it amounts to this—I get no real sleep at all, I simply go on with another man's life.'

I had to laugh then, but I soon checked myself as I saw that he was ruffled.

'Do you know anything at all about corn and oats and dried peas and that sort of thing?' I inquired.

He laughed in his turn.

'My dear man, as Baxter I'm a bally authority. Only my knowledge doesn't pass out of the dream with me. I know all this must sound perfectly incredible to you. But if it doesn't—what do you make of it?'

I made the usual fatuous jokes about drink and late suppers and left him. His story recurred to my mind two days later when I was looking up a train to Swindon. I was hastily looking through the ABC, and naturally came to the T's before the S's. And suddenly, as I was in the act of turning some pages, the name Thurlbury caught my eye.

Thurlbury, it seemed, was in Warwickshire, and had a population of 6,410. I was a little surprised to see it until I had thought the matter over. Then it occurred to me that Thissler, if he had invented the story about his dreams, would naturally have made it as circumstantial as possible by preparing the details first. It would not have surprised me to find that there was a Baxter, corn merchant of that town, who was also an alderman. There are such things as directories.

A week later I ran across Thissler once more, and being reminded of his extraordinary story, told him that the town of Thurlbury actually existed.

'I know it does,' he said, a gleam of excitement in his eyes. 'I took your tip and looked it up. As soon as I can spare a day off I'm going down there, and if I can find such a man as Baxter I'm going to introduce myself to him. Wouldn't it be extraordinary if, as soon as he goes to sleep, he becomes *me*!'

We both laughed at the far-fetched absurdity of the idea, but there was a note of seriousness in his tone.

'How are Clara and Ethel?' I inquired.

'Oh, quite fit, thanks,' he answered with a grin. 'But just before I woke up this morning I had to give Ethel a pretty healthy wigging for going to the pictures with a man who hadn't been properly introduced to her. Can you beat it?'

I said I couldn't and wasn't going to try. And thereafter he formed a habit of sidling up to me and telling me half seriously, half in amusement, all that Mrs Baxter and Ethel and Clara had been doing. As I have already stated, it began to bore me after a time, and consequently I avoided him as much as possible. He was very busy in those days, and was continually expressing his regret at being unable to steal the time to pay a visit to Thurlbury.

It must have been five or six weeks after he first told me of the strange affair when one evening he came round to my place looking white and haggard.

'I want you to do me a favour,' he said—'a pretty big one. I want you to sit up with me all night, play chess, cards, any old thing, drink black coffee, and stop me from going to sleep.'

'Why on earth?' I demanded.

'Because I daren't. Last night I had my usual continuation of the same dream, and as Baxter I fell down in my shop in a sort of fit. I simply can't tell you how perfectly horrible I felt. They carried me to bed and fetched a doctor. I overheard him tell my wife—I mean Mrs Baxter, of course—that I couldn't live for more than a few hours. I didn't feel like it either. So, don't you see?—I simply daren't go to sleep tonight and continue that dream.'

There was no mistaking the man's sincerity, although I tried to laugh away his terrors.

'Why,' I said, 'if you dreamed again tonight you'd only *dream* that you died.'

'I won't risk it!' he said hoarsely.

I knew now, by his whole manner, that this dream-story of his was not a piece of conscious invention on his part. And although I thought his fears were shadowy, I am a humane man who can sympathise with another's terrors. I was never a glutton for sleep, but although I like my small share, I willingly agreed to sit up all night with him and keep him awake.

It was about the dullest night I ever spent. I hate draughts and chess and such card games as two can play. Thissler dared not read nor permit me to read. And so we swilled black coffee and played interminable games of chess which would have disgraced children of seven. At last came the merciful dawn, and breakfast, and we parted company, I to bed, and he to the office, looking wan and hollow-eyed.

The following morning he was round at my place before breakfast, his eyes staring with excitement, his cheeks and forehead flushed.

'Well,' I said, 'did you venture on some sleep last night.'

'I did', he answered, 'and I didn't dream a thing. You'll know why when you've seen this. Look!'

He had with him a copy of the *Daily Wire* open in the middle and then folded twice across. He pointed at a column split into very small news paragraphs, and I looked where his thumbnail dug into the paper.

'*Alderman Baxter,*' I read, '*a corn merchant of Thurlbury, and twice mayor of that borough, died at his residence early yesterday morning after a brief illness. He will be remembered for much philanthropic work in connection with his native town.*'

The words seemed to lose themselves in a haze under my eyes.

'Good Lord!' I said softly. 'This is beyond everything I've ever heard of!'

'I wonder,' said Thissler, his eyes suddenly moistening with awe— 'I wonder what would have happened to me if I'd gone to sleep that night?'

THE GREEN
BUNGALOW

Foul deeds will rise,
Though all the earth o'erwhelm them, to men's eyes.

WHEN Freeceland arranged nearly to have a nervous breakdown
and so acquire medical backing for a month's rest in the middle of
the winter he overlooked the fact that his Chief might exhibit some
curiosity as to where he was going.

Freeceland had a Government appointment; he was assistant vice-
something or other in a Government office, and sick leave was easy
enough to obtain. He had, however, to make some decent pretensions
to being ill, and the medical certificate he laid before his Chief might
have led one to suspect that he was not long for this world. He must
have complete rest and complete quiet in some extremely bracing place.
Freeceland admitted that he had thought of Brighton.

'Brighton,' said the Chief, 'is not quiet, nor is it bracing. The Hove
end is even relaxing. I'll lend you my bungalow at Reed Bay.'

'It's awfully good of you,' said the wretched Freeceland, whose mind
had been running in the direction of golf and occasional theatres.

'Reed Bay,' continued the Chief, 'is just the place for you. It's bracing; there's an east wind enough to cut your head off this time of the
year. It's quiet enough, too, in the summer. This time of the year one
might describe it as God-forsaken. There are no amusements, of course,
and there isn't any golf; but then you couldn't play golf if there was.
Hardly anybody lives on the beach this time of the year, so you won't
be worried by neighbours, and it's miles away from anywhere. My dear
fellow, it's the very place for you.'

Almost before he knew it Freeceland had allowed himself to be bullied into accepting the loan of The Green Bungalow. He returned home

in a state of mind that it were kindest to call 'dissatisfied', and his wife and his wife's sister prepared regretfully to accompany him. I looked in upon them after dinner that night and announced my intention of coming, too, adding that I was not so inhuman as to allow them to go into exile without a fourth for auction-bridge.

The real reason was that Doris Dreever lived in one of the bungalows, and her people, partly from an eccentric love of the place and partly from economy, remained there during the winter. I had met Doris there the previous summer.

I cheered the Freecelands up a little by telling them about the Dreevers. Then Freeceland exclaimed:

'Oh, by Jove! and we shall see something of Hartley. He's got a cottage on the Downs, about a mile inland.'

'It won't be so much like exile after all,' said I. 'Who's Hartley?'

'A very good chap, but a bit of a recluse, and no wonder. He's had a rotten time. No harm in telling you, since all the world knows it. About twelve years ago he was tried for murder.'

'Really? And acquitted, I suppose?'

'Yes,' said Freeceland, 'but acquitted in such a way that a lot of people cut him. He didn't prove himself innocent, but the Crown hadn't quite enough evidence to hang him. If it had been anything less than murder he'd have been convicted, and convicted wrongfully. When you meet him you'll agree with me that he couldn't hurt a fly.'

'That sort of thing,' said I, 'is enough to sour any man.'

'I feel sorry for him already,' said Gertrude Freeceland. 'I shall be glad to meet him.'

Next day I wrote to the Dreevers, sending the keys of the Green Bungalow, telling them more or less what was going to happen, and begging them to engage an efficient charwoman. Thus when four days later we went down to Reed Bay we found fires lit and tea awaiting us.

Directly after tea I went round to the Dreevers, and brought Doris back with me to supper. In the ordinary way, I suppose, the Dreevers should have waited two or three days and paid a twenty-minutes' call; but there is no such thing as convention on the beach.

The front door of the bungalow opened straight into a sitting-room—a cross between a dining-room and a morning-room. Opposite was a door leading into the dining-room, and to left and right were other doors leading respectively to the kitchen and a bedroom, for the bungalow, being only of one storey, and intended to accommodate a number, was inclined to be rambling.

Doris and the Freecelands—who immediately showed symptoms of

liking each other—and I had just settled ourselves comfortably around
the fire when a curious thing happened.

The dining-room wall shook violently as if something struggled
against it. A loud, metallic clang sounded on the wall close to the roof.
Then the latch clicked, and the door, which opened into the room where
we were sitting, was violently flung open.

'Oh, come in!' cried Gertrude Freeceland, laughing.

Freeceland jumped up.

'That's deuced odd!' he said.

It was. I was sitting nearest the door with my back to it, and as it
flew open I had an impression that reminded me of a certain black
day in the Ypres salient, just before I received the wounds which got
me my discharge from the Army. I had not heard the coming of the
shell that burst beside me in the mud, but for the fraction of a second
I had a queer feeling of something heavy hurtling down on me. As
that door flew open I felt it again, and flinched. 'Nerves,' one would
say; and 'nerves' I was willing to believe it then.

Freeceland pushed past me and gazed into the next room.

'Nothing there,' he said.

'Wonder what it was,' cried Julia, his sister-in-law, who wore, like
the rest of us, rather a startled look.

'Wind!' said Freeceland. 'You can't expect a place like this, with
hardly any foundations, and built entirely of timber, to behave itself
like a brick house. Still, it made me jump for the moment.'

Apparently our nerves were, for some reason or other, a little
unstrung. Shell-shock had left me particularly susceptible to sudden
noises, and the others seemed quite as disturbed. Later we all jumped
again, and I opened the door and looked in to discover that the new
disturbance was occasioned by the charwoman who was gravely laying supper.

When at last we were summoned in for the meal I made a discovery
which had eluded me at tea.

'Why,' I exclaimed, 'this room is an old railway-carriage.'

Gertrude laughed.

'Hadn't you noticed that before?' she exclaimed. 'And a first-class
compartment too. Look at the ceiling.'

I looked up and saw that it was arched, and covered with rather
dirty, cream-coloured lincrusta, such as is used to cover the ceilings
of some first-class railway-coaches.

It was not so strange that I had not noticed it before. Furniture and
decorations had wrought miracles of alteration. The long rows of win-

dows were completely covered by green curtains. Above them was a shelf lined with books. A curtain reaching to the floor entirely concealed the door. But between the shelf and the windows the communication chain still remained, and it was hanging down in a loose coil as if it had recently been pulled.

'Funny!' said Freeceland. 'I could have sworn the chain wasn't hanging down like that at teatime.'

'That,' suggested Doris, 'is what we must have heard rattle against the top of the partition. It must have slipped down.'

I rose and pulled it up again. Then I jerked it down, and it took quite a perceptible effort on my part.

'Don't see how this thing could slip,' said I.

I went to the door and pulled aside the curtain. It was very obviously the door of a railway-coach. There, in faded black numerals, just below the window, was the number 6787.

There was no need to tell any of the others that I felt uncomfortable about the room, and the fact that it had once been a railway-coach made me still more uneasy. My nerves were far from sound, and I tried to put down my sensations to their vagaries. I had never before accounted myself a superstitious man, but I could not help wondering if that particular coach had any special history. It was not difficult to account for noises, or even for the sudden opening of the door, but I did not see why that chain, which was so rusty that it was difficult to pull down through its narrow grooves, should drop of its own accord.

It had dropped, however, and it continued to drop. If we pulled it up at night we found it down in the morning; also the door of the room was always open.

We spent the next three or four days in laziness—reading, playing bridge, and taking short walks. I saw Doris as often as I decently could, and Freeceland paid his friend, Hartley, a visit. We exchanged calls with the Dreevers, but Doris, lured by me, came oftener than her people—at least once a day.

On the afternoon of the fourth day I met Doris in the village, and had to decline an invitation to her people's bungalow on the following night.

'You see,' I said, 'a man named Hartley is coming to dinner. It wouldn't matter so much if I wasn't there when anybody else came, but I don't want it to look as if I don't want to meet the man.'

I told her what I knew of Hartley's history, and Doris, who knew him by sight, nodded agreement with me.

'It's terribly hard luck on him,' she said. 'I must say he doesn't look like a murderer.'

'What does a murderer look like?' I asked her mischievously.

Doris did not know; she was only positive that Mr Hartley did not look like one, and that was good enough. I took her back with me to tea at the bungalow where Gertrude and Julia were alone, Freeceland having taken the train into the nearest large town with the intention of begging, borrowing, or stealing one or more bottles of whisky.

After tea, which was served in the front room, I led Doris through the railway-coach dining-room into the beach-garden beyond.

It is hardly necessary that I should intrude my personal affairs into this story, but it would be as well to mention that on our return I was not in a condition of mind to pay much attention to Gertrude and Julia. Doris had said 'Perhaps' several times in answer to my questions, and finally 'Yes.' When at last we returned I was rather less observant than a bat. I did, however, notice, in a subconscious sort of way, that something seemed rather wrong with Julia and very wrong with Gertrude.

Well, man is a selfish animal and I did not pay much heed to them. Doris having consented to take me and mine, including the piece of shrapnel that had yet to work its way out of my back, I took little interest in anyone else's affairs. We said nothing to them about ours, and Doris refused to stay to supper, having, I suppose, something to think about.

I saw her home, and returned to be pounced upon by Gertrude. Freeceland had not yet come back.

'John,' she cried, 'don't for heaven's sake laugh at me, but this place is haunted.'

I myself had fancied something of the same kind, but never dared to put it into words. Gertrude's doing so gave me a queer shock.

'John knows,' said Julia. 'I could see he knew.'

'There is,' I admitted, 'something queer about the place, but—'

'There are no "buts",' Gertrude interrupted. 'Don't let's be afraid of giving things their names. The bungalow is haunted.'

I sat down.

'Well,' said I, 'don't tell Vicky (Freeceland). His nerves are a bit wonky, you know.'

'Vicky knows, only he won't admit even to himself that he knows. He's that kind.'

I lit a pipe. 'What's been happening now?' I asked as soon as it was going. 'Any more noises?'

'I've *seen* something,' Gertrude said quietly but impressively. 'When you and Doris went into the garden I thought you were in the next room. We stopped here because we didn't want to—er—to interrupt you.'

Gertrude paused and smiled wanly. All unstrung as she was then she was still capable of a certain archness.

'Presently we both heard a noise in the next room like two people struggling and banging against the wall. I thought you two were squabbling over something in fun. I've seen you handle that poor girl as if you were both playing Rugby football, and looked in to remind you that there was glass behind those curtains. The room was dark, and—well, two people *were* there struggling—two men. They were very shadowy and indistinct, but I saw them for a moment, and then somehow I seemed to lose them.'

'Lose them! How?'

'I don't know. I couldn't see them any more, but they were there. They pressed close against me and past me, gasping and panting, and then—then the door burst open of its own accord. Julia saw that happen.'

I looked at Julia. Clearly she did not doubt one word of her sister's narrative.

'You're quite sure?' I began puffing laboriously.

'You know,' said Gertrude, 'that I am quite sure.'

After that there was nothing more to be said.

Next evening Hartley duly arrived; and just before he came Freeceland said something that set me thinking.

'I say,' he exclaimed, 'I'd forgotten about the dining-room being an old railway-coach. I hope it won't upset poor Hartley.'

'Why should it?' Julia asked.

'Because the murder of which he was accused took place in one.'

It set me thinking, although I had no right to think. If what naturally occurred to me were true it would be a strange coincidence. Still, all things considered, it would have been strange if I had not wondered a little.

When Hartley came he proved to be a very florid man with glasses, about fifty years of age, I should think, but his fair hair had retained its colour and had scarcely thinned. He somehow gave me the impression of a man who suffered from heart trouble, and just as I came to that conclusion he told us that he did.

The suddenness of the tragedy made it all the more appalling and grotesque. Hartley had scarcely been inside the bungalow five minutes when it happened.

'Whisky's good for the heart,' said Freeceland with a smile. 'I managed to "wangle" two precious bottles yesterday. Come along in and have a spot, you two men.'

He lit a candle and preceded us into the dining-room. I went last and closed the door. Candle in hand, Freeceland marched over to the sideboard, and Hartley looked about him.

Even in that dim, wavering light I saw him change colour.

'Why,' he said, even as I had done, 'this is an old railway-carriage.'

Neither of us made answer, and Hartley smiled rather horribly as if to reassure himself. His hands moved nervously towards his throat.

'I shall be glad of a whisky,' he faltered. 'I'm not—feeling—very fit.'

I think we were both embarrassed. Freeceland was busying himself in getting out the bottle, but I had no such occupation.

'Are the glasses here?' I asked rather fatuously, and drew the curtain aside from the door to grope for the handle, preparatory to going out.

A sort of gasp from Hartley caused me to turn my gaze upon him. His eyes were huge, bulging, horrible. His gaze was directed upon the door at the spot where my moving the curtain had exposed the number—6787.

'My God!' he cried faintly, and almost protestingly, 'my God!'

I can't say precisely what followed. Somehow the candle went out. Freeceland doesn't think he dropped it or blew it out, but he cannot be sure. Simultaneous with the sudden darkness came the crash of a heavy body falling.

'What's the matter?' I cried out. 'What are you two struggling over?'

'Don't be a fool! We aren't struggling!' said Freeceland's voice, high and agitated. 'Come here, quick!'

But two people *were* struggling there in the darkness. They brushed against me and past me, locked in a struggle for life or death. The door flew open, apparently of its own accord, and a panel of light from the next room fell across the floor. It showed Hartley lying prone and still, his face yellow and wax-like, and—well, the reverse of peaceful. It never did look peaceful, that face. When I knelt beside him he was quite dead. Heart-failure, of course.

We had the curiosity to go to the British Museum and read in some old newspapers an account of Hartley's trial. He had been accused of murdering a rival in business by half-throttling him in a railway-coach and flinging him out on to the line, thus breaking his neck. The victim had managed to pull the communication chain, but the train stopped too late. The number of the coach was not given, but we are pretty certain that it was 6787.

THE ATTIC

Before the war, Stanley Forbes and Raymond Telford used to play Rugby football together for a small and unimportant club, now defunct, which rented a playing-pitch near Wimbledon. They had nothing very much in common, save that they formed the left wing of the three-quarter line, and shared common triumphs and failures every Saturday afternoon during the season.

The club consisted mainly of young men who had 'jobs' in London offices and had more money to spend at the weekends than at any other time. After matches it was customary for the team to pay a protracted call at the nearest house of entertainment, and afterwards go up to the West End, there to dine inexpensively and go on to a music-hall. They saw little of one another save on the field, and at these subsequent mild debauches.

However, Forbes and Telford discovered that only the length of a short street separated their respective business premises, and this led to their lunching together two or three times a week, talking of past and forthcoming matches, and working out schemes for attack and defence. Forbes worked in the office of a firm of chartered accountants, and Telford was articled clerk to a long established firm of solicitors. They were of much the same age, their prospects in life were about equal, and, in a quiet, unostentatious way, each was more than a little impressed with his own importance. It is more than likely that the tacit rivalry between them was at the root of this casual friendship. They never boasted openly to each other of what they had done or were going to do; there was a slight strain of subtlety in both of them; but each was firmly convinced that he was the better man and would wrest more out of the world than the other.

It is more than likely that the memory of this old rivalry, after a decade had passed, was the cause of Telford suddenly writing to Forbes and inviting him to come down and stay with him for a week or two. Telford had come into money, and had bought a partnership in a firm practising at Horlington, in the New Forest. He was proud of the big house he had recently bought and the pretty young wife he had recently married.

The war, which had killed the football club—and, incidentally, most of its members—had separated Forbes and Telford. They were gazetted to different regiments, and came out with honours easy, each having won the MC and attained the temporary rank of captain. Neither played football again after the war. They were getting 'thirty-ish,' when most men prefer to become spectators; and Telford had in his leg that which put an end to all serious athletics. Having settled in the Moat House, which stood actually in the Forest, whence he drove himself to the High Street office every morning and afternoon, he fell to wondering how 'old Forbes' was getting on, and at last, obeyed an impulse to write and ask him and invite him down. That was in the spring of 1924.

Forbes was not at all averse to meeting Telford and comparing notes. He was unmarried, but unlikely to remain so indefinitely, and he, too, could boast of some success. He also was now a partner, and his firm, which specialised in making war on the income-tax commissioners, was prospering exceedingly. He was overdue to take a holiday, and he accepted the invitation very much in the spirit in which it was made. He drove himself down in a brand-new car on the Tuesday of the week preceding Easter.

If there had once been a moat around Telford's house, there was no sign of it now. Instead, there was an old red wall, ten feet high or more, up which closely trimmed ivy climbed in places, which completely hid house and gardens from the road and lent the place not so much an air of privacy as one of secrecy. The wide gates were of solid timber set in an arch; and a little door further down the wall—which, when open, showed nothing more satisfying than a path which lost itself immediately in a dense shrubbery—gave access to servants and tradesmen.

'Pretentious, but dark and damp, I should think,' thought Forbes, as he got out of the car and pushed open the heavy gates.

On the inside was a small lodge, and a woman came out to close the gates behind him as he drove through. The house, just visible through the fledgeling trees, was scarcely fifty yards distant. He followed the windings of the short drive, and came to a halt on fresh gravel before the front door.

The house was long, three-storied, creeper-clad, and of a slightly depressing aspect. Forbes recognised Jacobean architecture, and at the same time wondered what a lawyer in a country practice could want with a house of such a size. For one idle moment he speculated on its past and on the intentions of those who had designed and built it. While nobody but an estate agent could have described it as a country mansion, it was too large to be called a hunting-box. Then the door opened and Raymond Telford, looking scarcely a day older after ten years, came out with a grin of welcome and a cheery hail.

An hour later, over tea in the drawing-room—dispensed by the frail, dainty wisp of a girl who had been Mrs Telford for the past two years— he learned how his host had come to acquire the house.

'Of course,' said Gladys Telford, 'we and the furniture are simply lost here. We don't use the top floor at all, and keep it empty except for one attic which we use as a box-room. The servants sleep on the same floor as ourselves, in order to save work. It's a lot too big for us, but we shan't be here for ever. We shall be selling it.'

'I'm hoping to make a clear couple of thousand on the deal before I've done,' remarked Telford, with quite his old air of suppressed but conscious cleverness.

'I hope you'll prosper to such an extent that you'll soon find it too small for you,' Forbes said.

Gladys laughed.

'I'm afraid not. We're a very modest couple. At least, I'm trying to teach Ray to be modest. But, of course, when he decided to go into business in Horlington we had to find somewhere to live, and it wasn't so easy as it seems. As a residential district this part of the world is enjoying something of a boom. We found that there were practically no moderate-sized houses to be had, and those on the market were an appalling price. And this place was as cheap for its size as the smaller houses were dear.'

'Most people,' explained Telford, 'are poor nowadays, and they've got to think about upkeep and servants. They find it saves 'em money in the long run to pay a bit extra for a small place and save on the cost of running it. Houses of this size, which are too big for the New Poor and not big enough for the New Rich, are a bit of a drug on the market.'

'And Ray thought,' continued Gladys, obviously proud of her husband's acumen, 'that if we bought this place cheap and lived in it for a while, values would begin to readjust themselves. We could then sell the Moat House at a profit and buy a small house for very much less than we should have to pay now. Without using the top floor, it's not a difficult house to run. I manage quite well with two maids.'

Telford gave Forbes that quiet, knowing smile which, in the old days, had always reminded him of a wink, and Forbes laughed and said:

'You were always steeped in low cunning. But when the time comes you won't be able to persuade Mrs Telford to go. It's too charming.'

He had already been over the house, and he spoke sincerely. It was melancholy, but still charming. It was rich in beams and panels, and these things Forbes reverenced. For a permanent residence he preferred a modern house, but it was only right and proper that he should have friends who were able to provide him with a complete change.

'You don't feel that it's like a prison, then?' Mrs Telford asked.

'Like a—— Oh, you mean the wall? Well, on the outside I did rather wonder. But one doesn't seem to notice the wall here. Does it go completely all round?'

'Oh, yes. At the back there's just a little wicket gate which leads into the orchard and pitiable-looking broken bottles cemented to the top. I wonder who built it, and why?'

'Some old guy who got fed up with the sight of his fellow men, I suppose,' Telford laughed. 'I wonder how young Derek will like it. That reminds me. Tomorrow, my dear!'

Mrs Telford smiled.

'I hadn't forgotten. The three-eighteen train, isn't it? You've a fellow guest, Mr Forbes, and I hope you won't let him bore you. My young brother is coming home from school. He hasn't had a home of his own since mother died, so he goes around spending his holidays with different relatives. This is his first visit here.'

'Good,' said Forbes. 'I like boys. How old is he?'

'Fifteen,' Telford said. 'He's at Hurlborough, and he's going to cost me a fiver if he gets Seconds at cricket this year, which I think he very likely may. He's a bright lad. If you know anything about wireless or electricity, for heaven's sake don't let on to him, or he'll plague the life out of you.'

'I'll retaliate,' said Forbes, 'by telling him all about accountancy.'

After tea, Telford took out his two-seater and bore the guest away to the little Country Club in Horlington, where the élite, consisting mostly of retired warriors, assembled to play bridge in the early evenings.

On the way home for dinner, Forbes said:

'It's suddenly struck me. If you ever do sell that house I know exactly who you'll sell it to.'

'Who?'

'Somebody who's going to start a school.'

Telford laughed over the steering-wheel.

'That's rather bright of you,' he said. 'I'd thought of that already. Matter of fact, it has been a school. Years and years ago, though, and not within living memory. Not much chance of the kids breaking out, eh?'

Dinner was a little more elaborate than Forbes had expected. He knew instinctively that his hosts lived more simply when they were alone, and the succession of courses secretly annoyed him, not merely because they hinted at vulgar display, but because he realised that they must have cost his hostess a great deal of trouble. Gladys Telford was very jolly and simple, and he wanted her somehow to be made aware that all this fuss on his behalf was quite unnecessary. But Telford was a good host, and after Gladys had crossed the hall to the drawing-room he crowned the evening by producing an old vintage port and a very old brandy.

It was when they were on their way to rejoin Gladys that Forbes halted in the middle of the hall and stood listening.

High up, and coming seemingly from the very roof of the house, he heard the shaken, rending sound of a child sobbing. The sounds varied. Sobs became a low wail, ending in a paroxysm like a muffled scream, changing again to hard, tearing sobs. Infinitely distressing, with their suggestion of the direst bodily or mental anguish, the sounds came straight to him down the well of the staircase.

'Good lord!' he exclaimed. 'What's that?'

'That,' said Telford with a chuckle, 'is our ghost.'

He pinched Forbes' elbow and gave him a gentle push towards the drawing-room.

'Stanley's just been hearing our ghost,' he remarked to Gladys, who had risen to ring for the coffee.

'Yes,' she said indifferently, 'I noticed it as I came through.'

Forbes looked from one to the other and laughed weakly.

'But what on earth is it?' he asked. 'It sounds exactly like a child——'

'I know! I know! It frightened us to death when we first heard it.'

'It's a ghost,' said Gladys, turning away from the bell, 'that comes to warn us. But that's quite usual among ghosts, isn't it?'

Forbes smiled, and continued to look puzzled. They were plainly teasing him.

'But what is it?' he asked. 'And what does it warn you against?'

'Rain,' said Telford. 'It means that the wind's gone round to the south or west. Our ghost is actually a chimney-cowl which needs something done to it. When it spins one way it doesn't make a noise, but when it spins the other way we get *that*.'

'Well, it sounds most uncanny,' Forbes remarked, sitting down opposite his hostess. 'I could have sworn you'd got some frightened child shut up in one of the attics.'

'Quite ghostly, isn't it?' Gladys laughed. 'We never believed in ghosts, but we thought at first we'd got one. We soon found out that it was the chimney-cowl, but it scared us at first.'

'You must have thought it was the ghost of one of the kids who were here when the house was a school?' Forbes suggested.

Husband and wife exchanged smiling glances.

'We never thought of that,' Telford said. 'What I call a nice, cheerful suggestion! Pity you weren't here to remind us the first time we heard it. It would have made going up to bed seem still more adventurous.'

For the moment Forbes was disinclined to let the subject drop.

'You hear it in the day, then?' he asked.

'Not to notice,' Telford returned indifferently. 'Plenty of other noises then. Besides, during the day one takes no notice of sounds which seem pretty ominous at night.'

When Forbes went up to bed the house was silent.

'Wind's dropped or changed again,' he remarked to Telford. But he was hardly in bed when the sobbing and crying, which now seemed to come from close overhead, broke out again. He lay listening, conscious of a vague uneasiness and a quicker beating of the heart.

'If that's a cowl,' he thought, 'I'll eat it.'

Presently he jumped out of bed, wetted his index-finger, and held his hand out in the night air.

'H'm!' he muttered, withdrawing his hand over the sash. 'Wind seems to be nor'-east. Ray was wrong.'

He stood irresolute a moment, cold and strangely uncomfortable.

'Still,' he thought, 'if it's a chimney-cowl it's a chimney-cowl, and that finishes it. And if they're satisfied, why shouldn't I be?'

He went back to bed, but he did not fall asleep until the sobbing noise had ceased and the house was quiet.

The following afternoon brought upon the scene Master Derek Wilson in the black coat and dark trousers which were the uniform of school servitude, and the customary 'going-away' bowler hat. He was a tall, dark, fresh-faced boy with a friendly grin and a very happy laugh. He brought with him two periodicals, one devoted to wireless and the other to motorcycling, and, after having been introduced to Forbes, followed his luggage upstairs to array himself in gorgeous tweeds. He came down again whistling, full of high spirits, and demanded to be allowed to explore. Telford was not yet home from the office, so Forbes accompanied him.

'Thank everything the bally spring term's over,' he remarked to Forbes. 'Hockey and Lent is a ghastly combination. Gladys looks fit. How's old Ray? Had an invite to go and stay with a chap in my house whose people live in Earl's Court, but I wanted to have a look at this stately home of England which Gladys and Ray have got hold of. Besides, there's nothing to do in London now, and you want such bags of money.'

'Which nobody seems to have nowadays,' Forbes remarked.

'Especially when you've got trustees,' Derek added cryptically.

On the whole, he struck Forbes as being quite a nice boy, who could be enthusiastic without gushing and seemed easy to please and entertain. He liked the house, and was glad that it contained no wireless set. He would put one up while he was there. He had never been in the New Forest before, and was glad of the opportunity to explore it. Forbes earned his gratitude by promising to take him around in his car while Telford was away at the office. Indeed, the boy seemed perfectly happy in his surroundings and in the prospects held forth to him for the holidays.

Before going to bed that night he was warned about the chimney-cowl, but the peace of the house was not disturbed. Forbes, coming down early on the morning following, found Derek out on the drive talking to Robinson the old gardener. Derek greeted him with a grin and a wave of the hand.

'Robinson says this place used to be a school,' he said. 'Did you know?'

'I'd heard so. Must be pleasant for you to feel that you're still living in the odour of learning?'

'Oh, that must be near a 'undred years ago, sir,' said the literal Robinson. 'My gran'father used to tell me about it when I were a nipper. All sorts of stories he used to tell me. The man as kept the school used to starve the boys and beat 'em something 'orrible.'

'Good old Squeers!' laughed Derek, safe in his generation. 'That's the stuff to give 'em.'

'Well,' said Robinson seriously, 'as a matter of fact he were rather like that man Squeers as you reads about in Dickens, and this were just the same sort of school. There was no 'olidays, and people used to send boys here just to get rid of 'em. Something bad happened at last—I never 'eard rightly what it was—and Hicks, the man who kept the school, run away.'

'More than the boys could—with this wall around them,' commented Forbes. 'Derek, my lad, be thankful that you're twentieth-century vintage.'

The boy laughed.

'Oh, I wouldn't have stayed here with old Squeers,' he said. 'I'd have got away somehow, although it 'ud take a cat burglar to get out. And, talking of cat burglars, I believe old Robinson's one.'

'Me!' chuckled Robinson, who was sixty and rheumatic.

'Yes, you! What were you burying under the wall last night at the back of the house, at the kitchen garden end? Midnight, too! It looked suspicious.'

Robinson looked blank and Forbes chuckled.

'Robinson,' Forbes said, 'doesn't believe in working overtime.'

'Well, somebody was digging away like blazes. It wasn't you, and it wasn't Ray, because you'd just come up to bed. I was standing look-ing out of the window——'

'Smoking, I s'pose?' interpolated Forbes.

'Ssh! Not a word to Ray! Anyhow, I was looking straight across the garden. You know what a fine bright night it was. There was hardly a breath of wind and everything was quite still, so that the sight of something moving caught my attention at once. It was a man digging away like steam at the foot of the wall close to the biggest pear-tree. I couldn't see him very clearly, but quite clearly enough to know what he was up to, and he was either burying something or digging some-thing up. I thought it was a bit funny, and nearly went and told Ray. And then I thought it might be only somebody burying rubbish out of the kitchen, in which case I would look rather an ass, and you and Gladys and Ray would pull my leg about it all the hols. After a bit a cloud came up, and I wouldn't see him any more, so I waffled off to bed.'

Robinson was slightly up in arms. It was *his* garden, and he could not listen unmoved to this tale of unauthorized digging.

'*Where* did you say this was goin' on, sir?' he asked.

'Come along,' said Derek, 'and I'll show you. Dash! There goes the gong. Never mind. We've got time.'

He led the way around the side of the house, across the dewy lawn at the back, and on through the kitchen garden to the boundary wall.

'There you are,' he said, pointing. 'In that corner.'

Forbes and Robinson followed him and looked down. The crust of the earth was solid, hard, smooth, and stiffly knit. Robinson laughed.

'You been dreaming, young sir,' he said.'That earth ain't been turned since I been here, and you can see for yourself it weren't turned last night.'

The boy looked blank.

'But I swear——' he began, and then broke off. 'Yes, it was here, too. It's the only part of the wall you can see from my window because of the trees. And I marked the place by this old pear-tree.'

Forbes laughed and punched him lightly on the shoulder.

'Come on to breakfast,' he said. 'You were dreaming.'

'I wasn't! I ought to know.'

'Well, if you weren't, you saw the shadows of the trees moving about. You and your cat burglars and people burying things at midnight! You'll be seeing ghosts next!'

During the day the incident was forgotten by all except Derek.

The next morning ushered in a torrent of rain which went thrashing through the leaves in the garden and beat upon the windows of the breakfast-room.

'I expected this,' said Telford, rubbing his hands. 'Heard our ghost again last night. That old chimney-cowl nearly always lets us know. Where's Derek?'

The maid who came in with the coffee-pot at that moment remarked that she thought Master Derek had gone out. She had been to his room with a cup of tea and found it empty and his clothes gone.

'He's gone for a walk in the Forest,' Telford remarked, 'and he's probably taking shelter somewhere out of the rain. Better keep something hot for him. It won't be much; only a heavy shower.'

But the clouds passed over and still no Derek appeared. Telford drove off to the office and, as time passed, Gladys Telford began to grow anxious. Midday at last brought the second post, and, most surprisingly, a letter from Derek bearing the local postmark. Gladys opened it, frowned and stared. Then she read the contents aloud to Forbes.

'Dear Gladys,— You'll think it horribly low-down of me for bunking off like this, but I can't help it. I don't want to tell you why I'm going— at least not yet. I'm catching the first train to London, and scribbling this note to you on the platform. I can't stay in your house another minute, so I'm off to stay with Lindley's people at Earl's Court. They asked me, so it will be quite all right. Don't think I'm a beast. I can't help doing this. Love. DEREK.

'Well, what on earth do you think of that?' Gladys exclaimed.

Forbes uttered a baffled laugh.

'It beats me. Why, only last night he was talking about going down to Hurst Castle, and I promised to run him down to Keyhaven in the car.'

'It's not a bit like Derek.'

'People,' said Forbes reflectively, 'when they leave a house in a hurry generally write a note there and then. Funny idea to write one on the station and post it. What time does the first train go?'

'Five o'clock. And the station's two and a half miles away. Why, the boy must have got up in the middle of the night. Look at the handwriting— how shaky it is.'

'The boy's been scared stiff by something.' Forbes almost said, but he looked at Gladys and checked himself in time.

'I wonder,' he said, rather unsteadily, 'if that chimney-cowl upset him.'

Gladys shook her head.

'We warned him what to expect. Besides, Derek wouldn't be such a baby.'

At that moment a maid appeared with a buff envelope on a salver, and inquired if there was an answer. The telegram was brief and to the point.

'Derek arrived safely. Bringing him back to you tomorrow.— LINDLEY.'

'Well, that's that!' said Gladys. 'Poor Derek! I wonder what Ray will say about it?'

Telford said very little about it to his wife, but he was plainly very much annoyed. To have his hospitality slighted pricked him in his most vulnerable spot. Privately to Forbes he held forth long and sulphurously.

'Damned bad-mannered little beast! After all we've done for him! To go sneaking off like that. I'll never have him in the house again. When this Lindley brings him back I'll send him off somewhere for the rest of his holidays. I'm finished with him!'

Forbes had his own opinion about Derek's conduct, or, rather, vague and uncomfortable theories had begun to form in his mind. He, too, had heard those noises, so terribly like a child in an extremity of woe, on the preceding night.

The chimney-cowl? Was it? Could a chimney-cowl really produce sounds so completely and utterly human? Because the chimney-cowl certainly made noises at times, the Telfords and their servants, all hard-headed and practical folk, were completely satisfied that all sounds, otherwise unaccountable, proceeded from it.

He did not believe in manifestations of the supernatural, but his scepticism was not bigoted. The Telfords said in effect: 'There is no child in the house, there are no such things as ghosts, and therefore it must be the chimney-cowl.' Forbes did not go all the way with them. Apparently nobody had gone up to the attics in the dark to make sure, unless—— Here came a thought which set his nerves tingling unpleasantly and strangely chilled him. Nobody had gone to investigate, *unless Derek had.*

Forbes could not help remembering that the house had once been used as a school by a scoundrel who starved and ill-treated unwanted and friendless children. In his walled-in house in the New Forest he had been as immune from observation as the Yorkshire schoolmasters whom Dickens pilloried. At last there had been a scandal and the man had run away. What scandal? It was buried now in the limbo of lost things, whence, in all human probability, it would never be dug up again. But certain it was that the walls of this sad old house had once heard the cries and sobs of maltreated children which now the chimney-cowl—*was* it the chimney-cowl?—so strangely imitated.

But he said nothing to the Telfords. They would have laughed at him or heard him not too patiently. The following day, Good Friday, would bring Derek back, doubtless with a tale which would confirm or disprove the unpleasant suspicions which were taking doubtful shape in his imagination.

That night Forbes slept soundly for an hour or two, and then woke for no reason that he could guess. The sounds which he heard faintly and seemed to be proceeding from the floor above—sounds like the moaning and crying of a child—were not loud enough to have wakened him. But now that he was awake he lay listening, while awe and fear struggled with a rising sense of shame.

He wanted to investigate, and wanted not to. Courage urged him on, fear held him back, and shame looked on and sneered.

Derek had dared to go up to those attics. He was almost sure now that Derek had gone. Derek was a boy, he a man, and he was holding back. Shame stung him to activity at last. He cursed himself, got out of bed, felt for dressing-gown and slippers, and shuffled out on to the landing.

The staircase leading to the attics was a narrow, straight, steep flight. There was no window on the top landing, and the stairhead was lost in darkness. Somewhere quite close a child sobbed and moaned, and, while his heart gave a warning of the tighter hold of fear, he could have sworn that it was a human voice.

It was not until he faced the wall of darkness above him that he realized that he had neglected to bring candle or matches. He shook the pocket of his dressing-gown in vain. He hesitated, realizing that if he went back to his room to procure a light his resolution would waver and desert him. Slowly he mounted the stairs—one, two, three, four of them. Then the sobbing became a muffled wail which died into silence, and he looked up.

Something moved in the darkness at the top of the stairs. It seemed suddenly to be pierced by a faint light, as the moon is sometimes seen looking through murky clouds not dense enough to hide it. While every nerve cried out upon the outrage thus done to his senses he beheld the figure of a man about to descend.

He did not notice what clothes the Thing appeared to wear, although he will carry to his grave the memory of the thin, attenuated hands. But it was the face which visited all his subsequent bad dreams—a face almost grotesquely evil, long and livid, and splashed across the right cheek with a hideous red discoloration of the skin. The eye were small, closely set, and smouldered as if with some evil fire. The knowledge—the certain knowledge—that he was faced with something not of this world was sufficient to drive Forbes to an extremity of terror, but it was the indescribable vileness of the Thing which momentarily bereft him of his wits and atrophied all his nerves of motion.

Agony drew out time, spending it like a miser. Whole minutes while the descending feet passed from stair to stair. Somewhere, deep down in Forbes' tortured brain, the machinery still worked. The Thing was descending and would pass him—would pass him on stairs so narrow that one human being could scarcely crowd past another. The prospect of close proximity, of actual touch, gave him another push along the road leading to madness. He struggled to move as one in a nightmare struggles to wake. Mercifully, something seemed to snap, leaving him free to spring backwards, to sprawl and plunge at the foot of the stairs, and thence to rush for his bedroom, where he turned on the friendly electric light before pressing his face into his pillow.

It is not necessary to this account to describe how he spent what remained of that long night. He came down in the morning looking the sick man that he felt himself to be. The Telfords asked him what was the matter, and, strangely, he felt that he could not tell them. Drearily he felt that he did not know how to begin to tell them. He could now only wait for Derek.

Derek arrived at three in the afternoon, white-faced, after a drive of a hundred miles through crisp, spring weather in an open car. He came accompanied by a grey, dapper, middle-aged man, who gave his name as Colonel Lindley.

'I expect you've heard of me?' he said to Telford with a faint smile. 'My boy and Derek are friends at school. I invited Derek to spend the Easter holidays with us, but found that you had forestalled me. I should be very glad to have him, but I did not like the way he had left you without any explanation, so I have brought him back to tell you his story like a man.'

Telford was looking at the boy in no friendly way; and Derek, white and fidgeting, kept his gaze bent downwards.

'If,' continued Colonel Lindley, with a tactful glance at Gladys, 'Derek and I could have a word with you alone—'

'I don't think that's at all necessary, Colonel Lindley. My wife is his sister. Derek can have nothing to complain of in the way he has been treated here.'

'Certainly not. But I was thinking that if Mrs Telford were nervous— To put it bluntly, the fact is that Derek thinks he's seen a ghost.'

Derek looked up at the faint sound of derision which came from his brother-in-law's lips. The boy's eyes suddenly flashed.

'Yes, you dare to laugh!' he cried. 'You go through what I went through and then see if you laugh!'

'There, old chap!' said the colonel, and touched his arm. 'Mr Telford,' he continued, 'whatever you and I may believe on the subject of apparitions, and whatever the explanation may be, it is quite evident that poor old Derek has had a bad shock. His nerves are all to pieces. Aren't they, old man? I know you would not wish to keep with you a boy who is badly scared of the house, and I trust I was not officious in promising that he should return with me. Meanwhile, he owes you an explanation. Apart from that, I think you will agree that there are reasons why you should hear his story.'

The pinched, white face of the boy touched Telford in spite of himself.

'Well, what did you see, Derek?' he asked, not unkindly.

For the moment it looked as if Derek were about to cry.

'I can't,' he muttered, with a queer, half-hysterical petulance, 'I can't talk about it!'

Forbes drew nearer to the boy.

'Never mind, old man,' he said unsteadily. 'They'll believe you. I saw him, too.'

For the moment every pair of eyes were on Forbes. Telford uttered an exclamation and a faint cry came from Derek.

'You!' he gasped. 'You've seen him? What—the little boy?'

'No; the man.'

The boy struggled and choked.

'Oh, he was *worse!* It was him that finished me. Did you see that red mark on his face? A port wine mark they call it, don't they? Tell them you saw that, and then they'll believe—'

'I saw it,' said Forbes unsteadily, 'and I'm not likely to forget it.'

'Good lord!' said Telford, just above his breath.

Derek drew a deep breath and seemed to gain courage.

'I'll try to tell you what happened,' he said. 'You'll remember I didn't go to bed until you did the night before last. And when I got to my room there was a book I wanted to finish, so I sat up reading for about an hour. I'd only just got into bed when I heard that dreadful crying noise which you said was the chimney-cowl.' He paused and swallowed. 'Well, it wasn't!' he added laconically.

'Where was I? Oh, yes, I know! I lay and listened, and the more I listened the more I felt sure that it wasn't the chimney-cowl. I some-how felt that there was a kid in one of those attics, and I had to go and see. A real kid, I thought it was. I swear I never thought about ghosts.

'Well, I got to the top of the attic stairs, and the sound seemed to come from the room at the end. It was pitch dark, and I had to feel my way along. In the dark I tumbled against a door and pushed it open, and then—I don't know why I didn't faint, but I just stood still and felt as if I were dead.

'The room was just light—a faint greenish light it was, and I don't know where it came from. It was quite bare except for a table and a chair. On the chair before the table there was a boy, sitting. He looked about twelve or thirteen, and he was dressed like a kid in those old pictures of Dickens' stories—only he was dirty and ragged and his hair was rather long. He was crying terribly and his eyes were all swollen.

He looked up at me at once, and I shall never forget the look in his eyes. Then he went on writing.

'I forgot to tell you he was writing something. I can't tell you everything at once, just as I saw it. There were one or two mouldy old books on the table and some bits of paper, and the boy was writing with one of those old quill pens—an ordinary white feather.

'I knew he wasn't real—I mean real like ourselves—but I tried to talk to him and found I couldn't say a word. Presently, when he'd finished writing, he looked at me again as if he wanted something. Then he got up, still crying and moaning, and went over to the window and slipped the piece of paper he'd been writing on through a crack in the window-seat. It must have been a very narrow crack, for the paper kept on bending and he had to tease it through. And all the time he kept on looking round at me as if to make sure that I was watching him.

'When he'd done, he came away from the window-seat, still looking at me, and suddenly his face changed. Before I could wonder why, something brushed past me. It was a tall, thin man in black—oh, a horrible beast—with a great red mark on his cheek. He was carrying a thick stick, and he made a rush straight at the boy. I heard the boy scream. Then, I suppose, I must have fainted, for I woke up presently on the bare floor, and the room was all dark.

'I don't remember getting back to my bedroom. I think I must have jumped or fallen downstairs, for I found myself bruised all over. The only thing I could think of was getting out of the house. I didn't even want you, Ray, or Gladys. You couldn't have helped, and you'd have kept me talking, and you mightn't have let me go, and then I should have gone mad. I had to get straight out of the house or go mad. I gathered my clothes up in a bundle and put them on in the front drive. I'd forgotten my tie, and I found I'd left a sock behind, but I didn't care. I wasn't going back for them. I bought a tie and a pair of socks in London before going on to Colonel Lindley's. I walked to the station and found it all shut up, but I climbed the railings and sat on the platform until the first train came in. The booking-clerk, when he came, gave me a bit of paper and an envelope and sold me a stamp, so I wrote to Gladys, but it was no use trying to say what had happened. You must have thought me an awful beast, but I couldn't help it. And I'm going back with Colonel Lindley, if you don't mind. I'd rather die than sleep another night here.'

Derek came abruptly to the end of his story, and looked up gratefully into Forbes' face, as Forbes laid a steadying hand on his shoulder. Nobody spoke at first. In the face of that story, which seemed so incredible and yet rang so true, nothing could have been said which would not have sounded ridiculously inadequate. Telford was the first to speak.

'I think we'll take a look at that attic,' he said gruffly.

'I'm not coming with you!' Derek cried out.

'All right, old chap,' his brother-in-law said soothingly. 'The attic at the end, you said?'

'At the end on the left,' muttered the boy.

'Right! Colonel Lindley—'

'I should like to come with you, if I may,' the colonel replied simply.

Gladys put her arm around her brother. The hand which patted his shoulder shook a little. 'You stay down here with me, old thing,' she said.

Telford led the way upstairs, and it was he who pushed open the attic door.

'This must be the one,' he said. 'H'm! No table or chair here, you see. I knew there wasn't.'

'I didn't expect to see any,' Forbes remarked dryly.

The room was bare save for the dust which rose up chokingly from the boards under their feet. In the empty shell of the room their voices sounded strange and hollow.

Colonel Lindley walked over to the window.

'There's certainly a window-seat,' he remarked, 'and there are plenty of cracks in it.'

Telford followed, and laid his hand on the surface of the seat.

'I suppose we'd better have this off,' he said 'I'll go down and get some tools from the kitchen.'

'You'll have to smash it,' said Forbes. 'Get an axe.'

Telford left them and went downstairs. He returned presently with tools, including an axe, and it was the axe which eventually did the work of destruction.

The box-like space underneath was full of the dust and débris of ages. Splinters and scraps of mortar had found their way there. Forbes pulled the rubbish out in handfuls, and exclaimed suddenly on seeing a dirty and discoloured scrap of paper. He held it to the light, gently stroking the dirt away with his thumbs.

The removal of the dirt showed faint, pink, ruled lines which served to show that the paper had once been torn from an account-book or exercise-book. On it something was written in faded black ink. The writing was round and childish, but so faint that it was not easy to decipher. The three men bent over it, picking out words and slowly stringing them together.

The writing was in the form of a statement. Punctuated and with the spelling amended, it was as follows:

I have been locked in this room for a punishment five days and five nights. Mr Hicks comes and beats me something cruel. I think he means to kill me. I think my uncle wants me to be dead. If I die here nobody will ever know, because Mr Cawland, the usher, is as bad as Mr Hicks, and they will tell the boys that I have been sent away. So I have written this down and I am going to put it through a crack in the window-ledge, so as perhaps it will be found some day, and then people will know all about it.

(Signed) JOHN THIRKHILL.

The three men looked at one another. For a little while there was only the sound of breathing.

Telford still struggled not to believe.

'Is this a hoax, or what is it?' he said presently, as if to himself. 'I mean—a boy might easily write such a statement, without any real cause. And when he was let out at the end of his punishment he wouldn't be able to recover this scrap of paper from the place where we found it.'

Forbes made an impatient gesture.

'In the face of what Derek has told us,' he began, 'there seems to be only—'

'I know. It's incredible, but it seems almost conclusive. What do you think, Colonel Lindley?'

'I think it's murder most foul. We must inform the police—'

'Murder most foul in the eighteen-thirties or thereabouts,' Forbes interrupted gently. 'Too late now, Hicks'—he shuddered—'Hicks has gone to his own place long since. No man can avenge little John Thirkhill now.'

Telford passed a hand over his damp brow.

'I feel queer and sick,' he said. 'I didn't believe . . . There's nothing we can do now, then? Except get out of this accursed house. Nothing else we can do?'

'Yes,' said Forbes gently, 'there's just one thing. Perhaps when we've done that we shan't hear—your chimney-cowl—any more.'

'Ah!' exclaimed Telford, and flinched.

'Your gardener isn't about, is he?'

'No, he gets a day off. He may be down at the lodge or he may not. Why?'

'It doesn't matter. I want some garden tools—just a spade and a pick. Don't you remember Derek looked out of his window one night and said he saw somebody digging. I know the spot because he took me there.'

Derek heard the three men leave the house.

'Where are they going?' he asked.

'I don't know.' Gladys' arm was still about his shoulders. 'I don't expect they'll be long. Don't worry, old thing.'

She felt a tremor go through him.

'I know,' he said, with a sudden intuition. 'They're going out to dig. They're going to dig in the garden.'

They were not very long gone. The earth was soft, and they found what they sought four feet below the surface. They came back silent and white and grave, and none looked straight into Derek's face.

'Have you—have you found anything?' the boy asked jerkily.

'We'll tell you—all about it—some day, old man,' Telford stammered.

'Yes, don't tell me—yet.'

The boy crossed over to Colonel Lindley, touched his arm, and looked up piteously into his face.

'Are you ready to go now, Colonel Lindley?' he asked.

THE TICKING OF THE CLOCK

HEBDEN showed me to my room, and crossed it to pull the chintz curtains wider and thus give me the full benefit of the view across the water meadows. It was seven o'clock by summer-time, the sun was still fairly high, and the inhabitants of the rookery at the end of the garden had not yet thought of returning home.

The room was unpretentious but comfortable, and although it contained little besides necessities it had none of the uncompromising inhospitality of a hotel bedroom. There was, for instance, a table on the right-hand side of the bed which bore an assortment of the right kind of bedside books, such as Pepys' Diary, Chaucer's poems, and some of the works of Pater, Henry James, Meredith, and Stevenson. Hebden was not one of those people who thought that cheap and nasty pictures and ornaments were better than none at all. The mantelpiece was bare save for one article, and that was an article of utility.

I have called it an article of utility, for so I thought it at first, but I would now correct myself as, a moment or two later, I had to correct my first impression. Those cheap little alarm clocks are certainly not ornamental, but they are generally most useful. This one was of a type such as are manufactured in Germany and Switzerland and sold here in England by the thousand at the cost of a few shillings each, principally for use in servants' bedrooms. The watch on my wrist had been a persistent rebel for the past three weeks, and I was at first glad of the presence of this unsightly instrument for the measurement of time. And then I noticed that it was as silent as my own watch, and, although I knew the present time to be seven or thereabouts, the two hands mutely insisted that it was one minute after nine.

I walked across, picked it up, and began to wind it. The mechanism responded with a noise like that of a check winch on a fishing-rod.

'Got the exact time?' I asked Hebden. 'I think I've got some sand in my watch, so I may as well get this chap going.'

He turned abruptly.

'Oh, you're not trying to get that thing going?' he asked. 'You'll be lucky if you do.' He came over and stood behind me. 'It hasn't gone for these six years and more, and there isn't a clock-repairer who's been able to make it go, although a round dozen have tried their hands.'

'You seem to have taken some trouble over it,' I remarked, wondering why he had taken such pains over three or four shillingsworth of mass production.

'What's the matter with it?'

He laughed shortly.

'Well, none of the experts know, but I think I have an inkling. It simply won't go, and that's that. I just had it looked at to see if anyone could advance a scientific reason why it had stopped and couldn't be restarted, and none could. Perhaps you're lucky in a way. Like nearly all these cheap clocks it had a terrible tick, and you'd have thrown it out of the window or at least banished it to the landing. But I keep it because there's a story behind it. It used to belong to Martin Hornbin.'

I was interested at once. Most of us have a morbid streak in us. Hence the money taken at the entrance to the Chamber of Horrors at any waxworks show.

'Of course!' I murmured. 'I was forgetting that you were mixed up in that affair.'

He laughed good-humouredly.

'Mixed up in that affair! I like that. Considering that I didn't appear on the scene until nearly a year later. Yet I suppose in a way I was. It's just possible that I threw the last ounce into the scale which decided a man's fate, and thereby caused a sort of nine days' wonder. I don't often tell the story, because if a man calls me a liar my first instinct is to punch his head, and I don't want life to become one continuous scrap.'

'I won't call you a liar,' I said.

'Thanks!' He laughed and looked down on me. 'Well, even if you did, you wouldn't be big enough to hit. And, besides, you're my guest. Well, if you really want the story I don't mind breaking a rule in your favour. You'll think I've got Ananias beaten still and cold, but there's Dr Brewin to support me, if you care to trouble to write and ask him. And there's still the old clock here. There's an hour to spare before dinner. You'll find me downstairs when you're ready, and I'll tell you all about it over a pipe in the garden.'

I was downstairs at the end of five minutes, when I found him waiting for me, and we walked out into the patches of late sunlight and the long shadows of the scented garden. There was a little preamble while we lit our pipes, and he pointed out to me certain examples of his skill as a horticulturalist; then, while we paced the long middle lawn, he told me the story which I am about to re-tell. I cannot, of course, be completely accurate, but I shall use his own words to the best of my recollection.

You know (he said) what happened to me after the war? I'd been one of those fellows who left school in July, 1914, and found themselves in khaki by the middle of August. When peace came along I was nearly twenty-three, with no profession except soldiering, so I stuck in the Service as long as possible. Then, after a year or two, the popular passion for economy got me stuck on the Reserve of Officers and decanted me on a hard, cold world with two or three hundred pounds and no prospects for the future. That was before I came into Aunt Elinor's legacy, and, although I'd got a microscopical income of my own, I had to learn to do something in order to spread butter on my bread.

Those were the days when every ex-soldier wanted a life in the open air. No stuffy offices, no long hours of routine, but something healthy and strenuous, so that a man could go on feeling that he was a man. Lord knows how many gratuities went west in miserable little poultry farms, run by fellows who knew no more about chickens and eggs than that there was some sort of intimate relation between the two. Poultry farming had been a bit blown on by the time I left the Army, or I might have gone in for it; but I did the next worst, and got myself taken on as a pupil at fruit-growing and French gardening.

The man who took me on was an old R.E. Colonel. Sappers can do anything except pass a searching test of sanity, and what old Felmer didn't know about his job you could find room for in the stop-press column of a newspaper on Saturday night. He had acres and acres, all beautifully kept, and grew wonderful stuff; but even then I don't think it would have paid without us pupils.

There were half a dozen of us pupils, and none of us lived with old Felmer. We had to find lodgings for ourselves, and be 'on parade' at godless hours in the morning. We worked pretty well all the time it was light, with the very shortest breaks for meals and so forth. All the other pupils were ex-officers, and we formed a little community of our own and had practically nothing to do with the rest of the village.

I don't mean that we were stand-offish or ungregarious, but we hadn't much time for associating with other people. By the time we'd knocked off for the day we generally wanted to fall straight into bed and lose consciousness. Sometimes we raided the village pub, but nobody beside ourselves seemed to come into the stuffy little parlour at the back, where beer was a penny a pint dearer than in the tap-room. I'm giving you these details to show how it was that I didn't hear much village gossip or local scandal.

You know already that I got digs at Hornbin's farm. I knew, of course, that there was a certain amount of talk going on about him. He was a tall, lean, leathery, grey-whiskered old sinner of fifty or more, and the second Mrs Hornbin was quite a girl, with a sullen sort of rustic prettiness. She'd been his wife for six months, although the first Mrs Hornbin had been dead scarcely a year. In that part of the country they love funerals and wreaths and deep mourning, and they were just the sort of people to resent a second marriage in indecent haste—as they would call it. So although I knew the Hornbins were unpopular I put it down to the old man's aversion to celibacy and the young woman's readiness to meet him half way. But they made me pretty comfortable, and the rest was no business of mine.

Well, now I can start telling you about that clock. I found it in my bedroom on the night of my arrival, and wondered how I was going to endure having it in the room. Like most of those cheap tin clocks it had a very brisk and appallingly loud tick. It was like having a wood-pecker in the room. However, it didn't trouble me as much as I expect-ed, for on most subsequent nights I was so dog-tired that I could have slept with a thousand similar clocks all around me. I was always promising myself that I'd buy another, but I had little time and few opportunities, and when I had time and opportunity I somehow always forgot.

Like all clocks with a loud, quick tick, it used to 'talk'. After the alarum had gone off in the morning it used to say: *'Get-up, get-up, get-up, get-up,'* until I was irritated into getting out of bed and busying myself with dressing, so that I needn't hear it. It used to talk in a dreary and never-ending iambic rhythm, by which I mean to say that the accentuation always seemed to come on the second beat. On Sunday, when I wasn't compelled to rise early, I used to lie in bed and hear it tell me so. *'It's-Sunday, it's-Sunday, it's-Sunday,'* it used to say. After a bit I found that by exercising my will and imagination I could make the clock seem to say any short sentence over and over again, provided, of course, that the words were suited to the clock's rhythm; and when I had once idly pretended that the clock was actually saying the word, or words, that I wanted it to say it was strange how human the voice began to sound.

But until I started teaching it to say things—and I can't describe myself any better—the clock, like a badly trained parrot, seemed to know only two sentences. *'You're-awake, you're-awake, you're-awake,'* it used to say before I went to sleep or when I woke in the night, and in the morning there was that irritating *'Get-up, get-up, get-up.'* However, after a while, when sometimes I lay idly imagining that it was repeating to me a phrase of my own invention, I noticed subtle changes in it at times. I don't know much about clocks, but I imagine that, especially with the cheap variety, their action is apt to hasten or slow. At any rate, I would sometimes hear a loud click from its interior and then the rhythm would change, so that the words *I* imagined I was hearing changed too, and there was nothing but a garbled balderdash until I invented some short sentence suitable to the altered beats of time. I dare say you'll think this was a witless sort of amusement and a sign of incipient lunacy, but shut any tired man up in a room with a clock like that breaking in upon his thoughts, and I think, if he were honest, he'd have the same sort of confession to make.

Anyhow, I'm telling you the facts and you can think what you like. If you think that I was on the way to going off my head, there was a time when I should have been disposed to agree with you, as you shall hear. But as yet you haven't begun to hear why.

I came home dead tired as usual on a certain evening, had my supper, nodded and drowsed over the local evening paper, and blundered upstairs to bed. The old 'grandfather' in the parlour said that it was half past nine, but the clock in my room had run down and stopped two or three hours since, and I altered the hands, wound it up and set the alarum for the morning. And while I was doing this I received the most extraordinary impression.

Briefly, I felt that the clock *wanted* to talk to me, that it had some message to convey. When the postman has called I don't know if you have ever picked up a letter lying face downwards, and, although the envelope was unfamiliar, known instinctively that it was for you and contained news of great interest or importance? I have. And on those occasions I have been conscious of what people call Personality. Well, that's how I felt about that clock.

I don't mean that the clock itself seemed to have personality or anything analogous to personality, but just as I had picked up letters and known instinctively that here were connecting links between some strong personality and my own, so did I feel about that clock. It had suddenly become a connecting link between some other entity and me. It was a means of communication as ink and paper are means of communication, and I will swear that in touching it I was conscious of an influence which was baleful and sinister and unhappy.

The impression couldn't have lasted more than a second, for I had a dread of becoming morbid, and while I undressed I declined to listen to the loud chattering of the clock. But once in bed, and composing myself for sleep I had to listen, and, as usual, the clock began 'talking.' And tonight it said something which it had never said before. It said, *'Kate-speaking, Kate-speaking, Kate-speaking,'* the same words over and over and over.

The thing irritated me at first, and then almost set me laughing when I wondered how my subconscious mind could have invented such rubbish. I didn't, as far as I was aware, know anybody named Kate.

I tried presently to imagine that the clock was saying something else, and this time I failed. It persisted in this one idiotic series of repetitions, and at last I had to bury my head under the clothes to shut out the sound.

It may have been this uncomfortable and unhealthy way of getting sleep which caused me to wake in the middle of the night. The clock seemed to be ticking a little slower, and now it seemed to say very distinctly: *'I-died-here, I-died-here, I-died-here.'*

Now mine was the best bedroom in the house, and I had always had a kind of idea that the first Mrs Hornbin had died in it. The thought had never worried me because I hadn't known the lady, I didn't believe in haunted rooms, and anyhow hundreds of people must have died in every bedroom in a very old house. But I must admit that I went hot and cold all over. Of course, I wouldn't admit for a moment to myself that what I heard could be anything but the clock ticking out words which my own imagination had, so to speak, put into its mouth. But I didn't like my subconsciousness playing me that kind of trick. Eventually I got to sleep somehow and woke in the morning feeling jaded and tired.

On the following night the clock was on its best behaviour when I entered my room. *'You're-awake, you're-awake, you're-awake,'* it seemed to say to me as I lay in bed, listening. I hadn't to listen very long either, for falling asleep was as easy that night as coasting down a hill on a bicycle. I don't know what woke me between one and two, but wake I did, and with a very disagreeable sensation. A voice which sounded as human as my own was talking in the room, and it was saying only one word and a very unpleasant word at that. As dreary and monotonous as the note of a single chapel bell, but with a droning sadness impossible to describe, the Voice was saying, *'Mur-dered, mur-dered, mur-dered.'*

In an instant I was sweating all over, and although I seemed to wake to full consciousness I swear that it took me an appreciable time to realise that I was listening to no human voice but merely the ticking of the clock. It kept slowly ticking out that one word, and if you want to know what a beastly word it really is, just shut yourself up in the dark and repeat it to yourself slowly for a few times.

I sat up in bed there, staring at the clock, and went on sweating. It may seem very absurd to you, but I daren't even get up and put the clock outside. I was afraid to touch the thing.

I don't know how long I endured the Chinese torture of having that word drilled into my head. It must have been half an hour at least. At the end of that time, when I was expecting every moment to go raving mad, something in the thing's innards gave a click, and the ticks came quicker. It gave up droning out *'Mur-dered,'* but the new word it seemed to have learned wasn't much better. *'Ar-sen-ic, ar-sen-ic, ar-sen-ic'* was the new word.

Well, I don't know how I got to sleep that night, but somehow I managed to lose consciousness, and woke in the morning—when the alarum went off—feeling pretty cheap. To be frank, I was in a dead funk. It didn't occur to me seriously that the clock might be a means by which Somebody or Something was able to communicate with me. I thought, naturally enough, that my mind was going. And yet, *'Kate speaking—I died here—mur-dered—arsenic'*—well, it did make some kind of sense, didn't it?

The thought that I was going batty haunted me all day, so when I knocked off work that night I went straight and saw Dr Brewin, whom I hadn't met before. He was quite a young chap with an unprofessional manner when dealing with men of his own sort and age.

'Well,' he said, 'and what do you think is the matter with you?'

'I think,' I answered, 'that I'm going mad.'

'Literally?'

'Literally.'

He laughed good-humouredly and reassuringly.

'Well, that's a good symptom,' he said. 'Most people who are going that way haven't the least idea of it. Sit down and tell me all about it.'

I did. I told him what I've just told you. He gave me a smile which was somehow sly and yet penetrating.

'Ah!' he said. 'Who's been listening to local scandal?'

'I haven't—if you mean that for me,' I said.

'Oh! But I thought you lodged with the Hornbins!'

'So I do, but they'd hardly talk scandal about themselves. I suppose you think that because I knew the old man had married again so soon after his first wife's death—'

'My dear sir,' he interrupted me, 'do you mean to tell me that you've been here for months and not heard anything said about old Hornbin?'

I told him I hadn't; and why. Still he seemed not inclined to believe me.

'I'm going to trust you not to let this go any further,' he said presently. 'I wasn't here when the first Mrs Hornbin died. Old Wake had the practice, and he was treating Mrs Hornbin for some gastric trouble. He was a dying man himself at the time, and perhaps didn't trouble much when Mrs Hornbin died suddenly. He signed the certificate without making an examination. From what I can hear the symptoms were not incompatible with arsenic poisoning, and local opinion is to the effect that Mrs Hornbin would have got better if he hadn't helped her into the next world.'

He paused and we stared at each other.

'I'm a doctor,' he continued. 'I don't profess to know anything about spirits. I don't believe in them and I don't disbelieve. But suppose there were such things and one of them wanted to send a message—as poor Mrs Hornbin might be supposed to want to send one—I don't see why she shouldn't use that clock if she couldn't speak for herself.'

It was a ghastly thought, but it was comforting to know that he saw no signs of lunacy in me.

'What's to be done?' I asked.

'I don't know. I've had half a mind to look into the matter a long time ago. Local gossip, you know. It won't have been the first time that local gossip's been the cause of an exhumation. But I've done nothing yet, because I really haven't had sufficient cause to meddle. But now—well, I think I shall go and see the Chief Constable. You've just about turned the scale.'

'And what'll happen?' I asked, with a funny tight feeling in my throat.

'Oh, if he thinks as I do there'll be a post-mortem. It'll all be done quietly and privately. Another little job for Dr Bee.'

He meant, of course, the great pathologist whose name was, and still is, a household word. I went home comforted, but more mystified than ever, and I couldn't help shrinking from the sight of old Hornbin in the kitchen. After what I'd heard the man began to look to me like a murderer.

When I got to my room that night, what do you think that infernal clock was saying? It was ticking away triumphantly and saying:

'They've got him! They've got him! They've got him!'

I put it out on the landing and risked not waking in time. And in doing so I almost dropped it, because I couldn't bear the feel of the thing.

Well, you know most of the rest. They came and arrested Hornbin about a fortnight later. The woman was found to have died of arsenic poisoning, and suspicion, followed by proof, settled on her husband.

Of course, I had to leave the farm then, but I took the clock with me as a souvenir.

They hanged Hornbin at Wandsworth at nine o'clock one morning. You can see for yourself what time the clock stopped. It hasn't gone again from that day to this.

THE IMPERTURBABLE
TUCKER

IT could only have happened in a large town parish, whose ill-defined boundaries were known only to the vicar and the parish clerk, if even to them. And it happened on Christmas Eve, which means that the weather was muggy and wet, and that everybody with any desire or pretentions to sing carols—and many who had neither—were out and after their neighbours' legal tender.

The official carol singers, comprising certain male voices from the church choir, led by Mr Thomas Tucker, were, of course, doing better business than their rivals.

The reasons for this were many and good. The noises they produced were less painful to sensitive ears. They had *locus standi*. And where Mr Tucker observed no symptoms of generosity he was able to plead that all the monies were to be handed direct to a most deserving cause.

Apart from the facts that he had a baritone voice of sorts, and could reach the compass of a sailor having teeth out without gas, there seemed no very good reason why Thomas Tucker should be a member of the church choir.

Many people questioned why he was, although the answer was quite simple. It was simply because he was a creature of habit and had been made to join the choir as a small boy. His mother had conveyed him to all the practices by the left ear—which even now protruded a little more than the right—until the habit was so engrafted on him that he could be trusted to go alone.

For similar reasons he was now a butcher. He had been apprenticed to the trade in days when his fancy had lightly turned to the High Seas and to deeds of doubtful ethics under a flag which he was wont to call the Jolly Ole Roger. He had become a full-blown butcher simply because everybody else connected with that particular shop had died, and because he had heard that the only pirates left were certain Asiatic gentlemen who lived principally on rats, birds' nests and unwanted dogs.

He was not only a person with whom habit soon became unaltera- ble nature, but one to whom nothing came amiss. He was phlegmatic as a waxwork figure, and people said that it was impossible to shock, surprise or scare him. How true this may be the reader must presently judge for himself.

Tucker and his band of singers had been out some two hours ere they came to a curious old house, once of some pretensions, hiding away from its new and perky neighbours behind a red wall enclosing a bedraggled garden. Two or three members of the choir halted before the rusty gate and debated as to whether the house came within the parish boundary.

'Doesn't matter,' said Tucker. 'People who live in it won't know either.'

And he pushed open the creaking gate and led the procession up the path. They formed a semicircle in front of the hall door of the dingy old house that showed not a light anywhere.

'I b'lieve it's empty,' said the leading tenor.

'Soon see,' said Tucker. 'Good King Wenceslas.'

They got as far as the good king's lavish order for pine logs, when they suddenly stopped, Tucker finishing the verse alone. No lights had appeared, and all except Tucker were convinced that they were wast- ing their breath on an empty house.

Hoarsely they pointed out this probability once more to Tucker, who had otherwise, from force of habit, gone through with the carol to the bitter end and possibly begun another.

'Soon see,' said Tucker. 'Wait a sec.'

He strode to the steps and walked up to the door. There was a great black handle which slipped back under pressure, and Tucker pushed the door open before him.

'Don't be a fool!' hissed a voice. 'You can't walk in.'

'I have,' said Tucker, and he closed the door behind him.

At first it seemed to him that the house really was empty. There were no-lights in the front rooms, as he had already seen from without, and the place smelt of dust and decay. But nothing less than a com- plete inspection of the premises would satisfy him; and largesse would certainly be demanded of any human being.

He was on his way to the servants' quarters when he noticed that a door on his left was thinly framed by a bluish light stealing through its chinks. Tucker pushed open the door without knocking and entered the room beyond.

The room was small and almost devoid of furniture. It was lit by a candle which burned strangely, and gave the wan bluish light which had attracted him.

In a far corner a villainous-looking old man was on his knees before a great chest. The old man was clad in rags, and the wicked leering face above his dirty white beard would have inspired a mediaeval designer of gargoyles.

But in spite of his rags the chest was full of gold pieces which ran like sand through his long, crooked fingers, and chinked wickedly as they dropped. The scene was weird enough, and sufficiently awe-inspiring to appal the stoutest heart.

'Evenin'', said Tucker.

The old man's wicked eyes blazed at him.

'Stranger,' he said in deep, hollow tones, 'what do you here?'

'Collecting,' said Tucker. 'Ain't you heard the carol-singers?'

'No!'

'Ah, you ought to have been round in the front. Will you go round or shall I bring 'em in here?'

'Do you know whom you address?' cried the old man in an awful voice. 'I am Devloe, the miser.'

'Pleased to meet you,' said Tucker. 'Subscriptions, however small, are invited. You don't seem to have anything less than Jimmy O'Goblins in that box. So much the better.'

'You will get nought from me,' cried the old man angrily.

'I bet I do. Buck up. Then we'll sing to you. Will you have "Noel" or "Hark the Herald"?'

'The only music I delight in is the tinkling of these little coins which are my heart's blood to me.'

'Quite nice,' Tucker agreed, 'I wish I had a few of 'em. Come on. It's Christmas time, and this is a good cause.'

'Never,' cried the old man, 'have I ever given anything away.'

'Time you did, then,' said Tucker.

'This is tainted gold.'

'Can't help that,' said Tucker. 'We've got two company promoters in our congregation, and there'd be a row if the verger didn't pass 'em the plate.'

'Every penny of this was wrung from the poor—'

'And I bet it wanted some wringing,' said Tucker. 'You ought to see the money I've got out on my books.'

'Except what was stolen by violence.'

'Ah, that's easier,' said Tucker.

'I have committed bigamy, theft, arson, forgery.'

'Really,' said Tucker, faintly interested.

'And two murders!' thundered the old man.

'You have been a bit of a nib, haven't you?' said Tucker agreeably. 'But think what a comfort it will be to you to know that you've contributed—'

A look of hopelessness dawned in the old man's wicked eyes.

'Will nothing frighten you away from here?' he demanded.

'Not that I know of.'

'And you will not go?'

'Not until you've subscribed—'

The old man interrupted him with a loud groan.

'Take a coin, then,' he said resignedly. 'Stay, I will find you the smallest. Anything to get rid—'

'Hold hard,' said Tucker. 'You needn't be mean about it. Remember it's for an excellent cause.'

'What cause?'

'The Church Warming Fund,' said Tucker.

A terrible cry emanated from the top of the old man's beard. He dropped the lid of the chest and held it down as firmly as he could with his thin hands.

'Look here!' he exclaimed. 'There *are* limits, you know. I told you the kind of life I led. Well, I died years ago, and if you think I'm going to subscribe to any kind of *warming* fund—'

Words suddenly failed him, and so, seemingly, did everything else. The light and the apparition—for an apparition Tucker now knew it to be—vanished in a flash.

'There now!' Tucker murmured.

He lingered to strike a match and see if the treasure chest had also vanished. Finding that it had, he murmured, 'There's a pity!' and went out to rejoin his fellow carol-singers.

'Any luck?' someone shouted, as he reappeared.

Tucker shook his head.

'Found an old man, but I couldn't get nothing out of him.'

'Why didn't you tell 'im to go to blazes?' somebody demanded.

'Wasn't necessary,' said Tucker. 'Come on. Next house.'

THE BOY WITH RED HAIR

AFTER the little corner shop had been broken into, and Henry Gilkes killed by a blow over the head from a jemmy, and a week's takings abstracted from a drawer in the parlour, the intelligentsia of Scotland Yard, which was presently asked to take an interest in the affair, agreed with the county police that it was the work of a beginner.

Most aggravating of all the aggravating circumstances attached to the case was the fact that the assassin had actually been seen, but little Frank Gilkes, who had rushed downstairs after his father on that tragic night, was almost worse than useless to the big, patient man who plagued him hour after hour with question after question.

Poor little Frank Gilkes was only nine years old, and the detectives had need of their patience, for he had an impediment in his speech which his terrible late experiences had not tended to alleviate. He had heard a noise downstairs, his father had rushed down, and he had got up and run down after his father. Grim reconstructions in the very room inevitably followed. His father was lying *there*, and the other man stood *here* with an iron bar in his hand. He was a big, tall man with dreadful eyes. No, he c-c-couldn't say how the man was dressed, and he h-h-hadn't seen him before. And that was all they were ever able to get from the boy.

The shop stood at a corner of a row of small villas on the outskirts of a small and depressing provincial town. Cigarettes and sweets and groceries were to be bought there, and the word groceries embraced an assortment of articles ranging from bootlaces to slices of cold meat. It was a useful shop for anybody in the immediate neighbourhood who had suddenly run short of something, and the slipshod housekeeping of the local matrons had been the gain of Henry Gilkes. They were for ever popping in—as they termed it—for sugar, or tea, or 'popped in' for sweets, and their husbands for Woodbines and Players. The shop was seldom empty, although only the more discerning realised the comparative magnitude of Henry Gilkes' apparently modest business.

Gilkes was in the habit of banking on Thursday mornings, and the robbery and murder had taken place on a Wednesday night, when more money was likely to be found on the premises than at any other time. It took, therefore, no great effort of deduction to assume that the wanted man knew Gilkes and his habits. For the rest, the crime was stamped all over with the hall-mark of the amateur. But the big man with the dreadful eyes was never found, and the hounds of the law bayed on false scent after false scent, and slowly relinquished the chase. Within a year the murderer had an undisputed place in the shadowy gallery of undiscovered criminals.

Ernest Peckham was not a big man, although he looked big to a boy of nine. Nor were his eyes dreadful, except at that time when he first wore the stigmata of Cain. Normally they were deep blue eyes, merry and kindly and utterly deceptive, and they went well with a round, chubby, rosy face. He was not more than five feet four in height, generous when he had the means, fond of animals, attractive to women, and generally popular in his restricted circle. As is quite common in such cases, he was the last man who could be suspected of such a crime; and it was a fact that nobody ever did suspect him.

The man was then twenty-nine, and he called himself a canvasser. He lived at Calby Cross, five miles distant from the site of the Weybury murder. He spent his days touting in the mean streets of half a dozen towns and villages, trying with varying success to induce working-class women to buy cheap finery, drapery, blankets, and flashy jewellery on the instalment system. He was good at his work, having an attractive smile, and a flair for telling the kind of joke which was best appreciated. When instalments lapsed he was no more harsh than the firm of Levy & Garstein compelled him to be. Everybody liked young Ernie Peckham.

It is not altogether a good thing for a man earning two pounds ten a week to taste the sweets of popularity. Such compliments as he received he must return in the same liquid measure. Moreover, there were horses which, much more often than not, belied the written word of the newspaper prophet, and football teams whose sudden lapses of form perpetually defeated his purpose of naming four home and one away.

So it happened that early one January he shared with the firm of Levy & Garstein a difficulty in balancing his accounts, and another was sent in his place to tempt the working-class wives and daughters to part from their shillings. He found himself a cipher in the published returns of the unemployed, and spent a long month practically without beer and tobacco, while he got deeper and deeper into debt with his landlady.

He had no thought at first of visiting that shop at the corner of Gaylard Road, Weybury, or of doing anything else which might put him on the wrong side of the law. He had never imagined himself to be anything but honest. But as one long and dreary day followed another, an incident which lingered in his memory burned deeper and deeper into his consciousness.

On a certain Thursday morning, not many weeks since, he had gone from door to door through the meaner streets of Weybury, and, finding himself short of cigarettes, he had entered the little general shop at the corner of Gaylard Road. He had to wait his turn to be served, for the shop was crowded. Above the babble of gossiping women he heard a voice at the counter, and saw a messenger from the public-house across the road holding out a five-pound note. 'Please, Mr Gilkes, could you change this?'

Mr Gilkes, filling a narrow valley between two mountains of tins on the counter, shook his head.

'Sorry, you're unlucky,' he said genially. 'I've just banked right up. Thursdays is my day. Come an hour ago and I could have done it—or a hundred if you'd liked. Wait a moment, though. I've taken some since, and I'll just look to make sure.'

He hurried through an open doorway into the room behind the shop. Taking no particular interest in the proceedings, Peckham heard the unlocking of a flimsy drawer. Then the shopman returned.

'Sorry,' he said. 'Can't do more than two-ten. Send the rest over later, if you like. Now if you'd come yesterday, or earlier—'

And now, weeks later, Ernest Peckham began to think seriously about that little shop. It was so easy! And a Wednesday night was obviously the time. Change a hundred on a Wednesday, could he? Lucky man. Still, for a long time Peckham did no more than think, and went about looking in vain for another job.

Queenie Smith, who worked at the laundry, was the innocent cause of his making up his mind. He was fairly confident that she loved him, but there were four or five other fellows after her, and in these days you never knew quite where you were with a girl. And it wasn't to be expected that a girl was going to wait for ever for a bloke who was out of work. Meanwhile, there was Gilkes' shop—always Gilkes' shop—and it was so easy.

Quite a number of ugly crimes have been committed by men normally and conventionally in love with decent women. Only the Recording Angel knows how many undetected thieves and murderers have subsequently become model husbands. Ernest Peckham had no thought of killing, and the crowbar which he took with him was intended merely for the common purposes of burglary. He rode over on a bicycle that Wednesday night, and hid it in a field close to Gaylard Road.

Ten thousand times during the following weeks he assured himself that he hadn't meant to kill Gilkes. He had just lost his head and struck out. The fool shouldn't have interfered just as he was preparing to go.

It was all like a nightmare to remember, vague and terrible and shadowy—that which had happened in the little room, his dashing back into the road, and his mad ride through loneliness and darkness, with Gaylard Road waking behind him in a tumult of screams and shouts and the blowing of police whistles. The police never found out about the bicycle. He was safe back at Calby Cross while they still hunted the town and the adjacent fields.

Only one incident remained distinct in the man's memory, and one face looked out clearly through the hellish mists of nightmare. It was not the dead man's face. Never afterwards was he to close his eyes without seeing a little boy in a flannel nightshirt, who appeared in a doorway, mouthing and stammering—a little boy with red hair and a chalk-white face.

Fear multiplied the man's brutality. 'I ought to have done the kid in, too! He'll be my death for this!' Afterwards he could never understand why he had spared the boy, or why he had killed the father, for no frightened man understands his secret springs of action. There remained the ghastly fact that he had left behind a witness who might some day weave a rope for his neck.

The boy's red hair and his impediment of speech added a thousand-fold to the terror which chance had lent to his pathetic personality. He stood beside the door, staring through dilated eyes, and trying to say something. 'You—you—you,' and, 'Oh——oh—oh,' and then, 'What—what—what.' A meaningless stuttering and gasping, grief and horror and fear all trying at once to find expression—no more than that. But he heard the words persistently as one hears voices in delirium, and to the end of his days he was haunted not by the man whom he had killed, but by the boy whom he had spared.

He was scarcely reassured when he read in the papers the boy's description of him. 'That kid'll be my death,' he told himself hopelessly time and again. But he was not a big man, as the child had described him, and his eyes, although the glass showed him their anxiety, were not dreadful.

The takings of the robbery amounted to some few shillings short of a hundred and twenty-six pounds, nearly all of which was in Treasury notes. The notes were nearly all old ones, culled from here, there, and everywhere, and he was confident that they were untraceable. Except for the boy he would have felt perfectly safe.

Ernest Peckham developed caution and found himself possessed of an unsuspected fund of low cunning. He conquered the instinct which bade him vanish from the neighbourhood, realising that this would be the surest way to attract suspicion, and he was very careful to continue to appear penniless. He continued to cadge for drinks and fags in his favourite public-houses.

He grew more confident as time went on, and recovered still more of his nerve; but the sight of a policeman always chilled him, and he could not endure seeing red hair or hearing a person stammer. Also he picked up an odd job or two, and this gave him an excuse for breaking in a little on his secret hoard of money.

A few weeks later the Lincolnshire Handicap was run, and, prior to the race, the newspapers published the fact that a North-country bookmaker had backed his own discredited horse to win him a fortune. Ernest Peckham put a shilling each way on the horse with two different street bookmakers, and told everybody that he had backed it. When White Bud had won at sixty-six to one he had every excuse for appearing in funds. After all, one has not to plunge very desperately on a sixty-six-to-one chance to win a hundred pounds or so. Fortune, at that time, and for a long while later, seemed persistently to favour the evildoer.

Now that he was able to make use of his money openly, Peckham set himself up in business as a tallyman. He knew the tricks of the trade, and he had a ready-made clientele. He became a thorn in the sensitive flesh of Messrs Levy and Garstein. He bought a second-hand Ford car in order to cover more ground, and a year later he married Queenie Smith. He was safe now—safe except for the red-haired boy who stammered.

The boy continued to haunt Peckham. He was not a superstitious man,

but he lived in the shadow of his own doom, and endured all the ago-
nies of a thousand different anticipations. Sometimes in imagination
he stood in the dock and heard the boy stammering his story from
the witness-box. Sometimes he projected himself into the future, and
the boy, grown into a man, recognised his father's assassin and took
summary vengeance in a hundred different and ghastly ways. Once
he woke up and heard himself mutter aloud:

'That kid'll be the death of me yet.'

His wife had roused and had asked sleepily:

'What kid?'

He stared at her, aghast, and then recovered his composure.

'That kid down at Simpson's who's always messing about with the
Ford. Took the reed out of the 'ooter the other day. Nice thing that
might have been for me—goin' round a corner.'

His superstition grew rather than diminished. If one of the women
whom he had visited had any impediment of speech, or if she came
to the door with a red-haired child clinging to her skirt, he was careful
never to call at the same house again.

He prospered, and was outwardly happy, but the fear lingered and
grew. 'That kid'll be the death of me yet. I know! I know!' And the
sight of a policeman sauntering along a road, or standing at a corner
with alert eyes for every passing face, still turned his heart to water.
He knew the folly of his fears. He was safe now—safe except for that
boy, who might not recognise him if they met face to face, and could
prove nothing if he did.

It was on a summer afternoon, four and a half years after the Weybury murder, that Ernest Peckham returned home from his round early
in the afternoon, to be greeted by his wife, who wore a portentous air
of mystery.

'Policeman's been round to see you, Ern,' she announced.

He felt his jaw drop and his cheeks whiten.

'What does he want?' he jerked out.

'Not knowing, can't say. He didn't tell me, and it don't pay to ask
questions. You ain't been stopped on the road, have you? Your licence
ain't run out, or anything?'

'No.' He felt suddenly sick and ill. 'No; everything's all in order.'
He was thinking: 'That kid—he's spotted me and told! He'll be my
death—that kid!'

'Well, you won't have long to wait,' his wife continued. 'He'll be
round again at four o'clock. I told him you'd be in by then.'

He turned upon her fiercely.

'Then you didn't ought to have told him anything of the sort. I shan't be in—see! I'm goin' out again. And when he comes round, you just ask him what it's all about—see!'

His wife laughed aloud.

'You *are* a fool, Ern,' she said, 'to get all 'ot and bothered over nothing. I believe I know what it is. He's 'erd you 'aven't took out a licence for the dog. That'll be seven-and-six, my lad, even if they don't fine you.'

Peckham lurched towards the door.

'You find out what he wants,' he said. 'Ask him straight out, and then tell me.'

The Ford was still outside. He clambered in and drove away, with the sweat pouring off his forehead. That was it, undoubtedly—the dog licence. Only he could not bear the thought of being at home when the policeman came back, of enduring the moment or two which would elapse before the man stated his business. He was quite aware of the folly of driving away. If it were the Other Thing, he was already in worse case than a trapped rat. But his nerves would not let him stay.

He drove wildly, recklessly, scarcely noticing that he was heading straight for Weybury. But the thought would not have troubled him. He had done business in the town a hundred times in the last few years, choosing always those hours when he knew the children would be in school. They would still be in school; it wasn't four yet.

They came out even as he entered the outskirts of the town. A triangle on the left of the road, with a notice beneath it, warned him, and he slackened speed a little, but only a little. He was moving at thirty miles an hour when half a dozen boys ran out through an iron gateway, kicking a tennis ball into the road.

Half angrily and half desperately he snatched at the bulb of the horn. All save one of the boys started and leaped back on to the pavement. The last ran, stooping, to recover the ball. Down the road, on the other side, came humming a laden motor-coach.

For the second time in his life Ernest Peckham lost his head. On the first occasion he had taken life; this time he spared it at the greatest of all costs. He struck the charabanc almost bonnet to bonnet, and he died that night in the cottage hospital.

'I knew that kid 'ud be the death of me,' were the last words he muttered to the nurse. Knowing no better, she thought that he had made a deliberate and heroic choice. You may find on his tombstone the text beginning: 'Greater love hath no man.'

The boy who was the cause of the accident gave evidence at the inquest. The coroner was very kind to him, remembering a previous tragedy. He was a red-haired boy, named Gilkes, and he stammered painfully.

THE GARDEN OF FANCY

I CANNOT clearly recall how the conversation began; I only remember that we suddenly found ourselves immersed in a topic which has a great fascination for all who own to a strain of mysticism. We spoke of people who dreamed vividly of houses, villages, and even towns which they had never been to, and dreamed so vividly that they were familiar with the smallest details of their visionary haunts.

It was a Sunday afternoon, and the club lounge was deserted except for the four of us who were week-end visitors to London. We were something more than mere club acquaintances, and it was a happy chance which had thus drawn us together to dispel one another's boredom.

'I think I know what you fellows mean,' said Pewsey, the artist, absently filling a pipe. 'Chap comes to a strange place, stares, and exclaims: "Why, I've been here before!" And yet he knows he hasn't. That's not at all uncommon—'

'No, I don't mean that at all,' Ford interrupted. 'In fact, I mean just the opposite. Going to a strange place for the first time and recognising it may be put down to a hundred different causes. Inherited memory—that's a bit far-fetched, of course—but there's self-hypnotism, and the possibility of having seen and forgotten pictures of the place, or having heard it minutely described. In those cases a man does not *remember* the place. He only thinks he recognises it when he sees it. We're speaking of people who dream in detail of places they have never been to—'

'And afterwards find the places of their dreams?' Pewsey asked.

'Not necessarily. Indeed, I never heard of an instance. I believe these dream-places are always non-existent in fact.'

'Don't be so sure,' remarked Harlow, the novelist. 'I should have believed that these dream-places were non-existent if I hadn't had some personal experience.'

We all looked at him to see if he were smiling, as indeed he was, but it was not the smile he wore when he indulged in the gentle pastime of pulling legs.

'You mean,' asked Pewsey, 'that you dreamed of a place you had never seen nor heard of, and afterwards you actually saw it?'

'No, I don't mean that.'

'Then how can you say you've had personal experience?'

Harlow laughed good-naturedly.

'It sounds paradoxical, I know,' he remarked; 'but it is nevertheless true. I've often thought of making a short story of it, but I can't write short stories. I can only work satisfactorily on a large canvas. Besides, there are some important links missing which I don't suppose will ever be found. As it stands, the tale is only a jumble of queerness, unexplained, and, I truly believe, inexplicable. It seems wholly improbable; and, besides, people like their fiction neatly rounded off, without any loose ends—worked out and proved, like a sum in arithemetic.'

'Never mind,' drawled Ford, with a faint air of superiority, 'we aren't the public. Let's hear the story and judge for ourselves.'

'All right,' said Harlow good-naturedly; 'but I warn you you won't believe me or be able to make head or tail of it. But it's solid fact; indeed, it was through this queer business that I first met my wife.'

We all laughed.

'Well, that's conventional enough for any work of fiction,' I remarked. 'I've read a hundred stories which began like that.'

'Yes,' said Harlow; 'but I'll wager they didn't end like this one. Well, if you want to hear, I suppose there's no harm in telling you.'

Although (said Harlow) I needn't inflict on you the whole story of my life, I am afraid it will be necessary to bore you with a few bits of autobiography. I was the only son of my parents, and my father was a retired Army man, and terribly poor. My people settled down in a pokey little six-roomed villa at Hewstone, in Berkshire, so that, when I grew old enough, they might contrive to send me to Hurlborough, which was my father's old school.

You know Hurlborough, of course. Some of the wealthiest families in the country had their sons there, but I should think, if the truth were known, there was a large proportion of boys whose parents had scraped and saved and made similar sacrifices to those made by my own father and mother.

There always was and always will be a great deal of snobbery below the surface of a public school. The richer boys set a certain standard which the rest of us had to follow as best we could. Hardly any fellow exhibited the bad form to boast about his father's money, but, on the other hand, their poorer brethren lived in terror lest the poverty of their homes should be discovered. One never openly bragged, but one bragged by inference. One casually mentioned certan good times enjoyed during the holidays, which left it to be inferred that one's people had spent a lot of money. We saw through one another, but we respected one another's poses, always remembering our own.

Roughly, the school was divided into those who could say they had hunted or shot or been to Switzerland during the Christmas holidays, and those who could not. One was terrified lest one's father should arrive on Speech Day wearing the wrong kind of hat. I dare say things have altered now. I am speaking of long before the War. Nowadays it is rather *chic* to be poor. It wasn't then. A funny, snobbish, clannish lot of little beasts we were; in fact, we were just ordinary boys of an awkward age.

I made plenty of friends. Automatically we sorted ourselves into sets. And perhaps the boy I liked most, for no particular reason, was a youngster of my own age who bore the commonplace name of Thompson. He was in my House, played in the same games, began in the same division of the same Form as myself, and, while I remained, we moved up the school together. It was as well that we were friends, because circumstance had seemed to ordain that we were to be inseparable.

He was a small fat boy with one of those cheeky, good natured faces which nobody can help taking to on sight. He had a natural gift for ragging which amounted almost to genius, and he was perpetually in hot water. A queer phenomenon he has always seemed to me—a natural clown with depths, intelligence, sympathy, and decent instincts. In any event I should always have remembered him as the coolest and most colossal liar I have ever met.

Don't misunderstand me. He was not an offensive liar. He never slandered, and he never lied with the least hope of being believed. I suppose really the offensive thing about a lie is the motive behind it. Thompson's motive was plainly to amuse. It was as if he had entered into a tacit bargain with the rest of us: it amused him to spin his yarns, and it amused us to listen. The only trouble was that if by any chance any of his milder reminiscences had some vague foundation on fact it was impossible to tell.

We knew that Thompson's father was a parson, and his status in the Church was a little vague, since Thompson sometimes described his reverend sire as a rector, sometimes as a dean, and sometimes as a suffragan bishop. As a matter of fact, the Reverend Thompson was senior curate of a large church in a suburb of London, and poor as any of the mice which may have inhabited it. Thompson had very little to say about his father but plenty to say about his uncle, who was, by inference, a county magnate with almost incredible wealth.

'Oh,' Thompson would say, when asked where he was going to spend the next holidays, 'part of the time, I suppose, I shall be down at my uncle's place. It really is a ripping show. You ought to see it!' And his eyes would light up.

There was nothing Thompson enjoyed more than telling us about his uncle's place. He had quite a gift for describing things, and he described his uncle's place so often and so minutely that most of us knew it as if we had actually paid a visit there.

The house apparently stood with its left shoulder to the main entrance and quite close the road. There were huge wrought-iron gates which opened in the middle. Over them hung a shield of arms and a lamp. There was 'a funny kind of bird' on the shield.

'You ought to know what kind of bird it is,' I once said to Thompson. 'It must be your crest too, you know.'

Thompson shook his head. He could get out of most tight corners. 'Uncle on my mother's side, y'know. Named Villiers.'

To continue, the house was built of stone, but so smothered with creepers that you could hardly see it. It had five gables. If you went up the short drive you could, instead of going straight on up to the house, turn to the left and go down a walk with box trees on one side wonderfully cut. The first represented a peacock, the second a hippogriff, the third an acorn, and the fourth a giant mushroom. Going on further you came to a tennis court raised on a bank some five feet above the ordinary garden level. Those box trees took hold on my imagination, which is probably why I remembered his description of the garden in such minute detail.

Curiously enough, Thompson never described the inside of the house. 'Oh,' he would say, vaguely, 'it's all right inside!' When asked to say where this desirable property was situated, he would reply: 'Place called Little Lynn down in Hampshire. You wouldn't know it.'

I looked in vain for Little Lynn on the map, but I did find it in a novel which Thompson had been reading. This, you will say, exploded the myth so far as I was concerned. In a sense it did. But Thompson described the place so often, and never varied in his details, that I for one suspected a vague foundation on fact. My theory was that Thompson had actually seen such a house and gardens from the outside, and they had taken such a hold on his fancy that he had generously presented them, in imagination, to one of his uncles.

All this, it may be urged, is very trivial, and but for the sequel I should be wasting my breath and your attention. I want you to understand that Thompson told me about this old house and garden so often and in such minute detail that I never forgot it and could almost hypnotise myself into believing that I had seen them.

I left school before Thompson. My father's death when I was sixteen and a half necessitated my immediate removal. The state of the family exchequer made it necessary for me to begin to pull my weight. I had won an English prize, and I could write schoolboy essays, so I was naturally considered a heaven-born journalist. Within a month influence had obtained for me a berth on the *Hewstone Weekly Argus*. There I learned my trade, in a sort of way, and at twenty-one I got my chance in London on the *Daily Leader*.

I never really cared for journalism; I had always intended to be a novelist. Journalism provided me with bread-and-butter while I was learning the other craft. I had very little fun and very little recreation. All that time I hardly saw an Old Hurlburian, and hadn't the least idea what had become of old Thompson.

By the time I was twenty-five I had launched two novels on an unsuspecting world. I lost on both these because I had had to pay for the typing; and my publisher complained that he was ruined. Then, while I was still on the *Leader* I wrote *White Sunday*, and woke one morning to find myself in clover.

I don't know what made *White Sunday* go as it did. I've written better and worse since, but everything I've done that can be called a success, I owe to the success of that one book. It has always mystified me, and it almost frightened me at the time. From a month after the date of publication it started selling in thousands.

Well, there was I, a newspaper man earning six pounds a week— and not bad pay in those days—who suddenly found himself a popular novelist and a 'made' man, as I considered the meaning of 'made' in those days. All I had to do was to chuck the *Leader*, go and live where I liked, and sit down and write another one. But the *Leader* provided me with bread-and-butter, and, although I certainly gave notice of my resignation, I was in no hurry to leave the paper until my royalties began to trickle in. I was so innocent in those days that it never occurred to me to tap the publishers for a bit on account. So, although potentially rich, I was still poor, and carried on in the ordinary way.

White Sunday had been going strong for about two months when, one morning, I was shyly approached by Miss Harding. I just knew her by sight and name. She was a shorthand-typist, one of the chief's secretaries, a neat, dark, shy little thing.

'Mr Harlow,' she said, 'my fiancé asked me to speak to you, and offer you his congratulations on the success of your book. He used to be at school with you, and wonders if you would remember him.'

Naturally I asked his name, and she said: 'Thompson.'

'What, old Tommy'?' I laughed. 'Well, I'm hanged! I'm awfully glad to hear of him again. Where is he, and what's he doing?'

'He's in a bank,' she said. 'Just now he's living in rooms at Streatham, but as soon as we're married we're going to live at Golders Green.'

'I'd love to see him again,' I said.

'I'll give you his address if you like,' she said, obviously glad to see me so pleased.

She did, too. I made a note of it and lost it immediately afterwards. I was a great deal preoccupied in those days.

'I'll bring you a photograph of him tomorrow,' Miss Harding promised. 'I don't think you'll find he's altered very much. He says he hasn't.'

She was as good as her word, and for once Thompson had told the truth about himself. The photograph was quite a recent one, but I should have recognised it anywhere. The same fat, good-natured face I used to know so well grinned at me from the glazed surface.

'You can keep it, if you like,' said Miss Harding. 'I've got another exactly like it.'

So straight it went into my breast pocket.

They knew at the office that I was only marking time, and the news editor, who was a good fellow, made things as easy for me as he could. About three days later I was sent down to Cornwall on a murder story. You remember the Penbirro murder? They didn't catch the man until six months afterwards. There wasn't very much story while the affair was still a mystery, and we Pressmen who invaded the village simply ate our heads off and did nothing. Situated as I was, it was an ideal job. I put in about five hours a day on the successor to *White Sunday*.

And now the really queer part of the story begins. Four miles out of Penbirro is a little place called Glynt, with an old church and a wishing-well, and one or two things worth seeing from an archaelogical point of view. That part of the world was strange to me, and I did a bit of exploring by way of recreation. So one afternoon—a scorching June afternoon it was—I walked over to Glynt.

I'd almost reached the village when I stopped by some big iron gates outside a house and immediately had that curious sensation which Pewsey spoke of. I knew that I hadn't been in that part of the world before, and yet I felt that I recognized the house and gardens. But in my case there was an explanation, and I struck it almost at once. I thought I knew it, because Thompson had described it to me so often in the old days.

There was the gabled, Elizabethan house of creeper-clad stone with its shoulder turned to the gate. There were the box trees cut exactly as Thompson had described—the peacock, the hippogriff, the acorn, and the mushroom. And there, in the middle distance was the raised tennis court enclosed by iron posts and netting. Over the gate was the shield of arms. I knew nothing about heraldry, and I didn't know until later that the freakish bird was supposed to be a raven. Here, to be brief, was the house which Thompson had so often described, complete, so far as I could see, in every detail. He had said that it belonged to his uncle in Hampshire, but here it was in south Cornwall.

Well, my curiosity was fairly roused, and I couldn't help smiling at the thought that Thompson had, for once, been telling something like the truth. That he had erred in the matter of geography simply showed that to tell the exact truth about anything was just outside the compass of his ability. As to whether the place really belonged to his uncle—or had belonged to his uncle—there was only one way to make sure, and that was to go up to the front door and inquire. It was a broiling afternoon, and I was hot and thirsty. If one of Thompson's relatives really lived there it occurred to me that there might be a welcome for me and a cup of tea. It was a rather queer sort of call to make, but shyness is not one of the failings of your average Pressman. So I pushed open the gate and went up to the front door and rang the bell. Within a few moments the door was opened to me by a smart parlourmaid. I inquired for her master and handed her my card.

I stood waiting in the hall while she transferred my card to a salver and turned away. But she hadn't taken two steps when a door opened, and out came a large, greyish man in flannels and an old blazer who looked at me inquiringly. The maid went up to him, offered him my card, and, with that still, small voice peculiar to parlourmaids, said: 'This gentleman wishes to see you, sir.'

He took the card, but did not look at it. He looked at me instead. The parlourmaid withdrew.

'Yes?' he said. 'What can I do for you?'

I suddenly found myself in rather a tight corner. It took a certain number of words even to begin to explain myself. While I spoke of a school friend who had described the house so minutely and said he used to stay there with his uncle, old Seymour—that turned out to be his name—looked more and more suspicious. Legitimately enough he was plainly wondering what I was leading up to, and he had a blunt direct manner which, I was soon to learn, belied his natural courtesy and kindness of heart.

'Well,' he demanded suddenly, 'what was the name of the boy who said he used to stay here?'

'Thompson,' I replied.

He made the least negative motion with his head.

'Never had a nephew named Thompson,' he said curtly. 'I don't know any Thompsons.'

'Then there must be some mistake,' I said, feeling more unhappy than ever. 'Forgive my asking, but have you been here long?'

'Born here,' he replied, with ominous brevity.

He really looked most intensely suspicious, as well he might. I might easily have been a burglar spying out the land. There had been a murder in the district ten days since. I began to make verbal manoeuvres to end what was up till then an unpleasant interview.

'Well,' I said, laughing uncomfortably, 'I am very sorry to have troubled you. Seeing the house which my friend had described I called in the hope of introducing myself to his people. As your grounds are so distinctive it seems very strange that there should be others like them.'

'Yes,' said Seymour briefly. He was twiddling my card in his fingers, and he glanced at it for the first time. Then his face changed, and he started and stared at me with half a smile.

'Are you Mr Raymond Harlow, the writer?' he asked.

I made a self-deprecatory noise of assent.

'The author of *White Sunday*?'

I admitted it and began to feel better.

'Yes,' he said, 'I've seen your photograph in the Press. It wasn't a very good one, if I may say so, or I should have recognized you sooner. A most extraordinary coincidence has brought you here, for my wife and daughter and I were all talking about you when you arrived. We have all been reading your book. It's most remarkable that you should have appeared out of the blue in an outlandish place like this just as we were talking about you.'

I explained that I was still a journalist, and that the murder in the next parish had been responsible for bringing me into that part of the world. We both of us began to talk with less restraint, and it ended in his asking me to have a cup of tea. 'I should find it difficult to make peace with my wife and daughter if I were to let you go without,' he confessed laughing.

Well, you can guess how it was. I was pretty young in those days, and new to my comparative fame. I didn't in the least mind being lionised. So I accompanied him into the drawing-room to meet Mrs Seymour and Eve, who, a year later, was to become my wife.

They were the kindest people in the world, with quick instincts for making friends. They flattered me outrageously, but their flattery appealed to something more than my baser instincts, because their liking for *White Sunday* was so obviously sincere. Within a very short time we were all laughing heartily at the extraordinary chance which had brought me to their house. They pressed me to stay to dinner, and over dinner I told the story of Thompson, and how he used to describe the gardens and the outside of the very house they were living in. We hit on what we thought was an obvious explanation. Thompson as a boy had been down that way on a holiday, had seen the house and been attracted by it, and the rest, after that, was entirely typical of Thompson.

After dinner we all went for a stroll in the gardens.

'We sha'n't see our ghost,' said Eve, slipping her hand inside her father's arm, 'because it's too early for him.'

'You've got a ghost, then?' I asked.

'Oh, yes!' said Seymour, so lightly that he might have been joking. 'We've got the most peculiar ghost in the world. Unlike any other sort of ghost, this one gets older. We've watched him grow up from a boy into a man.'

They all laughed, and Eve hastily added:

'Oh, yes, it's quite true! We've all seen him several times. We saw him first as a boy years ago, and, as father says, he's a man now. And he stays outside—he never comes into the house. This has been going on nearly ever since I can remember. He's quite pleasant for a ghost, but I do wish we knew what he wants.'

I don't know what made me do it, but something prompted me to pull Thompson's photograph out of my breast pocket.

'I suppose,' I said, 'this isn't your ghost, is it?'

They gathered around me to look, and immediately there was a shout of surprise from Seymour, and faint screams from Mrs Seymour and Eve. The ghost had been identified.

I hung on down at Penbirro as long as I could, but I was recalled at last. You may guess how anxious I was to meet Thompson. I had lost his address, but I knew I could always get it again from Miss Harding.

I've told you there were reasons why I haven't turned this into a short story. Coincidences are almost taboo, but in the freakish way things happen in real life, I ran into Thompson quite accidentally almost immediately on my return. I received my first cheque for royalties, a nice fat one, and bore it proudly off to the Temple Bar branch of the London and Suburban Bank to open an account there. I was just coming out of the manager's office when I spotted Thompson sitting at one of the desks in the body of the kirk, so to speak. He spotted me, too, and came over to the counter to speak, grinning all over his fat face. It was neither the time nor the place for a heart-to-heart talk, so I made a luncheon appointment with him. An hour or so later we were facing each other over a small table in Romano's, talking about old times. I went very warily to work with him.

'Well, Tommy,' I said, when we had exhausted each other's stock of O.H. news, 'do you still entertain your friends with little stories about yourself?'

He laughed and coloured.

'Oh, you needn't remind me of that,' he said. 'I'm a reformed character now. When I die I shall be able to walk arm-in-arm with the shade of George Washington. My object was solely to entertain, and I brightened many a young life.'

'I've never forgotten,' I said, 'about your uncle's house.'

He laughed uneasily. Plainly he thought I was taking advantage of his past failings.

'Well,' he returned, 'at least I didn't invent *that*. Well, not exactly.'

'Tommy,' I said, 'be plain with me.'

'I don't know that I can. As a matter of fact, I *dreamed* that house. I've been dreaming it all my life. I still go there in my dreams and roam about the gardens. I don't suppose there is any such place, and certainly no uncle of mine ever lived in it, if it does exist, but I didn't exactly *invent it*. Queer things, dreams, aren't they?'

But evidently he didn't yet know how queer dreams could be.

'Tommy,' I said suddenly, 'have you ever been to Cornwall at any period of your life?'

He shook his head.

'Will you swear that you haven't?'

He looked puzzled, but he gave the required oath seriously enough.

'Did any of your people ever come from that part of the world?'

'No; my father came of an Essex family, and my mother was Scotch. What makes you ask?'

After a little I told him what made me ask.

And there (said Harlow) the story ends; and you'll see why I haven't made use of it. According to all the canons of fiction we should have discovered that Thompson was related to the Seymours, or that Glynt House had once belonged to his people. And, moreover, Thompson, and not I, ought to have married Eve. From the story point of view it's hopelessly unsatisfactory.

We went into the matter most exhaustively. There was no point where we could discover that the respective family trees of the Thompsons and the Seymours touched branches. There was no reason at all that we could discover why Glynt House should have attracted Thompson. He had never seen it nor heard of it, yet he had dreamed of it, and sometimes while he slept his spirit had wandered free among its gardens. It is all quite inexplicable, and I think it is likely so to remain.

There is only one more curious point. A year or so later Thompson accompanied me down to stay with the Seymours, and saw for the first time the place of which he had dreamed and which he had actually 'haunted.' After that the 'hauntings' ceased. The Seymours are still living there, but they never see him now.

THE MYSTERY OF THE SEALED GARRET

P UNCTUALLY at ten o'clock—for the new policeman was not yet to be trusted—Billy Chignell went through his nightly ritual of crying 'Time, gentlemen!' in tones ranged between brisk joviality and reluctant severity. When he had ushered the last customer out into the night he put up the heavy bar and walked upstairs into the smoke-room.

He had four 'guests' sleeping under his roof that night, which, considering that the time of the year was early spring, was something approaching a record. Few visitors came to St. Fay, save in the summer, and most of those preferred the charms of the great new hotel, with its 'desirable situation' on the headland near the golf course. Most of the men who came to spend a night at the Schooner Inn were commercial travellers, and two or three in the course of a week was about the average number. Now chance had brought three all at once, and besides these there was Mr Dimsdale, who had been there a fortnight. Mr Dimsdale was a leisured, cultured, and extremely pleasant person in the late thirties, who cherished a delusion that there were trout in the upper reaches of the St. Fay river, and spent his days trying to catch them.

Billy Chignell, good sociable soul, liked nothing better than a glass and a chat in the smoke-room after hours with anybody who might be staying in the house.

He entered unobtrusively and sat himself on a chair near the door, for the four were engaged upon a discussion which had already waxed hot. Dimsdale, vaguely suspected by Billy Chignell of being a scholar and authority on most things, sat on a horsehair chair with an elbow resting on the table. His lips were set in a faint smile, which the landlord interpreted as a sign of suppressed amusement. Walters, a serious little man, who was something of a mystic and compelled by hard fate to vend frivolous articles beloved by womenfolk, sat simmering in a mild rage. Beside him, but a little to the rear, sat Dorley, the representative of a firm of wholesale haberdashers, smirking openly. He loved to see Walters under the lash of another's tongue, but lacked the wits himself to administer the lash. Chudd, who travelled for a firm of brush manufacturers, sat in the largest armchair and laid down the law with all the vigour of a man who relies upon noise and persistence in an argument rather than upon his own reasoning powers.

'It makes me sick,' he was saying—'right down sick, it does. How ever children, let alone grown men and women, can believe such fiddlefaddle beats me. Everybody who believes in spiritualism ought to be in a lunatic asylum, and those who go about trying to kid other people ought to get two years' hard for it. That's what I say, and I don't care who hears me say it. Ghosts—spirits—bah!'

He was a big man was Mr Chudd, with a very red face and neck. For the rest he was a blatant self-opinionated person, with hardly sufficient bovine intelligence to be aware that he was a bully.

The situation was perfectly clear to Billy Chignell before he had been ten seconds in the room. Little Walters, in the hope of starting some quiet and amicable discussion, had remarked how much talk of spiritualism one heard nowadays, and ventured his opinion that 'there might be something in it.' This had brought Chudd down upon him like a hundredweight of bricks, and he had proceeded to dispose of the denizens of the spirit world, using heavy sarcasm alternately with his table-thumping methods of reasoning. Dorley, with nods and half-words of encouragement, had egged him on, and Walters was having very much the worse of it, because Chudd, having much the louder voice, would not allow him to speak. Dimsdale was sitting quiet and saying nothing.

Billy Chignell disliked Chudd, who was noisy and would not brook the opinion which did not exactly coincide with his own. He did not think highly of Chudd's intelligence. For one thing, Chudd did not come from London—only from Bristol—and he was therefore not entitled to speak with the voice of authority.

Billy Chignell was a little disappointed to find that Chudd held the same views as himself. Not being a lawyer, he was unable to argue successfully against his own beliefs. He was, however, tolerant on the subject. If people wanted to believe in ghosts and such-like—well, they were welcome. One of his rooms was supposed to be haunted, and the stories which had reached his ears were strange and disturbing. He was inclined, lazily, to suppose that there must be some quite simple and natural explanation. He did not believe in ghosts, but he doubted his own courage, and so he had taken the line of least resistance and shut up the room. It was hardly ever needed.

'I've only just come in,' he remarked, 'but I'll lay Mr Chudd's been weighing in with some mighty heavy arguments against ghosts and spirits. I don't suppose any'll dare show themselves now.'

The delicate shaft of sarcasm glanced off the thick skin of the bag-man. Dimsdale, the angler, however, took advantage of the pause to enter into the discussion.

'Mr Chudd,' he said, 'hasn't favoured us with any arguments. We have heard him bang the table and shout and behave offensively, but no gems of reason have fallen from his lips. He has said Rubbish, and Bosh, and Nonsense, all of which are emphatic as an opinion, but unconvincing as an argument.'

Billy Chignell grinned delightedly, thankful that Chudd had found an antagonist who could take his measurements. Little Walters laughed and plucked up the courage to say:

'Yes, saying Rubbish and Bosh don't prove anything, Mr Chudd.'

Chudd's face flamed redder than ever. He was the natural enemy of men of Dimsdale's type. He conceived his intelligence to be the greater, but he had not what he called 'the gift of the gab.'

'Proof!' he cried. 'It don't want proof. If you said that two and two made five instead of four, it 'ud be rot, but nobody could prove it was rot, except by their own common-sense.'

'Oh, I see—that's the difficulty.' Dimsdale's voice was as smooth as milk. 'You are going by your own commonsense. But surely you don't expect other men to rely on your reasoning as an infallible guide. For instance, one of our leading scientists, one of the cleverest men in the land, is a confirmed believer in the things your intelligence puts to scorn. You may be a cleverer man, but I never heard of you before I met you, and if I had to pin my faith to one or the other of you I could not pin it to you.'

His speech ended in a mild uproar. Little Walters was bouncing about on his chair. Dorley, who observed that a greater man than Chudd was in the field, shamelessly changed sides and joined in the laughter. Chudd struggled to make his voice heard above the din, but for once in a way it was he who was shouted down.

'Yes,' he cried, as soon as he could make himself heard, 'and that man's as mad as a hatter.'

'Because he disagrees with you?'

'No, because he—he—everybody knows he's mad.'

Dimsdale shook his head slowly and regretfully.

'No,' he said , 'you have talked for a long time and been very rude, but nothing in the shape of legitimate argument has crossed your lips. Everybody does not believe—much less know—that that distinguished gentleman is mad. I am sure he is not. He may be a self-deceiver, but that again requires proof. You don't believe in a spirit-world partly because you think it beneath your dignity as a sober, hard-headed man of business to inquire into anything that sounds to you so childish. You don't want to believe in such things.'

'And half the people who do believe only believe because they want to. All the people who say they've seen ghosts, or talked with the dead, are liars—those that aren't mad.'

Dimsdale smiled.

'Yes,' he said, 'I'm afraid the worst enemy to the spiritualist is the liar. There are a lot of people going about who say they've seen ghosts, when they don't even imagine they have. They believe in such things and they want to convince other people. It may happen though that certain pig-headed people have had strange experiences which they won't talk about because they don't want to believe. Seeing isn't believing to a pig-headed man.'

Chudd sat upright and leaned a little forward.

'Do you believe in ghosts?' he challenged.

Nailed down by a direct question, Dimsdale smiled and shook his head.

'No—'

'Well, then, there you are.'

'Not at all. I don't disbelieve either. As a cautious man I take the middle course. I'm not anxious to be convinced. There's a room in this house that's supposed to be haunted, but I haven't plagued Mr Chignell to let me sleep in it.'

'A haunted room? In this house?'

Dorley and Walters repeated the words, and all eyes were turned upon the landlord.

'No there aren't,' he muttered. 'Aren't no such things.'

'Of course there ain't!' Chudd cried. 'Which room is it, boss?'

'Not the one where the murder happened?' Dorley inquired.

'It's shut up now,' said Chignell. 'I don't believe in ghosts, but there are folks who do, and I've got my living to make.'

'Did anybody see anything there?' Dimsdale asked.

'I dunno—there was complaints.'

'Complaints? What of?'

'Oh, all sorts of things. All imagination, I dare say. But there was complaints, so I shut it up. I can't afford to have people complaining in my house.'

'What's this about a murder?' Walters inquired eagerly. 'I didn't know there'd been one here.'

'It was some years back, just before I took the house,' Billy Chignell explained. 'A skipper it was. He'd just come ashore and he took a bed here for the night. It seems he'd had trouble with some of his crew—lascars and black men and such-like. Anyhow, he was found dead in bed in the morning—strangled! They never caught the man.'

'He must have been in this house the whole time,' Dorley exclaimed.

'No; they reckoned he'd managed to hide himself in the Black Horse, opposite, and crawled across from one window to the other. With the streets narrow, like they are here, and the upper storeys nearly meeting overhead, anybody could do it. The skipper had locked his door overnight, and it was found locked in the morning.'

'P'r'aps Mr Chudd 'ud like to spend the night there,' said Walters, grinning.

'I wouldn't mind.'

'No,' said Chignell. 'I don't want any complaints.'

'I sha'n't make any complaints.'

'I think Mr Chudd should certainly sleep there if he wishes,' Dimsdale put in. 'I wouldn't myself, because I don't disbelieve in ghosts.'

'Afraid!' said Chudd.

'Not necessarily. I don't go about in search of danger and discomfort, that is all. But you, as you definitely disbelieve, have nothing to fear.'

He looked sharply at Billy Chignell, who was preparing to utter a protest.

'I hate suggesting that our worthy host should be put to any trouble,' he continued, 'but it would be a matter of only a few minutes to have bedding put in that room. And if Mr Chudd is really anxious—'

'I am,' said Chudd, and he meant it.

The man was honest enough. He was quite convinced that he had nothing worse than a damp bed to fear. Give him a dry bed and he would be all right.

Billy Chignell hesitated. He had had complaints about the room, but he did not believe that it was haunted. He could not see of what advantage it would be to give Chudd the opportunity of crowing like a gamecock over the breakfast-table and pouring fresh scorn on the

credulity of weaker mortals. However, it was obvious that Dimsdale
wished it. Dimsdale was watching him now, anxiously, appealingly. He
found it hard to deny Dimsdale anything.

'All right,' he said, 'you can sleep there if you want, Mr Chudd.
Only you won't forget I did warn you that people have made complaints about that room.'

The room of evil repute assigned to Chudd proved to be a cheerless
and damp-smelling garret. It was in the old part of the house, which
means that portion which had escaped the hands of a previous owner
with a passion for renovation and reconstruction. The floor was on
a slant and the ceiling hung absurdly low—so low that a tall man had
to remember to bend his head as he passed under the long beam on
his way to the dressing-table.

The one window faced another window in the house opposite, and
the two were so near together that, by leaning well out, one could easily touch the outer sill of this opposite window. The thoroughfare below
was so narrow that an automobile could hardly squeeze through, and
the upper storeys of both houses projected, after the picturesque fashion
of mediaeval architecture.

Chudd held this to account for the air of depression—something
more than that of mere desuetude—which seemed present in the room.
It had never had, from year's end to year's end, one glimpse of the
sun. The house opposite shut it out as completely as if no window were
there at all. No wonder nervous and imaginative people had suffered
in such a room.

He whistled as he undressed in order to convince himself that he
was no nervous mouse of a man. But he did not whistle long, because
the atmosphere of the room seemed unresponsive. This feeling he found
difficult to analyse. It was a little as if he had made questionable jokes
in a company which declined to be amused and eyed him coldly. There
was no company present in this case, but he seemed to have aroused
some chilly and baleful consciousness.

'It's like singing comic songs in a vault,' he reflected, a little while
after he had ceased whistling. 'A chap doesn't want to believe in ghosts
to get the horrors in this room. If the sunlight could only get in—'

To do him justice, he was perfectly unafraid. He was barely conscious of the slight weakening of his nerves—a mere nothing. He put
down that, such as it was, to the brief story of the murder. Ugh! Easy
to imagine a murder happening there. His mind, slightly more alert
and imaginative than usual, conjured up an ugly picture of the sleep-

ing captain, lying on the very bed which he was about to enter, and some ugly shape, which had come out of the night, bending over him and crushing his throat with hooked, claw-like-fingers.

Before getting into bed he closed the lattice window, although ordinarily he was a great believer in the virtues of fresh air. He told himself that the room was already cold enough, and that the draught between the chimney and the door was sufficient to keep the room healthy. At the back of his mind he could not help remembering that it was through that same open window that the assassin had crept to strangle a man lying where he was going to lie.

The room was very dark when he had blown out the candle. The house opposite which shut out the sun by day, shut out all but a fitful glimmer of the dim moonlight. He looked long and intently, but could not see the window clearly, only a faint dimness which grew slowly beyond the posts at the foot of the bed.

'If anybody tries any tricks with me,' he thought savagely, clenching a great fist beneath the bedclothes, 'I'll smash 'em!'

It somehow comforted him to remind himself of his strength and manhood, although he would have denied that he stood in need of comfort. Three or four long minutes he lay, trying to define the shape of the window; then he turned over and lay on his side and tried to compose himself to sleep.

But that night sleep, which was usually so responsive to his wooing, played the jade with him and mocked him from a distance. He turned from side to side, restless and out of temper, and continued to toss and turn until—

Quite how it began he did not know. Perhaps it was no more than a creaking board which began that unreasonable nervousness which seemed to grow in him as quickly as the mango tree of the Indian juggler. Somewhere in the room a board did creak. There was nothing unusual in that, of course, and a hundred causes might have been assigned to it. Chudd, however, could not think of one. Lying there in the dark it did not seem right to him that a board should creak unless somebody trod on it. No, no; he wasn't afraid, only—only what made it creak?

He turned over in bed, and the board creaked again, as if in response to his movement. The breath he drew tingled and felt cold in his nostrils. His eyes were closed, and he had to summon resolution before he could open them. Perhaps the captain had heard that board creak—

His open eyes encountered nothing but the empty darkness and he breathed relief. Deciding that he must force himself somehow to go to sleep, he turned over once more. The board creaked again. This time he felt his heart beating, and one ear, pressed against the pillow, heard the loud, quick drumming of an artery. Damn that creaking board! If that wasn't enough to give a man the horrors, what was? It was as if there were somebody in the room—somebody who turned to look at him every time he moved on the bed. An unpleasant thought, that! To himself he fiercely denied that he was nervous, but he did not move, although he wanted to turn over again. Also, it was entirely his own affair if he chose to breathe more gently; it did not mean that he was afraid of attracting the attention of anything that might be taking cover in the darkness. Besides, there was nothing there.

He lay still until the posture tortured him; then he turned again. This time the board did not crack, but its not doing so, perversely enough, increased his discomfort. It seemed to prove that it was not his movement on the bed causing a slight pressure on the boards which had made the sound. He drew a long breath, and the board creaked again then, as if the sound of breathing had attracted unwelcome attention.

Chudd became conscious of feeling slightly damp. In the stillness he fancied he could hear something—something more than the blood singing in his veins. It sounded like a chorus of voices singing—a very long way off, low, but terribly distinct. All imagination he knew, but— He clenched his hands. He could not now disguise from himself the fact that he, Alfred Chudd, was nerve-ridden and afraid, and for no reason that the Alfred Chudd of normal times would accept for a reason. The breath came from his lips in a thin trickle of vapour, as if he released it grudgingly.

He lay and sweated, feebly battling against the invading waves of horror, and too engrossed in staving off a nightmare panic to curse himself for owning the weakness, which he had despised in other men. It was not merely the creaking of a board which had brought him to these straits, but because he was conscious—although not through the medium of any sense that he could name—of the presence of some horror, a vague, nameless beastliness for which there was no description in any human language.

Heavens! What was that! His heart bounded within him like a live thing, and every nerve in his body made for him a separate agony. That was no piece of imagination—that noise, that movement at the far end of the room. While his pulses still raced, he realised the meaning of the sound. The window had opened and was swinging in the night breeze that moaned along the narrow streets.

The window had opened! Yes, and when he had shut it before getting into bed he tried its firmness and been satisfied. It had taken pounds of pressure to shift it, but it had shifted. A strong draught invaded the room and breathing over his pillowed head cooled the sweat in his hair. The window had opened as—O God of pity!—as it had opened that night the captain—— No, no, he wouldn't, he daren't think about that.

The seconds lagged and became periods of eternity. He knew that his normal self would have risen and closed the window, but he dared not move. The least movement—even of a hand or limb beneath the bedclothes— seemed to attack the resentful gaze of countless unseen eyes out there in the darkness. If he got out of bed, surely they would all come clamouring around him.

In the midst of all the stealthy restlessness that seemed to be going on in the room, his hearing—or some other sense—made him aware of some other sound or movement that was definite and purposeful. Someone— something—was creeping towards him from the direction of the open window, slinking, huddled and crouched, along the carpet. Chudd was now wet through with sweat. He felt his hair stiffen and rise.

'This is nightmare,' he told himself; but in nightmare one cannot move, and Chudd was able, only he dared not.

But the climax was yet to come, and it came along moments later when something cold touched his cheeks and deftly and gently felt its way down to his windpipe. His tortured brain knew it to be a clammy hand with long bony fingers. They fastened on to his throat and broke the spell which had kept him lying still as a felled log. With his ecstasy of terror came the fighting courage of the cornered rat.

He uttered a harsh, gurgling cry as the fingers tightened on his windpipe in an agonising grip. As he writhed beneath it the strength of ten came to his aid. He lunged out, grunting with the effort, great smashing blows which struck the empty air. He tore the hands from his throat, and, with a snarling scream, struck again and again. Half rising, he lashed out like a madman, and toppled off the bed on to the floor in a huddle of bedclothes. His head struck the handle of the door as he picked himself up, and a moment later he had flung it open and half tripped, half staggered across the landing, trailing blankets and sheets behind him.

There was a horsehair sofa in the coffee-room; there was also an oil lamp which might be lit. He made his way there, and remained with a light burning until dawn was in the sky.

Alfred Chudd's appearance was such as to attract attention when, rather late, he made his appearance at the breakfast table. He looked pale and hollow-eyed and worse tempered than usual, and he kept his chin well down over his collar. Billy Chignell was in the room as he entered, the landlord having just brought in a fresh supply of bread-and-butter for the three already seated.

'Good morning, Mr Chudd,' he said, turning half round. 'I hope you slept all right.'

Chudd grunted an affirmative.

'No complaints about the room, I hope?'

Chudd, although not looking directly at them, was aware of four pairs of challenging eyes focused upon his face. He hesitated only for a moment. Now that the sun was shining into the coffee-room it was possible to conceive himself to have been the victim of a nightmare. Besides, the humiliation of telling his story was something not to be borne.

'No complaints,' he grunted.

'What?' exclaimed Dorley. 'You haven't seen the ghost?'

'Ghost be hanged!' exclaimed Chudd, in quite his old manner. 'If I'd been a madman or a liar I might have seen fifty. But I knew nothing would happen in that room, and nothing did happen. Pity I'm moving on to Bodmin today, or I'd sleep in it again and welcome.'

It did him good to talk in that vein, and as he continued the breakfast-table shook beneath his fist, and the room became highly uncomfortable for Mr Walters.

Dimsdale, who had been the first to come down to breakfast, was the first to leave the table. He went downstairs and into the outhouse at the back where he kept his rod ready jointed and his creel and tackle. Some march browns needed tying, and he came out into the light to thread the 'points'. Billy Chignell, emerging from the back door to shake a mat, saw him, dropped the mat, and made towards him. He was doing his best to grin and look severe at the same time, and his round, jolly face was oddly distorted in the effort.

'Doesn't it beat cock-fighting?' he asked, in a hoarse whisper. 'There's that there Chudd, he won't eat his words and he looks nearer dead than alive. He's had an awful night, and he won't say a word. If he doesn't believe in ghosts now—'

'I rather gathered from his shouting,' said Dimsdale, wetting the end of a point and holding a little brown fly up to the light, 'that he was still rather more than sceptical,'

The landlord's voice became a thought more serious. There was a note of respectful rebuke in the tone of it.

'Oh, Mr Dimsdale,' he said, 'it's been a rare lark. But you shouldn't have done it.'

'Done what? Dash it, my sight's getting very bad, or I'm very clumsy this morning.'

'Come, now, Mr Dimsdale, sir, it must have been you. Dorley and Walters wouldn't have dared. It beats me how you knew what the others complained of, for I know I didn't tell you. But I could tell what had happened to Chudd, although he did keep his chin well down. I could see the marks on his throat—bruises—all black and blue.'

Dimsdale lowered the fly and stared at Billy Chignell.

'Are you suggesting,' he asked, half laughing, 'that I went to that fellow's room last night and nearly throttled him?'

'I don't suppose you meant to nearly throttle him. But he won't forget it in a hurry.'

Dimsdale gazed at him in blank amazement.

'Well,' he said, 'I swear I never went near his room.'

Billy Chignell stared harder than ever.

'And I swear I didn't,' he said, 'and I'll take my solemn dying oath that Walters and Dorley didn't.'

They continued to stare at one another. The sunlight was very bright and warm and seemed to deny what was in their minds.

'The others,' said Billy Chignell, sinking his voice, 'all complained of the same thing. Somebody came in the night and tried to choke 'em, so they said. I didn't believe it, and I'm not going to say that I believe it now.'

'Nor am I,' said Dimsdale, and added, after a pause: 'Well, what are you going to do about it?'

'Do about it? I'm a plain man and I don't believe in ghosts or haunted rooms, and I don't want to. But I've got my living to get, and I can't afford to have people making complaints in my house, so I'm going to shut that room up again right away, and people can go down on their knees before I let them sleep in it again. As a plain man who doesn't pretend to understand some things—and doesn't want to—don't you think I'm right?'

'As another plain man,' Dimsdale answered. 'I'm rather inclined to think you are.'

FOR ONE NIGHT ONLY

I MET old Sydney Hippett in the 'Griffin' that Sunday evening. You know Sydney Hippett, the animal trainer, who, with his performing dogs and monkeys, has visited pretty near every music-hall in Britain? I was showing at the local Hip, for the coming week, and I'd just seen by the bill hanging up on the wall that Hippett was showing, too, when in he walked.

My own name doesn't matter, but I'm pretty well known to the public as Tom Gass, the Loquacious Comedian. I'm a good comedian, but no hand at writing a yarn. I shall have to tell it in my own way, and if that doesn't suit you, you needn't read it. After all, as Shakespeare didn't say, 'the story's the thing.'

I knew Hippett pretty well, or thought I did. We had a couple of drinks together, and he asked me where were my digs.

'Lottie Ludlow's down here,' he went on to say. 'You can see that by the bill, though. She's very sick because she can't find digs to suit her. Careless girl—Lottie. Never troubles about getting addresses while she's on tour. Simply blows down on a strange town and trusts to luck. Any room for her in your place?'

'I know there isn't,' I replied. 'I asked if they could fix up my pal, Gus Leyton, but the old ma told me she hadn't another vacant room in the place. By the way, Syd, you'd better come round for a bit of supper and a game of 'vanty' or something. Gus is coming, and I've managed to wangle a dozen of Bass and a bottle of Black and White.'

'Thanks,' he answered, 'I've got nothing on. What's the address, though?'

'Forty-one, Tutbury Road—quite near the station.'

His hand shook, and he spilt half that remained of his glass of Bass over the counter.

'Not me,' he answered vehemently. 'Not in these! I've been there before! They know me in that house!'

Well, I didn't ask questions. We're not all saints in the profession, and I knew Syd was no better than most. There must have been a lot of houses about the country in which he daren't show his head. The funny thing was, though, that I hadn't noticed a pretty girl about the place; but then, I'd only been in it for an hour or two.

We didn't speak for a minute or so, and then he asked abruptly:

'Who put you on to those digs? You haven't stayed there before?'

'Never shown here before,' I answered. 'I got the address from Lily Ginetta. She said they were quite reasonable and did her very well.'

At that moment I received a terrific slap on the back, and there was my pal, Gus Leyton, standing grinning behind me. With him was Dicky Cobbold. I daresay you've seen them on the halls. Gus is 'songs and imitations at the piano,' and Dicky kids the public that he's a ventriloquist.

'I've got fixed up,' said Gus. 'I'm with Dicky Cobbold. Not too bad a place. May I bring Dicky along with me to-night?'

'Do,' I answered. 'I asked Syd Hippett here, too, but he can't manage it.'

'Oh, he's a dirty dog!' Gus said, grinning. 'Always full up with engagements. How's the monkeys, Syd?'

'Still a darn sight better looking than you, and about twice as sensible,' he answered. With that he swallowed his drink, nodded to us, and walked out.

We all looked at each other and laughed when he'd gone.

'Queer fish, that,' Dicky said. 'Gets more and more unsociable.'

'Good animal trainer, though,' I said.

'Trains women pretty well, too,' said Gus. 'I've heard him talk to them, and heard the swish of the lash in his voice. Can't say I like the brute!'

Well, we'd all heard stories about Syd Hippett, but we weren't scandal-mongers, so we didn't start yarning. We had one more drink and then strolled along to my digs.

I had a bedroom and a sitting-room on the top floor but one, in a roomy old house which had seen better days before the old ma took it and let it out in lodgings for pros. It was a gloomy old place, but the rooms were large, and everything looked about as clean as one could expect.

The fire was burning up well when we arrived, and I lit the incandescent, and got out the bottles and glasses and a pack of cards.

'It wants about half-an-hour to the time I ordered supper,' I said, looking at the clock. 'Care for a game of something now to fill in the time? Nap or "vanty"?'

We agreed on 'vanty,' cut for the bank, and I won. The very first hand I laid down a 'natural' and drew double stakes from both of them.

'Tom's luck!' said Gus. 'Always wins at cards. Always finds the best digs. Always—'

'Yes, the digs are all right,' Dicky interrupted, 'so long as the ceiling doesn't come down while you're here.'

'Which it will,' said Gus, 'if the athlete overhead hops about like that very much longer.'

I looked up at the ceiling, which was full of cracks but looked safe enough for the time being. But overhead there was a soft bumping and thudding, which went on and on as if it never meant to stop. It did stop, while I was looking up, but went on again a few minutes later. It began to get on our nerves.

'What *is* that darned row?' exclaimed Dicky, who was then holding the bank. 'Did you say "twist?" Good, that's bust it! It isn't somebody up there with a hammer, is it?'

'Sounds more like some blithering idiot with a skipping-rope,' I said.

We all listened. Then Gus burst out laughing.

'Can't you tell what that is?' he asked. 'It's one of the pro's practising a dance. Who's staying here besides you?'

'Don't know,' I answered.

'Well, who's doing a dancing act down here this week? Lottie Ludlow?'

'She's not here,' I answered, 'Syd Hippett told me she was looking for digs, and that was after ma had told me the place was full.'

'Well,' said Gus, puzzled. 'Who else is doing a dancing act at the Hip, this week? It's a girl, too. A man wouldn't be as light as that on his feet.'

'Oh, what does it matter?' Dicky said, dealing the cards. 'We can ask the old ma who it is when she brings up the supper. If it doesn't stop then, Tom, you can send her a kind message.'

Mrs Pringold arrived with the supper-tray about half-an-hour later. During that half-hour the dancing overhead had been going on almost continuously. She was a thin woman, was Mrs Pringold, with almost a bluish tinge to her face—one of those women who always seem to be suffering from the cold. She hitched a dark shawl closer around her shoulders when she had put the tray on the table.

'It's easy to tell you've got a house full of pros, ma,' I said.

'Why?'

'Well, we can hear a *premiere danseuse* getting into training. You be careful she doesn't wear your linoleum out, ma.'

'And bring the ceiling down,' said Gus.

She looked at all three of us in turn. She seemed not to understand, but there was a queer look about her thin, cold face.

'Do you mean to say you can't hear somebody dancing?' Dicky exclaimed. 'There! Right overhead!'

She gave a quick glance up at the ceiling, and stood with her thin hands clasped, listening.

'I can hear something,' she said—and she'd have been deaf if she couldn't. 'It's the wind.'

'Wind! Rubbish!' I chipped in. 'It's somebody dancing or skipping. I don't mind it for a bit, but it'll have to stop sooner or later. Who's got the room overhead, ma?'

'Nobody,' she answered, turning towards the fire. 'It's an empty attic. Nobody's dancing there.'

'I thought you said you'd let all your rooms?' I said quickly.

'So I have—all I've got to let. I don't let that one. There's no furniture in it—not proper furniture. The wind often makes funny noises up there. The windows are all loose.'

'Let's go up and have a look,' I said. 'If that's not somebody jumping about I'll eat my hat.'

'The door's locked,' she answered. 'There can't be anybody there.'

Well, we had to let it go at that. As Gus said, the wind makes funny noises in old houses, and the old girl ought to know whether she'd got a dancing Dervish about the place or not. Then, while we were having supper the noise stopped, and it didn't break out again. I'd almost forgotten all about it by the time the two boys went.

They left me at half-past twelve, and at one I went to bed and fell asleep almost at once. At two—the luminous dial of my watch told me the time—I was broad awake again. I knew something had woke me and I hadn't to listen more than a moment to find out what it was.

The garret above must have been a long one, running the length of my bedroom and sitting room—I afterwards found out that it did— and there was the dancing, just above the ceiling, going on as merrily as ever.

Well, I'm not one of those who jib at a few inconveniences in lodgings. A chap must expect to have to put up with them. But to have somebody dancing overhead at two in the morning was a bit too thick.

So I jumped up, put on slippers and a dressing-gown, and groped my way to the stairs. I was pretty wild and I meant that the dancing lady—I was sure it was a girl—should have a piece of my mind.

I heard the dancing plainer than ever when I got on to the landing above. It was as dark as the inside of a tiger, but I blundered against a door, while I was feeling for one, and knocked. I got no answer. Whoever was inside took no notice whatever.

I found the handle and turned it, and just as the door came open in my hand, I remembered the landlady having told me it was locked. 'Old liar!' I thought. And 'old liar!' I thought again at the sight which met my eyes.

The window was broken, and through the starred gash the wind came rushing. Beyond I could see the moon and thin white clouds racing across it. And between me and the window a girl in a short dancing skirt pirouetted on her toes, holding out with both hands the ends of a long emerald-green cape.

She wore a little emerald-green bonnet, her short skirt was slashed with green, her shoes and stockings were white. Her face seemed very white, but I couldn't see it plainly because her back was towards what little light there was. But I thought—you know how quickly thoughts come into one's head—how like she was to Kitty O'Carr, a little comedienne and dancer I'd played with years ago. Her Irish get-up and dance was a crib on Kitty O'Carr's 'business'.

I only saw her for a matter of seconds, for a sudden gust of wind wrenched the door handle out of my hand and slammed the door in my face.

Well, I didn't open it again. I simply called through the chink: 'Do give it a rest to-night, my dear. Some of us want to get some sleep.'

She did stop then and I went down-stairs. I thought of asking her if she were Kitty, but I didn't. It wasn't the time or the place for talking, and I could find out easy enough next day. But when I got into bed again and started to think, I was a bit puzzled by things.

In the first place I couldn't understand a girl hopping about like that for hours on end without music. And I couldn't understand what had made the girl take a room with a broken window and hardly any furniture. And I couldn't for the life of me think why ma had denied there was anybody there, unless she was ashamed of letting such a room to a pro.

Then I started thinking of Kitty. Was it Kitty who had that room? I hadn't seen her for years. Somehow she seemed to have dropped out suddenly. I'd meant to inquire what had become of her, but always forgotten. It's not a bit unusual for a girl who's doing quite well in the profession to drop right out suddenly and never be heard of again.

In the end I decided that it couldn't be Kitty. At least, her name wasn't on the bills, and she always used to go on as a single turn. I made up my mind I'd find out who it was next morning, decided that ma was a 'holy friar,' and went to sleep.

Next morning, after breakfast, I ran upstairs and knocked at that attic door. As nobody answered me I opened it and looked in, and I saw at a glance that nobody could have lived in that room for years. The place was thick with dust, and I should imagine I'd been dreaming the night before if I hadn't seen the broken window and the few broken-down sticks of furniture.

I determined to say nothing to ma just then. Very likely she'd let the girl use the room to practise dancing, and denied that she'd done so to me, because I was objecting to the noise. But there was something very queer and unusual about the whole thing, and ma's manner had seemed very strange. I was bound to spot the girl at that afternoon's rehearsal, and, if she lived in some other part of the house, I made up my mind to walk home with her, confront ma with her, and say: 'What about the wind in the attic now?' or words to that effect.

That Monday afternoon's rehearsal was like any other Monday afternoon show. There was the usual grumbling over the order of the turns. The orchestra went through everybody's band-parts, and we came on and did part of a turn each to empty seats. But I didn't see the girl I'd seen dancing in the attic. Lottie Ludlow was the only dancing act, and she was a great fat girl who clattered about in clogs.

After I'd been on and managed to knock some sense into the conductor's head, I was standing in the wings talking to Gus and Dicky. I couldn't understand the business about that dancing girl, and I was beginning to feel a bit creepy over it. She couldn't have been 'on' anywhere else, as the Hippodrome was the only theatre in the town. I was thinking of the little Irish girl who used to sing and dance, and who looked like the girl I'd seen last night. So I turned round quite suddenly to Gus and said:

'By the way, what *has* become of Kitty O'Carr?'

The words were no sooner out of my mouth than I heard an oath behind me, and Syd Hippett pushed Gus and Dicky out of the way and planted himself in front of me.

'Do you want me to knock your ugly little head off?' he asked.

I didn't. And as Syd was about twice my size I couldn't have stopped him. I thought at first he was spoofing, and you could have knocked me over with a feather, I was so surprised. So I said: 'Keep your hair on, Syd. I'm not one of your monkeys.'

'Yes, you're beastly funny, aren't you?' he sneered. 'You be careful what you say and what names you mention, or I'll smash you!'

The others got in between us then, and told Syd not to be a fool, and pushed him away. And there was I, quite innocent of any intention to annoy him, and wondering what on earth I'd said that was out of place.

'You see,' Gus whispered to me a minute or two later, 'he thought you knew he was standing behind us, and I suppose he jumped to the conclusion that you were talking at him.'

'Talking *at* him! I asked what had become of Kitty O'Carr. How could I have been talking *at* him?'

'Don't pretend you don't know,' Gus said. 'You *must* remember. Everybody knows. By gum, I believe it happened in this very town, too!'

'Yes, it did happen here,' Dicky said gravely.

'What did?' I asked.

They both looked at me in bewilderment. Then Dicky said:

'It must have happened while you were doing that twelve months' tour in Canada and the States.'

'Ten years ago?'

'Yes, about then.'

'Well, what happened?'

'Syd Hippett was suposed to be going to marry Kitty O'Carr. She died in her digs somewhere in the town here, and Syd had to attend the inquest—that's all. Hullo! You're looking pretty queer all of a sudden.'

I leaned up against the electrician's ladder.

'I feel queer,' I said. 'You don't happen to have a flask of brandy on you, do you?'

An hour later I'd found some new digs, and went round to collect my props from the old ones.

'I'm sorry to leave you,' I told the old woman. 'I'm not very particular about my rooms. I can put up with half-cold food, the cat eating my supper, rats, mice and hard mattresses. But I draw the line at ghosts.'

She stared at me and fell back a step. Her cold-looking face went white, and her straight mouth dropped at the corners.

'You won't tell the others?' she said in a whisper. 'You won't ruin me?'

'I get called a liar quite often enough without spinning a yarn like this,' I told her.

'Besides, there's no ghost there,' she said, recovering herself. 'That noise you heard was made by the wind. I've been up to that attic a hundred times at night and seen nothing.'

'I've only been once,' I said, with a shiver, 'and I wasn't so lucky. And now, before I go, I want to know how Kitty O'Carr came to die in that room. You needn't tell me she didn't, because I know she did.'

She looked at me for a moment as if she couldn't speak. Then at last she said:

'If you won't tell the others—'

'The others all know,' I told her, 'but I want to hear from you.'

'They found out afterwards that she had a bad heart. The shock—'

'Begin at the beginning, please.'

'Oh, I suppose you know it all already,' she said wearily. 'Miss O'Carr had my big top room, the one I haven't let since. She was playing down here the same week as Mr Hippett. They were engaged. One night, home she comes from the theatre in high spirits, her turn having gone even better than usual. She'd come home in her stageclothes, make-up and all, with a water-proof over them. And so happy and light-hearted she was that she started doing one of her dances for me when I took up her supper tray. While she was jigging about the room, up comes the girl—I kept one then—with a note. It was from Mr Hippett. She took it from me and opened it and read it while she danced. Then, down she flopped on the floor, poor thing, and never moved again. She died dancing, as you might say. The note from Mr Hippett was read at the inquest, and a cruel note it was. It told her that he was going to marry some other woman; and I suppose she'd have been well shut of him, but girls don't look at these things in that light. The coroner said that her heart was in such a bad state—though perhaps she didn't know it—that she oughtn't to have danced at all, and the least shock was likely to send her off. That's all there is to tell you. It happened close upon ten years ago, as perhaps you've heard.'

And that's about all there is to it, as they say. I'm a comedian, and I don't profess to be able to tell stories—not this kind of story.

Syd Hippett is still touring the halls with his performing animals, and I'd sooner be dead than be any dog or monkey trained by him. He's a strong man and a brave man in a way, but there's one set of digs that he daren't set foot in. And, unless you're looking for trouble, don't mention to him the name of Kitty O'Carr or the address of the house I slept in for one night only.

FATHER OF THE MAN

WITHOUT stopping to wonder how he came to be there at all, Raymond Tallifer passed under a familiar archway and walked through a short stone passage into a long, cool corridor.

The place was as silent as an empty church; it held, in fact, an atmosphere like that of a deserted place of worship. It was paved with large square stones which rang underfoot and awoke echoes overhead, and which had been worn and hallowed by many generations of schoolboys. One side was lined by windows looking out upon the quadrangle, and for each window there was a little blaze in which the motes were playing and a distorted rectangle of light upon the far wall. This was hung with severe engravings depicting such subjects as the Forum at Rome, the ruins of Carthage, the circus at Pompeii. In the middle there was a board covered with red baize, to which many typed notices were pinned.

It was more than twenty years since Tallifer had stood in that corridor, and he was aware now of having happened upon a place which was barred and sealed against the access of time. He might have seen it an hour since for all the change apparent to him. An hour or a quarter of a century, it was all the same. The corridor had its own degree of coolness and its own subtle unseizable odour. This was neither quite the harsh smell of aggressive cleanliness associated with hospitals, nor the odour of an old building in the process of decaying, but a subtle blend of both combined with something unique and characteristic. Whatever changes had taken place in a mutable world during the past twenty-and-something years, the 'college stink' remained the same.

Tallifer was moved after a fashion which he would have been incapable of describing. His heartstrings became vocal, and quivered and wailed to an old, lost tune. He had not seen his old school since that last morning when he stood up in chapel to sing, 'Lord, dismiss us with Thy blessing,' with all the roads of the world lying open before him. However remiss they may be in their attentions to the dear old lady, there are few men who have not a deep and abiding love for their Alma Mater, and it is a pleasant emotional experience to return at long last and see the calm old face unchanged by any added line or wrinkle. Tallifer was an old Schoolhouse boy. It pleased him to think that, whatever changes might have overtaken the other houses—and he knew of two new ones since his day—Schoolhouse seemed as immutable as the pyramids.

It was a Saturday afternoon, enough in itself to account for the interior being deserted. From outside there came faint and far sounds, as sweet to Tallifer as the humming of bees—boys' voices and the hard, crisp impact of leather against bats. Tallifer walked to the west end of the corridor and thoughtfully climbed some stone steps. He supposed he should have called on the headmaster, but it amused him to walk about as if he were a boy once more. Sooner or later, he supposed, he would meet somebody, and then he would be able to explain.

Outside a door he paused with his hand on the latch. In his day this had given entrance to the House library, and he supposed it still did. He waited a moment before entering, trying to conjure a picture of the room as he had seen it last. It was here that he had first discovered for himself the delights of Sterne and the purple passages in Byron.

The latch clicked under his hand and the heavy door swung open before him. There were the same tables and cane-backed chairs and the same litter of magazines and newspapers. It seemed to him that even the same books stood on the cedar shelves, for here and there familiar bindings caught his gaze. Even the one occupant of the room, a boy who sat reading with his elbows on a table, and his head resting in his hands, looked strangely and even breath-takingly familiar to the visitor.

The boy looked up, and then rose with the easy smartness of a soldier coming to attention, and stood waiting with a shy boyish smile. He was about fourteen, and wore the regulation uniform of the lower school, a black coat, dark grey trousers, and Eton collar. The fact of the collar being worn outside proclaimed him to be in his first year.

'Sit down,' said Tallifer, wondering where he could have seen the youngster before, 'and don't mind me. I'm only an Old Boy come back to have a look round. Why aren't you at cricket?'

He put the question casually in a tone of civil inquiry, and the boy replied readily and smilingly.

'I crocked my knee, sir, so I got leave to fag. Of course, I could go out and watch, but the Firsts are playing away and the Seconds have only got a rotten match, so I thought I'd stay in and read. A chap at school doesn't get many chances of being alone, except some of the big fellows who have studies to themselves.'

Tallifer smiled.

'You like being alone, then?' he asked.

'Oh, no, not much, sir, but just now and then. A chap sometimes wants a chance to be quiet and think.'

'Ah,' said Tallifer, 'I remember feeling like that, too. It's an odd thing, but I remember doing exactly as you're doing when I was about your age. I'd crocked my knee and spent the afternoon here and—what's that book you're reading?'

'*Tom Brown's Schooldays*', answered the boy, and held it up for him to see.

Tallifer exclaimed aloud.

'Well,' he added, 'this is *too* remarkable! I remember that I started reading *Tom Brown's Schooldays* on that occasion, and I fell asleep over it and had a horrible dream which I couldn't remember when I woke up.'

The boy smiled broadly.

'Perhaps it bored you, sir. I don't think I like it very much. It may have been good when it was written, but it isn't a bit like school life today. But Mr Frankham, our English master, told us that everybody ought to read it, so I've begun.'

'Old Frankham still here, then?' thought Tallifer, smiling. 'I must go and look him up...Do you like being at school?' he asked aloud.

'Yes, I think so, sir,' the boy answered doubtfully, 'but it's different from what I expected it to be. Of course, I'd read the usual sort of stories in which the hero's a real wonder, and the butler's an ex-convict in league with one of the masters who is a crook, and the boys have the most wonderful rags which couldn't happen at any real school. We have rags, of course, and they're very funny ones, but they wouldn't seem a bit funny if we told anybody else about them, and nobody would think it worth while putting them in a book. And there's nobody here in the least like a hero, except Graceman—'

'Graceman!'

'Do you know him, sir? He's captain of the eleven; but there's never anything heroic for him to do, except knock up centuries sometimes.'

Tallifer stood staring hard and straight at the boy, gripping the edges of the table. And suddenly the boy coloured and looked abashed.

'I haven't been talking too much, have I?' he asked awkwardly.

'No, no! Go on, go on!'

'I feel that I could tell you things, things that I couldn't tell anybody else, not to my father or my mother or my best friend. I wonder why I can tell them to you.'

'Ah!' said Tallifer gently and very sadly. 'I think I know.'

'It's funny how we can't tell other people all about ourselves. I get thousands of thoughts and ambitions which aren't anything to be ashamed of, and yet I think I should die if anybody knew them—anybody but you. It's funny how little my father and mother really know about me, and I expect I know just as little about them. I couldn't bear that anybody should know how fond I am of Dick Saltash— except perhaps Dick himself, and then I couldn't stand it if he mentioned it. I don't know why, except that it would seem so sloppy and girlish.

'Dick's my friend. When I first met him here I thought we were going to live in a sort of school story, and that one of us was going to be the hero and the other the sort of second hero. I think I'd kill myself if any of the fellows knew that. But it wasn't like what we thought it was going to be, and neither of us is anything like a hero. Dick isn't because he funks Burns minor and gets out of fighting him. And I funk Burns minor too. I can't see the sense of fighting when you know you'll get beaten.

'In all the school stories the two boys who have had a fight shake hands and become friends for life, and it's always the bully who gets beaten. Even if I beat him I couldn't be friends with him, because he bounds horribly and I should think his people are cads. He doesn't bully like they do in the school stories, but he bags your books and breaks your pens and says rotten things, and when you get first to a fives court he comes and roots you out and swears blind he's bagged it first.

'Boys don't talk as they're made to talk in books. They've got much more sense than grown-up people think, they know more about things, and they're not so—healthy, I suppose is the word. They're very snobbish, too. There are thousands of things you must do, or you mustn't, for no reason at all, and there's the right and the wrong sorts of slang. School life isn't a bit like what I thought it was going to be like.'

'Nothing ever is,' said Tallifer, with a slow, sad smile; 'but I know how useless it is to tell you that. We paint our own pictures of the future, and then we have to scrape them out and paint others. But we continue so until the end, feeding on hope. What do you think you're going to do with your life, my boy?'

He looked up brightly.

'I know what I want to do,' he said. 'I couldn't tell anybody else, but I can tell you.'

Just for a moment Tallifer winced and leaned heavily on the table.

'No, don't tell me,' he said, with a catch in his voice, 'it isn't fair!' His face worked for a moment. 'Go on,' he said presently. 'I know that I am not a free agent. I know that I must listen.'

The boy uttered a high, clear laugh.

'I don't know what that means,' he said, 'Am I a free agent?'

'I have already told you that I am not, and you—— But you don't yet understand. Come, tell me! I know already what you are going to say, and I suppose I deserve to hear it.'

'Well,' began the boy, 'I want to be like Graceman when I'm his age, and afterwards I want to be a county cricketer and play for Surrey. Graceman will very likely be asked to play for Surrey during the holidays. He is going on to Oxford, and is almost certain of his Blue. So I should like to play for Surrey, too, when I'm old enough, and after that I want to be a soldier and win the V.C.

'I should be horribly ragged if the other fellows knew just that, and even Dick would rag me. But I can tell you. My father says he can't afford to send me into the Army, but he says there's almost certain to be war with Germany before many years, so then everybody will have to fight, and I may get a show. Oh, and I want to have a wonderful collection of stamps. Perhaps one day I'll buy a collection at a sale among a lot of old books, and there'll be a twopenny blue Mauritius in it, and Sydney views, and lots of triangular Capes.

'And afterwards I suppose I shall want to marry. I don't think much of girls, but fellows seem to when they get older, so I expect I'll be like all the rest. It wouldn't be so bad if I could find one who wasn't stupid, and had been brought up like a boy, and wouldn't mind racing me downhill on a bike and going to watch cricket and footer matches. And I want to live in an old house in the country, with panelled walls and a ghost, and find an old treasure in a secret hiding-place. And, of course, I want to have tons and tons of money, so that I can have a good time myself and be kind to the poor. And, of course, I want old Dick to live near me, and have a nice wife like mine. And I want to do heaps and heaps of noble and generous things without anybody ever thinking that I was pi. And I don't want ever to get old and die; and perhaps by the time I'm about forty they'll have invented something that'll let people go on living for as long as they like. And whatever happens, I want people to say of me, ''Well, he was a good sportsman and he always played the game.'''

Tallifer turned away, and for a moment his eyes were dim.

'Old chap,' he then said, 'it won't be a bit like that.'

The boy's face fell, but it lit up again after a moment.

'It might be,' he said. 'Nobody knows.'

Tallifer regarded him pitifully.

'I know,' he said, 'and not merely because I am forty and speaking to fourteen. You have learned already that nothing is as you expected it to be and hoped it would be, but you will go on cheating yourself until death steals your last breath out of your body. And your ambitions which would make most men laugh, and make me weep, you will shed as now you discard your outgrown clothes. And those with which you will replace them will be more reasonable and less worthy, but even these you will never attain, nor those which will follow and follow until the end.

'You will come to laugh at your dreams of playing county cricket, and give up the game when you find that you are, after all, only one of many thousands of muddlers. You will have your taste of war and endure the agony of having your courage tried and found wanting at your own tribunal. You will see in it nothing gallant nor soul-stirring, but a heart-sickening companionship with mud, vermin, and misery, long months of foulness and boredom punctuated by moments of indescribable terror. And you will win no V.C., but some small, tawdry decoration they will give you for having done, perhaps, a tithe of your duty.'

'How can you know all this?' the boy interrupted, hardly above a whisper.

'Let me go on. And your tom-boy sweetheart you will neither seek nor find, but you will kill the love of a good woman and go searching greedily for shams and base imitations, which are all that the world will have to offer you. Your idols will fall from their clay pedestals, and you will not pick them up nor have the courage to set others in their place, but sneer at yourself, because once you were their worshipper. What you call friendship now will some day come to be a myth to you; you will count as your friends those whose society is just endurable to you.

'You will never have your fine country home, nor will you be so simple and wholesome as to go and breathe God's pure air through a cottage window. You will live in the crowded places where men go to poison their souls and bodies. You will lose that clean taste in your mouth. You will feel the shackles upon you and have no will to break them, and drink to forget what you have become. You will play with unclean and unwholesome toys, and lose all taste for the sweeter things of life. And when you are scarcely past your youth you will come to the last hope of all—that God Who knows all and understands all human weaknesses may perhaps pardon all.'

And the boy looked at him piteously and raised a cry.

'It isn't true!' he cried. 'It can't be true! I am beginning to hate you, although I can tell you everything that is in my heart.'

'It is natural that you should hate me,' Tallifer answered, 'and it is true. Indeed, it has already happened, for time is not merely something that creeps around the edge of a clock; it is a plastic substance in the hands of the Almighty.'

The boy dropped his head between his hands.

'Who are you?' he asked.

'I will even tell you that,' said Tallifer, his voice vibrant with pity, 'for you will wake in a moment and mercifully forget. Yes, you will go on feeding on hope, and only remember that you had a bad dream which your first moment of waking sponged from your mind. And I must pity you, and you must hate me, and there is nothing in your heart which you cannot tell me, because I am you and you are me; because you are the boy I once was, and I am the man you will become.'

At that the boy screamed and recoiled, and his face was a mask of terror and loathing. But Tallifer stretched out his hands towards his lost youth, and in his heart there was a great tenderness, stronger than mother-love.

'No, no, don't hate me! Pity—pity—'

Another voice chimed in upon his own; a voice coming out of another world. And the boy slowly faded with the room, and the bookcases and the tables, and the last that Tallifer saw of him was the horror in his eyes.

The woman who was not Tallifer's wife had come into the room and awakened him. She was dressed to go out. In fact, she was on the stage, and due to set out for the evening performance. She was a hipless person, with a vapid and much-painted countenance. Tallifer blinked at her, at the familiar furniture of the flat dining-room, and at the coloured bottles and cocktail shaker which stood ready to hand on the bare, polished table.

'I wish you wouldn't mutter so much in your sleep,' she said. 'If I were you, I'd cut down the drinks a bit during the day. I'm just off. You might let me have my taxi fare. I haven't any change.'

He felt in his pocket for small silver and handed it to her. She turned towards the door.

'Don't forget,' she said, 'that you're meeting me after the show, and taking me to supper at the Eighty-Eight!'

'All right, Billie,' Tallifer muttered. 'Goodbye!'

He watched her go. Then he let his face sink between his hands, and groaned.

THE FOURTH WALL

W HEN Forran complained of pains in the head, a steadily declining appetite, and a growing difficulty in getting to sleep, his wife urged him to waste no more faith on the local practitioner and spend two guineas on a visit to some great man in Harley Street. And after two months of gentle bullying, and a miserable consciousness of growing worse instead of better, Forran went.

The Harley Street doctor earned his two guineas in as many minutes. When Forran left the house he found himself pledged to give up work for at least two months, and rest in some quiet and bracing part of the country.

Forran was one of three partners in a firm of solicitors, and as he was not a poor man it was not difficult for him to arrange for an eight or nine weeks' holiday. His idea was to take a furnished cottage within easy distance of some pike fishing, and where rough shooting might also be obtained. Mrs Forran was to accompany him.

At first, their plan was to go away by themselves, but it occurred to Forran that such an arrangement might be very dull for poor Betty, and Mrs Forran thought that a little company other than her own might be good for dear Jack. Thus it came about that Tom and Helen Marriott, Mrs Forran's brother and sister, were urged to join them.

At that time I was just beginning to realise that life without Helen would be worse than a lingering death; so I angled tactfully for an invitation, which eventually I received from Mrs Forran, who saw how it was with me. So we went away five strong, a happy little party, whose members could be relied upon to live for two months under the same roof without wearing upon each other.

Jack Forran saw the advertisement of the furnished cottage in a weekly paper devoted to such things, and Tom went down into Huntingdonshire to look at it. He returned full of ecstasies. He had never seen such a cottage, he said; and in five minutes we had caught his enthusiasm. It was very old, and had been endowed with the comforts of civilisation without losing its antiquity. It was furnished throughout with genuine old furniture, and the whole place contained nothing shoddy and not one jarring note. In a word, it was the cottage one often dreams of but seldom sees.

For the rest, Tom had to admit that it was miles from any town or village, but he argued that this seclusion was just what we wanted. Moreover, the Great Ouse was only half an hour's walk distant, and there, he told us, the wildfowl were crying aloud to be shot and the pike begging to be caught. So Jack, without wasting time, wrote to the London agent, and took this paragon of cottages for two months, antique furniture and all.

We arrived on a December evening, having driven five miles in a slow trap from a little village station on the branch line from Cambridge.

Our cottage stood just outside the region of the fens, but it had been built on the crest of what passes for a hill in that part of the country, and Tom guaranteed it to be fairly dry. In other respects we were prepared for disappointments, for we had begun to fear that he had made us expect too much. We got ready to fall upon him and find fault.

But when the door was opened to us, and one after another we crossed the threshold into a warm room flooded with soft light we were all ready to swear that Tom had done the place less than justice.

The door opened straight into the one large living room, and opposite to us a grandfather's clock ticked loudly and with elderly precision. On our right hand logs were burning on the wide, open hearth, in the ingles of which were chintz-covered seats. Already I fancied myself there with Helen, we two alone in the firelight, watching the grey smoke curling up into the wide chimney. Heavy beams supported the low ceiling, and one ran diagonally along the cream-washed wall, sloping downwards from the ceiling and disappearing behind the clock.

Beside the clock were two doors, one leading to the kitchen and the other to the stairs. There was another door on our left as we entered, and that led into a small apartment fitted up as a morning-room or study. These details are important in view of what follows.

Supper was ready, but we explored the rest of the cottage before sitting down to it. I don't think we met with one disappointment. There was even a bath-room. 'So,' Tom said to me triumphantly, 'you won't have to sponge yourself over, standing up on one leg in a kind of degraded frying pan.'

Mrs Forran had arranged for a woman to come in every morning and do the rough work, since there was no room there for a servant to sleep. The woman was present when we arrived, and had prepared a hot meal for us. Her younger sister had come, too, to keep her company.

This Mrs Lubbock was a stumpy, silent creature, seemingly very nervous and stupid, and it was hard to get more than a word out of her. She did not know to whom the cottage belonged, or so she said. A gentleman named Sellinger used to come and stop there, but him she had hardly seen, and knew nothing about. She looked nervously around her as she said this, and left as soon as we would let her, dragging her sister with her.

In the interval between her departure and our sitting down to the roast ham and fowls, Tom nodded to me to come into the kitchen. I did so, and he pointed to the inside of the door, on which a cross had been roughly drawn with a piece of white chalk. I looked at him and saw him smiling, his eye-brows lifted.

'That's that woman,' he remarked. 'Do you know what it means, Archie?'

'I suppose it means that she thinks the house is haunted,' I said. 'I should think the people round here are pretty superstitious. They generally are in these lonely places.'

Tom sank his voice.

'Don't say anything to Jack,' he whispered.

'Pooh! Jack doesn't believe in spooks. He's not such a fool.'

'Nevertheless, he's not himself these days, and we won't take any risks. Look out!'

He took out his handkerchief and smudged the chalk marks until the cross was obliterated.

'By Jove,' he added, 'this is "some" cottage! Ghost and all!'

'We ought to have a sweepstake,' I suggested. 'The money to go to the first who sees it.'

'Could we trust each other, do you think?' said Tom, and we both laughed.

It would be well to explain at once that none of us believed in what is commonly called the supernatural. We were normal, hard-headed people, even more sceptical concerning such things as ghosts than the average man in the street. At ordinary times we should have welcomed a ghost-story connected with our dwelling-place, but, as Tom had said,

Jack Forran was not quite himself.

During supper we criticised the cottage, and Jack was the only one who had something to say about it that fell short of praise.

'It's a ripping old place,' he said; 'but do you know it seems to me rather self-conscious of being a cottage.'

'What *do* you mean?' Mrs Forran laughed.

'I mean that everything about it—the furniture and all that—is so very "cottagey". It seems to keep on shouting at you: "I am a cottage. Everything in me is just right for a cottage." I don't express myself very well.'

Helen laughed.

'I know,' she said. 'You mean this room is, somehow, just a little stagey.'

'Stagey was just the very word I was trying to think of,' Jack said.

Tom, who was sitting opposite Helen and me, looked around him.

'Do you know,' he said, 'that this room is just like a scene on the stage. Try and imagine that wall over there—the fourth wall I think it's called—has been taken down. On the floor is a row of footlights. Beyond it's all dark, and there is row after row of blurred faces.'

Mrs Forran nodded, and we all looked round at the fourth wall.

'Yes, I can imagine all that,' she said.

'Well, then,' Tom continued, 'imagine yourself among the audience for a moment. You'd be looking on to the stage at a conventional stage-cottage sitting-room. That door leading to the little room would be the exit on the prompt side. There's no exit on the other side, but the space behind the chimney looks like one. Open hearth on right. Two doors at back, grandfather's clock, oak beams, everything complete.'

We all marvelled, because it was in very truth a perfect stage cottage, and I immediately experienced what I took to be the power of suggestion. I was sitting beside Helen, with my back to the fourth wall, and I felt that there was no wall there. Behind me was a row of bright footlights, and a sea of dim faces. I could feel hundreds of eyes upon me, and even suffered for the moment a mild kind of stage fright.

Now I am not one given to nerves, nor is my imagination in the ordinary way a particularly active one. But on that occasion it seemed to slip out of my control, and I imagined not only that the fourth wall was down, but that all our little party began to behave in a certain precise and self-conscious manner as if they were acting before an audience. And I, too, although I strove against it, became one of the mummers.

When we spoke we pitched our voices in a slightly higher key, and made our articulation clearer. We addressed each other not in our usual manner, but as rather stiff strangers who had been placed at the same table at an hotel. Our table manners lost their freedom. Jack, who was inclined to sprawl in his chair, sat up straight as a ramrod. Tom, who had a habit of playing with his breadcrumbs while he was not actually eating, sat between the courses with his hands under the table. The idea that the wall was down and the audience watching our every move-ment and listening to every word seemed to have worked ridiculously on the minds of us all.

We were talking primly in our stupid stage voices about something quite unimportant, when Tom, who had been silent for a while, sud-denly startled us. He raised his voice, and, looking over the heads of Helen and me, declaimed as follows:

'*When I do fall in love, Heaven help me—and her!*'

The voice was hardly his own; it was the sonorous, flexible voice of an actor. The words boomed from his lips, full of passion and sad-ness. I felt Helen start beside me. We had not been talking of love, and in the circumstances I had never heard a less pertinent speech. There was dead silence for nearly half a minute.

Then I felt a change come over me, as if a shadow had passed on from my mind. I felt no more the footlights behind me and the rows of faces, and suddenly set up a roar of laughter. Simultaneously all the others laughed. Once again we were old friends, supping privately and behaving naturally, no longer mummers on a stage. We laughed until the tears ran down our cheeks.

'Oh, Tom, you *idiot!*' Helen cried.

'What on earth made you say that?' Mrs Forran demanded, choking.

Tom regarded us all, smiling but slightly flushed.

'I don't know,' he said. 'It must have sounded frightfully mad. The words came into my head, and I just said them.'

Afterwards they became a catch-phrase with us. Now we all repeated them, imitating Tom's voice, until Mrs Forran sniffed audibly, and looked towards the fire.

'Can you smell anything burning?' she asked.

We all could. There was a heavy smell of smoke in the air. It was as if a part of the carpet were smouldering.

'A spark must have jumped out of the fire,' I said; and went to see.

But I could find nothing, although I searched the room, and presently the smell of burning went. We agreed that it was rather curious.

We had been at the cottage more than a week when, just after tea on a dark, drizzling evening, Tom begged me to come out for a walk with him. It was not inviting outside, and I was never glad to leave Helen, but the look in her brother's eyes made me aware that he had something to say to me. So I assented rather grudgingly, and put on my cap and ulster.

Up to then we had had a good time. I was always happy when I was near Helen; Jack was already much better, and everybody was delighted at the signs he displayed of an early recovery. Moreover, we had had plenty of sport with our guns, and Jack had landed an eleven-pound pike on a spinner.

All that marred our pleasure was that sensation of being on the stage, to which all of us had to confess. Generally it came on at supper, and then we made frantic efforts to behave like our normal selves. Fifty times a day we bullied Tom for giving voice to the suggestion, and thus affecting all of us.

There was also a mystery, which we had given up trying to solve. Regularly every evening at about the same time we smelt something burning, and always we searched for a smouldering splinter on the carpet, and never found it. Jack had a theory beginning, 'When the wind is in a certain quarter...' which we accepted, but only because a poor explanation is better than none to people who do not care for being mystified.

As Tom and I picked our way down the dark garden, sucking at our pipes, I knew instinctively that he wanted to talk to me about the cottage. For some reason I did not care to be too serious, and as we reached the road I imitated his voice, saying:

'When I do fall in love, Heaven help me—and her!'

He laughed, but not very mirthfully.

'Yes,' he said, 'that was dashed queer. Archie, my dear lad, there are a lot of things that are very queer. Have you any vices?'

'Such as?'

'Going downstairs at night and reading your immortal short stories aloud to yourself?'

'Me!' I exclaimed. 'Good Lord, no! Why?'

'Well, Jack had a jolly good night's sleep last night, so it wasn't he. It certainly wasn't I. And now you say it wasn't you. And it was a man's voice.'

I felt an uncomfortable, prickly feeling in my skin.

'What are you talking about?' I asked.

He hesitated a moment.

'Look here,' he said, 'Helen's had a fright. You know her room is over the dining-room? Well, it seems she woke up last night quite late, and heard a man's voice in the room underneath. It sounded quite plain—so plain that she could almost hear the words. It was like somebody reading aloud with a lot of expression. She didn't know the voice.'

Again I felt that prickly sensation in my skin.

'She must have been dreaming,' I said.

'My dear chap, a week ago I should have declared unhesitatingly that she *was* dreaming. But now I'm not so sure.'

'You say it was like somebody reading aloud?'

'Yes, with a lot of expression. An actor going through his part, for instance.'

He said this with an elaborate casualness, but I caught another note in his voice.

'Tom,' I said, 'don't be an idiot.'

He was silent for a short while. Presently he said:

'You don't believe in ghosts, of course?'

'No, I don't.'

'Nor did I until the last few days. It's no use howling me down, Archie, but there *is* something queer about that cottage. For instance, that sensation of being on the stage before an audience. We all get it at times. And the smell of burning. And the queer thing I said almost unconsciously that you all rag me about.'

I was already more than half convinced, but I tried to argue on the side of what I thought was sanity.

'Are you sure we haven't all caught nerves from poor old Jack?' I suggested.

'Nerves! Rubbish! Besides, old Jack is, luckily, the least affected by these things of all of us. That's because he doesn't believe in uncanny things, and he doesn't know all that we know. Helen told nobody but me about the man she heard reading, simply because she wanted it kept from Jack. And he doesn't know about the cross we found on the kitchen door. If anything happens to give him a bad shock—well, you know what the result might be. I think we ought to try to get him away.'

Still I argued.

'The cross we found on the kitchen door proves that the silly old charwoman thought the cottage was haunted. And you know what country people are.'

Tom looked at me queerly.

'Look here, old chap,' he said, 'when we came here we didn't believe in such things. We all rather prided ourselves on being hard-headed. But now don't you think, after what has happened, that we might as well revise our views a little? Even if we would like to believe other-wise, don't for Heaven's sake let us shut our eyes to proofs. Super-natural or not, there is something confoundedly queer about the place we're living in. If Jack gets a bad shock it may send him mad. And poor Helen's frightened.'

Those two arguments were enough to make me see that we ought to leave the cottage. But the problem of how to get Jack to go was not easily solved. He was so thoroughly in love with his surroundings that no trivial objection would dislodge him, while to tell him the truth would simply defeat our own ends.

We talked this over for some time, but found no way out of the difficulty. Then Helen began to occupy all my thoughts, and I insisted on our going back. She was safe enough with Jack and Mrs Forran, but I felt somehow that my place was near her. And Tom grabbed me by the shoulder with his long fingers, and let me know by a peculiar chuckle that he understood.

The evening of the twenty-second of December will live long in my memory, and with good reason. Let me try to tell what happened plainly and straight-forwardly, without the omission of any important detail, and yet without exaggeration.

We had then occupied the cottage for about a fortnight, and since my walk in the rain with Tom—when he had confessed his sudden belief in 'ghosts'—nothing of importance had happened. We had experienced as usual the smell of burning, and the queer sensation of being on the stage, but Helen had heard no more voices, nor had there been any fresh phenomena.

After tea on that particular evening it was arranged that we should drive into St. Ives and do some shopping; but I, seeing a Heaven-sent opportunity to do some of the work which I had neglected of late, elected to stay behind. I will not pretend that I was not nervous, but I will stoutly maintain, until the last day I live, that my nerves played no part in deluding me.

At first, when I was left alone and sat down to write, I felt 'jumpy' and uncomfortable. But a couple of pipes soothed me, and I soon lost myself in my work. After a while my pen began to scrape, paused, and went on scraping in the old familiar way. The old grandfather's clock said 'tock-tock, tock-tock', until I got so used to his voice that it seemed to become part of the silence.

Work passes the time as quickly as play, and when I paused to light another pipe and looked up at the clock, I found, to my surprise, that

more than two hours had slipped away. It would not be very long before
the others returned, so I went on with my work at once, and became
absorbed in it for another half-hour.

Then quite suddenly I felt grow upon me that feeling of self-
consciousness that I was beginning to know so well. I felt that hundreds
of eyes were upon me, that hundreds of people were waiting to see
what I would do next, and hear what I would say. I felt the cold air
of fear in my nostrils, a dreadful sinking in the stomach, a prickly feeling
in the skin.

'Nerves!' I told myself; but I dared not raise my eyes. I sat still, with
my gaze bent down upon the uncompleted sentence, my pen shaking
in my fingers. The grandfather's clock ticked on slowly, and I sat quite
still, the slave of fear.

At last, and never so slowly and stealthily, I raised my eyes. They
rested upon the door leading into the morning-room, which stood ajar.
It was dark inside, but certain things were dimly visible, and those
things were unfamiliar.

I saw the half of a step-ladder, the corner of what looked like a rough
wooden shed, and a piece of rope dangling. My heart gave a great
leap, and then seemed to stop beating.

'Oh, my God!' was the thought that leaped into my brain. 'The
wings of a theatre!'

I moved my gaze round a little to the left, and instead of seeing the
wall—the fourth wall—I saw a space of semi-gloom. Beyond the carpet was a short space of bare boards, and then a row of footlights throwing up a yellow glare. In the gloom I saw faces, row upon row of them,
the curves of a dress circle and gallery with a glint of light on their
brass railings, and high up in a kind of dome a cluster of small lamps
was burning dimly.

I sprang up with a little cry, and stood facing the ghastly change
that had overtaken the wall. There was not a sound, but I was horribly conscious of the undivided attention of hundreds upon hundreds
of eyes and ears. And as I stood, dumb and quaking, my nostrils caught
an acrid whiff of smoke.

Simultaneously I heard a sharp scream behind me. A hoarse voice
shouted something inaudible. Heavy footfalls began to ring on hollow
boarding; I heard a hiss like an escape of steam, and the clatter of pails.

Then I spoke, and the voice sounded in no way like my own.

I said: '*If I do fall in love, Heaven help me—and her!*'

I uttered the words without realising their meaning, and because
I was powerless to do otherwise.

Then the faces of that ghastly audience dimmed, and finally vanished, cut off from me by a curtain of black smoke. The smoke was all around me in reeking clouds. It got into my eyes and my throat, and I fell forward, choking and gasping, on to my knees. An agony of suffocation tore me. As consciousness slipped away from me I have a dim memory of a great tongue of flame flickering a yard in front of my eyes...

It was Helen who found me lying on the floor. She had run in a little in advance of the others, and the sight of me, lying thus, gave her the greatest fright of her experience. What she said to me before I came round I never learned until we became engaged, and that is neither here nor there. After a minute the others came in, and I have a dim memory of being given brandy and led up to bed.

Next day I lied painfully to my fellow members of the household, assuring them that I was only the victim of a heart attack, the first of my experience. But later in the morning Tom came and sat on the edge of my bed, fixing me with a pair of quizzical eyes.

'Better now?' he asked.

'Much.'

'Then you can tell me what happened. Heart attack be hanged. I've already prepared Jack for what I'm going to tell him. We're going to clear out of this at once. Will you tell your story first, or shall I tell mine?'

I looked at him in surprise.

'Has anything fresh happened?'

'I found out something yesterday,' he answered. 'The cottage is supposed to be haunted, although nobody seems to know precisely in what way. But I've found out all about the man who used to live here, and it seems to fit in rather well with what we've all experienced. Shall I tell you?'

'Yes, do!'

'Well, then. Yesterday evening, while the others were buying groceries, I went in to an inn at St Ives to get a bottle of whisky. There was a farmer chap in the bar, and I started talking to him, and told him where we were stopping. He pricked up his ears at once, and asked if we'd seen the ghost. I told him no, and asked him about it. He said that the cottage was supposed to be haunted by a man named Sellinger, who had lived in it off and on for years.'

'An actor?'

'Yes, an actor. It seems he used to use the place always when he was resting. He was quite a celebrity in his way, although he was hardly known to the London stage. For years he'd been touring the provinces with a play called *The Heart of Annette*, in which he played the lead. There was a scene in the play which depicted the interior of an old cottage, and from that scene he copied the arrangement of the room downstairs in every detail.'

'Ah!' I said, and shuddered. Already I had a dim idea of what was coming.

'He loved this place,' Tom resumed, 'and every week-end he could spare he came down here. All his vacations, too, were spent here. You can imagine him going through his parts in that room downstairs.'

I nodded grimly. My imagination needed very little stimulation.

'About a year ago,' Tom continued, 'he met his death on the stage. He was playing at a theatre in the Midlands, and was in the middle of his scene in the cottage sitting-room when the stage caught fire. He was suffocated by the smoke. He had just said, "*If I fall in love, Heaven help me—and her!*" when the smoke and flame rushed in upon him. Those were his last words. Why, what's the matter, Archie?'

There is a theory that when a man loves the place he lives in, it remains imbued with his personality long after he has left it. There is another theory to the effect that the spirit of a very strong personality (such as the actor Sellinger had doubtless been) can impress upon the minds of living people mental pictures of places and incidents which have figured prominently in his life, and can even make them experience the sense of a certain smell—as of burning, for instance. The spirit could, indeed, on rare occasions actually 'control' a person still in the flesh, and make him utter words quite involuntarily. As to that, let each think as he will.

But we were practical people, and we did not theorise overmuch. We simply left the cottage and went to Malvern. Anybody may have that cottage at a very modest rental, but we do not recommend it. There may not be such things as ghosts, but there are a lot of things, pleasant and unpleasant, which are beyond our ken.

SELECT BIBLIOGRAPHY

The stories in this collection originally appeared as follows:

The Blue Magazine

April 1926: 'Crookback'

The Grand Magazine

November 1922: 'Warning Whispers'

Lloyd's Magazine

October 1920: 'The Recurring Tragedy'
November 1921: 'For One Night Only' (as 'The Dancing Lady')

The London Magazine

December 1915: 'The Fourth Wall'
May 1920: 'The Mystery of the Sealed Garret'
June 1926: 'The Garden of Fancy'
March 1929: 'The Boy with Red Hair'
May 1929: 'Father of the Man'
January 1930: 'For the Local Rag'
September 1930: 'The Little Blue Flames'

Passing Show Xmas Number

November 1924: 'The Imperturbable Tucker'

The Premier Magazine

June 1926: 'The Acquittal'
September 1926: 'The Attic'

May 1928: 'The Ticking of the Clock'

The Royal Magazine
January 1919: 'The Green Bungalow'

The 20-Story Magazine
October 1924: 'The Case of Thissler and Baxter'

ACKNOWLEDGEMENTS

Grateful thanks are due to the following for their help and enthusiasm at various time: Richard Dalby, Rosemary Pardoe, David Rowlands; Bill Lofts (of course), and Derek Adley; Bob Adey; George Locke; A. J. Flavell, Assistant Librarian at the Bodleian Library. I'm particularly grateful for the encouragement of my editor, Michael Cox, who, like me, felt that A. M. Burrage has for too long been a forgotten figure.

THE FLINT KNIFE

Further Spook Stories by E. F. Benson

Selected and introduced by Jack Adrian

'I hurled myself against the door: it creaked, the bolt snapped and it gave way, falling inward. There met me a buffet of hot air tainted with some rank smell, and round me was the roar of hosts of flies...'

Welcome to the world of E. F. Benson's ghost stories—a world far removed from the sunlit social intrigues of Tilling in the celebrated Mapp and Lucia novels.

All three Benson brothers—Arthur Christopher, Edward Frederic (Fred), and Robert Hugh—wrote supernatural fiction; but Fred, as in so much else, outdid the others.

Unlike his brothers' stories, Fred's have ghosts that bite—that are vengeful, predatory, and utterly malignant. Occasionally a shouted appeal to God, or a thrust with a crucifix, might scatter them to the four winds; but in the main they are unstoppable in their thirst for destruction.

Benson published four outstanding ghost-story collections in his lifetime, beginning with *The Room in the Tower* (1912) and ending with *More Spook Stories* in 1934. Now Jack Adrian has unearthed twelve new tales, none of them published in volume form before, and presents them here with three further stories from a little-known collection, *The Countess of Lowndes Square* (1920). The result confirms E. F. Benson's reputation as a master of the ghost story form.

'A marvellous page-turning collection. No admirer of E. F. Benson—and certainly no supernatural fiction enthusiast—will want to be without it.' —Michael Cox, co-editor of *The Oxford Book of English Ghost Stories*, author of *M. R. James: An Informal Portrait*.

IN THE DARK

Tales of Terror by E. Nesbit

Selected and introduced by Hugh Lamb

'She fell into my arms in a heap. I clasped her and kissed her, and called her by all her pet names, but I think I knew all the time that she was dead. Her hands were tightly clenched. In one of them she held something fast ... It was a grey marble finger.'

So ends one of the most famous of all English ghost stories—'Man-Size in Marble' by E. Nesbit, author of such classic books for children as *The Story of the Treasure Seekers* (1899) and *The Railway Children* (1906).

While Edith Nesbit's mainstream fiction has often been revived, her tales of terror—apart from one or two anthologized pieces—have fallen into unwarranted neglect. This collection now makes ample amends by bringing together fourteen excellent stories culled from *Grim Tales* and *Something Wrong* (1893) and from *Fear* (1910), including such forgotten gems as 'From the Dead', 'The Ebony Frame', 'The Head', and 'Hurst of Hurstcote'.

In the context of Edith Nesbit's life and marriage to the priapic Hubert Bland, these powerfully told tales, with their frequent sexual overtones, reflect deep seated fears and anxieties—in particular, childhood memories of seeing mummified corpses in a Bordeaux church ('skeletons with the flesh hardened on their bones, with their long dry hair hanging on each side of their brown faces') and a lifelong dread of being buried alive.

But these are more than attempts at personal exorcism. Edith Nesbit was a natural storyteller and her gifts are shown to the full in this collection which will do much to re-establish her as one of the most accomplished and entertaining ghost-story writers of the past hundred years.